TH

If evidence seems about to come to light that the late Professor Garvie-Brown of Edinburgh University had murdered seven wives, four of whom he had married bigamously, enriching himself by each marriage and dying regarded by his colleagues as a wonderful old man, what ought his descendants to do about it? What, particularly, ought they to do when the professor's eighth wife, who, astonishingly, survived him, shows signs of developing a conscience and of feeling that they should all do something for an obscure young man in London called Luke Latimer, who, she has discovered, is the sole surviving grandson of one of the bigamous wives?

Luke himself wants nobody to do anything for him. He is in a job that he likes and he wants to be left in peace to get on with it. He has not the slightest inclination to blackmail or in any way to bother his wealthy relations, among whom are a High Court judge, a doctor and another professor. But how are they to be sure of that? They only know that if the truth were to become publicly known, they would all be ruined.

Their fears of this, their fears of what Luke perhaps might do to them, together with the devious activities of a certain private detective, Gilbert Arne, draw Luke helplessly to Edinburgh, into their lives and their problems, and to the scene of an eighth murder.

Elizabeth Ferrars has never displayed to better effect her well-known skill in characterization and suspense.

**Also by the same author,
and available from Coronet:**

Alive and Dead
A Legal Fiction
Murder Among Friends

The Seven Sleepers

Elizabeth Ferrars

CORONET BOOKS
Hodder and Stoughton

British Library C.I.P.

Ferrars, Elizabeth
    The seven sleepers. – (Crime Club)
    I. Title II. Series
    813[F]

    ISBN 0-340-55138-0

Printed and bound in Great Britain for Hodder and Stoughton Paperbacks, a division of Hodder and Stoughton Ltd., Mill Road, Dunton Green, Sevenoaks, Kent TN13 2YA (Editorial Office: 47 Bedford Square, London WC1B 3DP) by Clays Ltd., St Ives plc.

CHAPTER I

IT WAS nearly five o'clock in the afternoon when the door-bell rang. If it had rung a few minutes later, Luke Latimer would not have been there to answer it, but would have gone out to work. Not that that would have seriously altered the course of events. Something had already been set in motion over which he was to have very little control. If he had not been there it would merely have delayed a little what was about to happen.

Luke was not expecting anyone. Not many visitors came to his dark little basement flat in Kentish Town. He thought that probably it was his landlady, who lived upstairs, and who perhaps wanted him to post a letter for her, or take her empties back to the grocer. She was seventy-two, lame, and inclined to make use of him.

In return, she often did little things for him, such as taking in his laundry parcel if he was out when the van came round, and reminding him that it was the day to put out the dustbin. She was a good landlady, as land-ladies go. All the same, Luke did not hurry particularly to open the door to her now, but finished doing what the doorbell had interrupted, pulling on his long-sleeved, black sweater and combing his hair.

With the sweater he was wearing narrow grey trousers and a rust-coloured shirt, in which he looked very slim and long-legged and almost distinguished. In fact, his height was six feet, but he looked taller because of his slender bones and their very thin covering of flesh. His hair was dark, straight and fairly long. This was not exactly from choice, or because it was in fashion, but simply because he could not remember to have it cut as often as he sincerely intended. His age was twenty-eight. He had a pale, sharp-featured face, which was good-looking in a haunted, under-nourished way, with wary green eyes and black brows.

As the bell rang again, he returned his comb to the pocket of a corduroy jacket that was hanging over the back of a chair, put on the jacket, strolled to the door and opened it.

It was not his landlady who stood there, but a short, stockily built man whom Luke had never seen before.

'Mr Latimer?' the man said.

'Yes,' Luke answered. Then, as the man did not speak again, but only stood there at the bottom of the steps which led down from the street, looking at him with a remarkably cold, piercing gaze, Luke added inquiringly, 'Er—?'

'Mr Luke Latimer?'

'Yes.'

'My name is Gilbert Arne,' the man said. 'I'm not selling anything, or buying anything, but I'd be grateful if I could have a few words with you.'

'I haven't much time, just at the moment,' Luke said. 'I've got to go out.'

He had taken an instantaneous dislike to the man because of that brazenly direct, chilly, grey stare, and also because of the look of bullying strength about his heavy shoulders, together with the smallness and whiteness of the hands at the end of his short, thick arms, and the smallness of his feet in their pointed, suède, elastic-sided shoes. Also, Luke's feeling had something to do with the shape of the cocky little tweed hat which the man wore perched high on his big head, a head that appeared to be poised on his shoulders without any neck, almost as if it had been put down there by accident and might roll off at any moment. His short, tweed coat hung open. Under it he wore a cheap, creased, grey suit, which was too tight for the lumpily muscular body inside it.

'I needn't keep you long,' the man said, 'but I think it could be to your advantage if you'd answer just a few questions.'

His face, tilted to look up at Luke's, was unusually large, with a jaw that looked as hard as a horse-shoe. His age was about forty-five.

'Can't it wait, whatever it is?' Luke said. 'I've really got to go out.'

The short man's response was a slight roughening of his voice, which before had been thin and flat. 'You *are* Mr Luke Latimer, I suppose?'

'Oh yes.'

'Can you prove it?'

'Can I——? Look, what the hell *is* this? What's it got to do with you?'

'Then you can't prove it?'

'Of course I can.'

'How? Have you any documents? Any envelope addressed to you? A driving licence?'

'Yes, I've got a driving licence,' Luke said, 'though as it happens I don't know where it's got to. I haven't a car. I don't drive these days. Actually I haven't driven since an accident I had. But I don't see why——'

'Ah, licence suspended,' the man said.

'It was not,' Luke replied angrily. 'There was no question of blame. A tree fell over in a storm and crashed on top of me.'

'I see, lost your nerve.'

Luke was about to deny it hotly, when he remembered that that was exactly what he had done.

'Well, sort of,' he admitted.

'Tough,' the man said. 'Life gets complicated nowadays if you can't drive. You ought to see someone about it.'

'See someone?'

'A psychiatrist, or one of those. They'd straighten you out.'

Luke's anger revived. He wondered why he should stand here, allowing a complete stranger to insult him by saying that he ought to see a psychiatrist.

'I don't want to be straightened out, I'm quite content as I am,' he said. 'And as it happens, everyone knows that a car in London is merely an inconvenience and a perfectly insane extravagance.'

'Well, if you've no driving licence, what about a passport, or don't you go abroad either?'

'I do—but what's this all about? By what right do you come here, demanding to see my passport? I've never heard anything like it. You can't come to a person's door, simply ring their bell and ask to see their passport. Even if you're from the police, you can't do that. This isn't a police state. Besides, I told you, I've got to go out. I'm on my way to work.'

'I know,' the man said. 'You work for Mrs Audrey Doubtfire of Good Neighbours, Ltd, 2 Watershed Lane, W.1. You're one of her staff of baby-sitters, dog-walkers, shoppers, and helpers and advisers on domestic problems generally. You've been working for her for three months. God knows why, when you're a perfectly qualified chartered accountant, but that's your business. Perhaps something went sour in the accounts. You see, you aren't a stranger to me, even if I am to you, Mr Latimer.' The man took off the jaunty little hat to which Luke had taken such a dislike, revealing that the straw-coloured hair under it was thinning. Running a hand over it, he all at once looked discouraged, bored and so tired that he had to stifle a yawn. 'And if only you'd ask me in and show me that passport, or some other proof of identity, we could get our business over in a minute, my guess is it would be to your advantage, and I could call it a day and be off home at a reasonable hour for a change. God, how I'd like that!'

Luke found himself standing aside and letting the man step past him into his home.

As soon as he had done it, Luke regretted it. It was with distaste and suspicion that he followed the stocky figure across the small dark hall of the flat and into the sitting-room. This was not a man for whom there was any place in Luke's life, a life which he found difficult enough to organize in any case. That accident had done something to him, apart from giving him concussion and breaking his leg. It had released in him all kinds of impulses, desires and ambitions which had been almost unknown to him before. Sometimes he wondered if it had left him a little insane. Alternatively, he thought, just possibly what he was experiencing was the onset of sanity, and if that were so, the turmoil would probably last longer and be more painful than if he were merely lapsing into lunacy.

Hence the importance to him of the undeniably rather undignified job that Mrs Doubtfire had given him. He had met her first in the waiting-room in the out-patients' ward of the hospital where each of them had recently spent some weeks, he because of the injuries in his accident, she for an operation on her spine. He had realized at once that she was an unusual, complex woman, shrewd, sharp-tongued, overbearing, at times unconvincingly, disingenuously flattering, yet at others almost furtively kind. For the job that she had offered him that very afternoon she paid him barely enough to keep body and soul together. But the work was really very undemanding, and sometimes actually interesting and pleasant, and so was like an extension of his convalescence, a state in which he ought to be able to rediscover himself, or come to terms with his strange new identity, before making up his mind whether or not to return to his old job.

His former employers, Curt and Broadley, had been commendably generous to him, saying that they would keep the

9

job open for him for a reasonable time. Not that he could imagine at present ever wanting to go back to it.

'Well,' Gilbert Arne said, 'that passport, please, or a birth certificate, or even an envelope addressed to you, or any darned thing. I'm not fussy.'

He was looking round Luke's sitting-room. It had once been the kitchen of the house, which was mid-Victorian, and situated in a drab but quiet street. The room was fairly large, and there was some good furniture in it, for Luke was a diligent and perspicacious frequenter of sale rooms. But the windows were small, barred, and only the tops of them were above the level of the pavement outside. There was no view from them except of the ankles of passers-by, and it was astonishing what a small percentage of these were worth looking at.

The room happened to be moderately tidy at the moment. Once a week Luke tidied and cleaned the whole flat and he had done this only two days ago, so there were not yet many specks of soot on the window-sills, not too many books had strayed from the bookshelves on to the chairs and floor, and the flowers to which he treated himself every Friday, when he had received his weekly pay-packet, were still fresh.

After a deliberate look round, Arne took a few steps to a table on which were a typewriter and a heap of type-script.

'Trying authorship?' he asked.

Luke thought the tone and the question so extremely patronizing and impertinent that he did not answer it. 'If you'll explain what you want . . .'

'That proof of identity.'

'I think I want some proof of yours first,' Luke said. 'I haven't the faintest idea who you are.'

'Fair enough.' The man took a wallet out of his jacket pocket, extracted a card and gave it to Luke. The words on the card were, 'Gilbert Arne, Confidential Inquiries,' followed by an address in Holborn.

'A private detective!' Luke exclaimed.

'It's taken you long enough to get around to it,' the man said. 'Now I'd have got it in one.'

'But what in God's name does a private detective want with me?'

'I just need to be sure who you are.'

'Yes, but . . .' In his confusion of mind, a possible explanation suddenly came to Luke. 'If it's anything to do with my work for Mrs Doubtfire, I must refer you to her. I can't discuss it at all. Naturally, doing the sort of work I do, I sometimes learn quite intimate things about other people, but I wouldn't dream of telling you anything—'

'Now wait, now wait!' Gilbert Arne interrupted irritably. 'It's nothing to do with your job. I just want to make sure, before reporting to my client, that you're Luke Latimer, the son of the late Laurence and Teresa Latimer.'

Luke put down the detective's card on the opened flap of a William and Mary writing desk, opened a drawer in the desk and took out his passport.

'Here you are.'

It contained the usual hang-dog photograph, which made him look more like a convicted felon than a man about to enjoy a holiday abroad, but still it was recognizable. Arne glanced at it and handed it back.

'And that makes you the grandson of a woman known as Lilian Garbury, née Potter,' he said.

Luke had just sat down at the table on which the typewriter stood. For a moment he sat there rigid. Then he came swiftly to his feet, his normally pale face flushing a dark red.

'So that's what you're after!' he shouted furiously. 'You're another of the people who's been digging up dirt about my grandmother. Well, you aren't going to get anything out of me. Get out! Get out!'

Gilbert Arne did not move.

Luke's voice grew even more strident and excited. 'Get out!'

A very faint shake of his large head was Arne's only response.

Luke struck the table before him violently, rather hurting his fist as he did so. He went on shouting. 'Why does this sort of thing have to go on happening? All right, my grandmother was murdered—everybody knows that. But what's that got to do with me? It isn't as if I remember her. I wasn't even born when it happened. Even my mother didn't remember her. She was only a few weeks old when her mother was killed. She was brought up by aunts. So why come plaguing me about it just because some damned fool of a journalist thinks up some new bloody theory about the murder? You'd think with the world in the state it's in he'd have enough other things to think about and could let the poor old woman rest in peace.'

'She wasn't old when she died—or poor,' Gilbert Arne remarked.

Luke sank back on to the chair. 'It happened getting on for fifty years ago,' he said. 'Why should you—why should anybody—think I can tell them anything about it? And what right have they to come asking me about it, even if I'd anything to tell?'

'Have you?'

'No, no, no! I'm telling you, no! And I won't answer any more damn' silly questions about what it did to my family life to have a murder in the family, and what I think it did to my own character, and do I think the tendency to commit murder might be hereditary, and have I ever felt any murderous impulses in myself? I won't answer anything!'

'Have you really been asked all those things?' Arne asked him, looking intrigued.

12

'All but, all but! It's what they were all getting at. First that journalist, Smithson, who spotted the similarity between the murders of those four women, and dragged all the dirt out into the open again, when people had had plenty of time to forget it. Then there was one of those true crime characters, who was writing a book about unsolved murders. Then there was someone who called himself a psychologist, also trying to cash in on Smithson's idea for some lectures he wanted to give. And they all asked disgustingly personal questions and wanted to see any mementoes I had of my grandmother. Mementoes of a murder—nice, cosy things to have around. I don't hoard mementoes anyway. I don't like clutter. I'm always throwing things away. So I hadn't got the knife she was stabbed with, or the nightdress she was wearing when it happened, or even a photograph of her. I've got nothing. And I'm not quite the naïve fool I was when all this started, and ready to talk without thinking about what I'm getting myself into. So if you don't want to waste any more of your own time and mine, you'd better go.'

'All right.' The detective turned towards the door. 'I think you've told me all I need to know.'

'Wait a minute!' Luke exclaimed impetuously. 'You can answer a few questions of mine before you go, can't you?'

Arne continued across the room. He walked with small, sedate steps, with his toes turned out, yet somehow he gave the impression of being poised on his little feet like an animal, ready to spring.

'I thought you were in a hurry,' he said in the doorway.

'I am, but I'm going to be late anyhow. I'll have to telephone and explain.'

'What do you want to know?'

'Why you came, of course—what you want.'

'I was asked to trace you, that's all. That's to say, to trace any living descendants of Lilian Garbury, Georgina

Goode, Maureen Gray and Edna Gleason, if any. You're familiar with those names, I suppose.'

'I am since Smithson started stirring things up. I was in hospital when he found me. He came to see me day after day, can you imagine that? I had to tell them not to let him in. Then he turned up here as soon as I got home. I was rather interested at first, but after a bit the whole thing made me sick. He was licking his chops, he felt he was a bloody genius, because he'd spotted the similarities in the murders of those four women. The fact that they were all stabbed during supposed robberies, that they'd all had a lot of jewellery stolen, which was heavily insured and which they'd only bought recently after their marriages, and that their husbands all had the christian name of Duncan, a surname beginning with G., all had Scots accents and all had alibis and all went abroad, faded out, and were never heard of again, very soon after the murders.' Luke stared broodingly across the room at Arne. 'And it all happened forty to fifty years ago, but it seems it's still worth raking about in the muck. You can still get paid for doing it. That seems really strange to me. You're getting paid, of course. And I suppose Smithson made quite a good thing out of the articles he wrote.'

'Well, it was penetrating of him to spot what no one else had—very penetrating,' Arne said. 'In my job you get to admire that kind of penetration. And if you care to know, you seem to be the only surviving descendant of any of those women. Your grandmother was the only one who lived long enough after her marriage to produce offspring. It's possible that it was because she was producing your mother that she was allowed to live so long.' He perched his little hat on the top of his head once more. 'Now I'll be off home and you can get on out to your work and forget I was ever here, if you want to, Mr Latimer. Thanks for your helpfulness.'

'But why *are* you here?' Luke asked. 'You still haven't told me. Who wanted you to trace me?'

A sardonic smile twitched at the detective's lips. 'You told me you don't give out confidential information about your clients, Mr Latimer. Very proper too. And neither do I. But I'll tell you one thing. I shouldn't be surprised if you get a pretty interesting letter one of these days.'

'Who from?'

'I'm telling you, aren't I, I can't tell you that. And perhaps you won't get it. You never know, people change their minds. So I'm only guessing. I'm only saying, I shouldn't be surprised if you got a letter. And if I were you, I'd pay it close attention. I'll make another guess, which is that with your nature you're likely to tear it up in little pieces and throw it in the waste-paper basket. But I really shouldn't. I'd pay it attention. Close attention. I think it might be distinctly to your advantage.'

He turned back to the door and went out. By the time that it had occurred to Luke to get to his feet and go hurrying after him, the detective had let himself out of the door of the flat and disappeared up the steps.

CHAPTER II

LUKE, ALONE once more in his sitting-room, raked his fingers through his over-long hair and tried to think of several things at once.

First, he must telephone the people with whose children he was sitting in for the evening, to warn them that he would be late in arriving, but that they should not panic. He was on his way. They could rest assured that they would be able to go out to their dinner party.

Next, he must fill his fountain-pen and see that there

was some paper in the briefcase that he always took with him when he went baby-sitting. For Gilbert Arne had been right, Luke was having a try at authorship. He was writing a novel. And on the occasions when the children of the household allowed him a quiet evening, he generally got several pages written, to be copied out on his typewriter next day.

Not that he often had a quiet evening. To his own surprise he was popular with children, and found that as a rule they demanded far more of his attention than they would have of their parents'. He had to read to them, play cards, snakes and ladders, chess, and sometimes even sing to the very young ones. Yet the most dominant thought in his mind just then, quite unaccountably, was of a black poodle.

He did not know why. Somehow the creature seemed to be connected with Gilbert Arne. Yet the man had not had the slightest resemblance to a poodle. Indeed, with his stolidity and stockiness, his light, thinning hair and heavy jaw, he could hardly have been less like one. Yet an image of the animal went on prancing in and out of Luke's mind all the way to St John's Wood, where he found his clients, in evening dress, and with a taxi waiting, in a growing mood of desperation, in case, after all, he might not be going to arrive.

It was only after the door had closed on them and their assurances that he would have a quiet evening, because the children were all in bed and fast asleep already, that he suddenly remembered that it had been in the form of a black poodle that Mephistopheles had first appeared to Faust.

Had the devil then entered his life?

A small, uneasy shudder went through Luke. He made up his mind simply to put the man's visit right out of his mind and not allow it to trouble him in any way. He had so many other things to think about nowadays. More and more things, which in the days before his accident he had never thought about at all, but which daily were acquiring more importance. For in that split second during the storm, when he had seen the tree begin to fall on him and before he hurtled into unconsciousness, he had recognized that if by some miracle his life were spared, everything that followed would be different.

And so it had been. Nothing, he found, could be taken for granted. The value of everything had to be tested, proved, taken very seriously, what was worthless discarded and what, often unexpectedly, turned out to be astonishingly precious, cherished and hoarded. It was very demanding on the imagination. At the same time, it was more interesting than anything that he had ever experienced before, and he resented interruptions in his absorption in the new process.

It was three days later that the first letter came.

The envelope was white and of good quality. The writing on it was small, spiky and full of character. It was positive. It expressed strength and self-confidence. While he was still only looking at his name and address on the envelope, before he had even realized that this was the letter prophesied by Gilbert Arne, Luke felt sure that it was bound to be of importance to him.

The letter was from a woman who signed herself Christina Garvie-Brown and the address at the top was in Heriot Row, Edinburgh. The letter was short.

'Dear Mr Latimer,

I hope you will forgive what may seem to you an intrusion. I am sure you have never heard of me. But there is a distinct possibility that we are distantly related, which makes me feel that I should like very much to make your acquaintance. It might be that I could to some extent right a wrong that has been done. This would give me some peace. Is it too much to ask that you should pay me a visit? I am elderly and not very well and the

17

thought of travelling to London, I confess, intimidates me. If you could come to see me I should be most grateful. And the sooner the better, as I have an important decision to take and your view of the situation might be of the greatest assistance to me.

Yours sincerely,
Christina Garvie-Brown.'

Luke, who was in his dressing-gown and had neither combed his hair nor shaved and was sitting by the gas fire, read the letter several times over his breakfast, which consisted of toast and cherry jam and a large quantity of strong coffee.

'Crazy,' was his first comment, spoken aloud.

Here was a woman practically telling him that she was old and ill and thinking of leaving him some money. And things like that did not happen. He did not know what the statistics were of people who were suddenly left money by complete strangers, but he was sure that their number was very small. And he would never be one of them. It would not be in character for him to get something for nothing.

His next comment was, 'Related? How the hell . . .?'

It was then that he remembered the visit of Gilbert Arne. So the supposed relationship must be somehow through his murdered grandmother, since it was to search for any living descendant of Lilian Garbury's that this woman had employed the detective. Luke began to frown at the letter. It had always been possible to pretend that he did not mind having had a murder in the family and sometimes even to show off a little about it in the sort of company where it seemed likely to raise his status, but in his heart he had always hated it profoundly and hated being reminded of it.

After another minute, just as Arne had said he would,

Luke tore the letter into little pieces and dropped them into the waste-paper basket.

It was a fortnight before the second letter came.

It had been a busy fortnight for Luke. Besides the usual baby-sitting and the writing of letters of advice for Mrs Doubtfire to sign to people who wanted to be told such things as where they could obtain shoes with double A toes and quadruple A heels, or have a picture identified that had been in the family for years and which a friend had said he was sure was valuable, or buy an old-fashioned pair of curling tongs, or find a pen-friend, he had had to try to find a furnished flat for a young girl to share with two or three others, and this had turned out a particularly difficult assignment. For the parents of the girl, who lived in Brighton, had kept writing letters to Mrs Doubtfire, demanding the strongest proofs of the respectability of the other girls, while the young girl herself had simply rejected everything that Luke had found for her on the simple grounds that it was frightful. And in the process of accompanying her from place to place, recognizing, he thought, that all she really wanted was to be allowed to find a place for herself, and sympathizing with her in this natural desire, Luke had fallen in love with her.

Not that this in itself had created difficulties. The girl appeared to enjoy the situation, even if she did not like the flats that Luke found for her, and had been ready to go out with him whenever he had an evening free of baby-sitting. But naturally there had not been much room in his life for thoughts about incomprehensible letters from Edinburgh. When the second letter came and he recognized the small, spiky writing, he felt inclined to throw it away without even opening it.

Yet while he felt this, his fingers were slitting the envelope open and there was actually an uneasy sort of eagerness in the way that he read the letter.

'Dear Mr Latimer,

I have felt very disappointed that my letter to you did not receive any reply. I assure you, it was not a frivolous communication. I most seriously wish to meet you. If you are unable for some reason to come to Edinburgh, please let me know. I will then essay the visit to London. Perhaps you could advise me of a good hotel. It is a number of years since I was last in London and I am told it has changed a great deal in recent times.

Yours sincerely,
Christina Garvie-Brown.'

'God!' Luke ejaculated in horror and made the beginning of a tear in the letter.

But before he had torn it right across, he checked himself, read it once more, folded it and put it into his wallet. Finishing his breakfast, he dressed, and after a hunt for the card which Gilbert Arne had left behind, he set off to find the detective's office in Holborn.

It was in one of the few remaining old houses in a street of tall office blocks. The house looked as if it were keeping the demolition squads at bay with difficulty. Perhaps the tail-end of a lease still protected it in its declining years. Declining it certainly was, with a tattooist on the ground floor, and above him a number of almost nameless little businesses, jammed cheek by jowl between partitions in what had once been handsome rooms. Yet the house still maintained a certain ragged, reckless dignity, as it would till it died and was carted away for decent burial.

Arne's office was on the second floor. Luke climbed the stairs, through a strange medley of smells, animal, vegetable and mineral, and knocked on the glass panel in a door, on which were the words, 'Gilbert Arne, Private Inquiries. Confidential Investigations. Please Walk In.'

Through a clatter of typewriting a shrill, feminine voice from inside shouted, 'Can't you read? Come in!'

Luke pushed his hair back from his gaunt face, carefully straightened his shoulders, turned the door-handle and entered the office.

It was very small, with another door opening out of it. At a metal desk with two telephones and a typewriter on it, sat a woman, young middle-aged, artificially blonde, with a deathly pale make-up on her long, bored face. She was dressed in a sort of tunic of mustard yellow, which reached about halfway down her solid thighs.

Without pausing in her typing, she asked indifferently, 'Have you an appointment?'

'No,' Luke said, 'but I've got to see him.'

'He doesn't often see people without an appointment,' she said.

'He came to see me without one,' Luke replied, 'and I saw him.'

She looked momentarily surprised by the logic of this answer, but she had one of those faces on which it is difficult for an expression to take root. In an instant it was as blank and bored as before.

'Well, he's in, for a change, so I'll see,' she said, putting out a hand to one of the telephones. 'What name do I say?'

'Latimer.'

She spoke into the telephone. 'A Mr Latimer to see you, Mr Arne.'

The instrument gurgled something back at her.

'All right,' she said, 'go on in, Mr Latimer.'

Luke opened the door into the inner office.

It was not very different from the outer office except that it was a little larger, had a larger desk, an armchair upholstered in imitation leather for the client, and one wall covered in metal filing cabinets. The room was inadequately warmed by a single bar of an electric heater that stood in the empty fireplace.

An unexpected touch was the picture over the mantelpiece. It was a large print of wild ducks rising from a lake into a salmon-coloured sunset. Did Gilbert Arne have dreams then, Luke wondered, of lonely places and undisturbed, golden evenings? Did the thought of wild life, savage and dangerous but innocent, sometimes distract him from the squalor of the human scene? Or had someone, his wife, for instance, simply given him the picture and had he not known what to do with the damned thing but hang it up? Had he a wife? Along with his new absorption in his own nature, Luke had recently developed an insatiable curiosity about other people.

Arne had risen from his desk and was holding out one of his little white hands. He was wearing the same grey, crumpled suit as when he had visited Luke.

'Good morning, Mr Latimer,' he said. 'Sit down. You know, I've had it at the back of my mind that you might be coming in to see me one day soon. On the other hand, I didn't feel sure which way you'd jump. I didn't feel I'd got you sized up. You're an individual, you know. Tailor-made, not off the peg, as it were. So I really didn't know. Will he or won't he react, I asked myself. Well, I take it this visit means you will.'

'I won't,' Luke said. 'I've come to tell you you've got to stop this persecution. You started it, so you've got to stop it, or—or I shall go to a solicitor.'

'And what good would that do you?' Arne sat down at his desk. His big head and heavy shoulders made him look much larger, sitting behind it, than when he had been standing up. 'What's this about persecution? I don't understand you.'

'Read that.' Luke took out of his wallet the letter that he had received that morning and slid it across the desk.

The detective read it in one quick glance, and seemed about to hand it back when he retained it, reading it over again with a frown, as if he were afraid that he had missed the point of it.

'No, I don't get it,' he said after a moment. 'It's quite a nice letter. What's wrong with it?'

'Read it, read it!' Luke said fiercely. 'This woman is actually threatening to come to London to pester me. How would you like that if you were me?'

'I gather it isn't the first letter she's written to you.'

'It's the second. In the first she claimed to be some sort of relation of mine and wrote some crazy stuff about righting a wrong that's been done, and asked me to go to Edinburgh. And now, because I didn't bother to answer, she's threatening to come here to find me. I ask you, how would you like that if it happened to you?'

'I might like it quite a lot, but then I know the lady better than you do.' There was irony in Arne's hard stare. 'She's rich.'

'She's mad, that's all I know about her,' Luke said. 'And for reasons best known to herself—if reason of any kind is known to her—she's picked on me to persecute with insane letters. Well, I don't like it. It's a totally unjustifiable invasion of my privacy. It's got to be stopped.'

'She isn't mad,' Arne said. 'I oughtn't to talk about the affairs of a client, but I don't see any harm coming of my telling you that. Or that, besides being sane and rich, she's widowed and childless. If I were you, I'd go straight off to Edinburgh. I shouldn't waste a day. That's my considered, quite disinterested advice. Not a day. I'd be off this afternoon.'

He flicked the letter back across the desk to Luke.

'I've a job,' Luke said. 'I couldn't go, even if I wanted to. Which I don't.'

He picked up the letter by one corner and dropped it into Arne's waste-paper basket.

Arne got up at once, retrieved the letter, folded it and held it out again to Luke.

23

'Keep it, Mr Latimer. You never know, you may find you want the address or telephone number. Or you may want it to show to that solicitor you were talking about.' He sat down again. 'Anyway, what have you got against answering her at least? As I told you the other day, I believe, I really honestly believe, it could be to your advantage.'

'Ha, ha!' Luke said hollowly. 'She wants to leave me all her money.'

'Not all of it—I shouldn't count on that—but some, maybe.'

'Is it likely? And I don't want to get involved. I don't much want to get involved with anyone at the moment, and least of all with strange old women in Edinburgh.'

'You're very prejudiced.' A look of worry crept into the steely eyes of the detective. He seemed to be truly anxious to find some way of penetrating Luke's antagonism. 'What more can I say than that if I were you I'd go? It's true I've only met the lady once, but I was favourably impressed. Perhaps she was a little imperious, but believe me, nothing to what a lot of rich old ladies are. At the same time, I admit, she was nervous and excited. But so are a lot of people when they meet a private detective for the first time. And she'd plainly something on her mind which she didn't mean to tell me anything about, which was unfortunate, because naturally I can work more efficiently when I'm not working in the dark—'

Luke interrupted. 'There you are—nervous, excited, worried. Obvious symptoms.'

'Prejudice,' Arne said with a sigh. 'It's probably my fault. Somehow I got off on the wrong foot with you the other evening. I could tell I had. I didn't know what I'd done, but I knew I'd handled you all wrong. Well, I'm sorry about it, and if you lose by it I'll be sorrier still, but I've done my part of the job, I found you, which was all I was paid to do. So now, since you don't seem to want the advice which I'm giving you free and for nothing and I'm very busy, perhaps you'd let me get on with my other work.'

'But you've got to stop the woman writing to me,' Luke said. 'You've got to stop her coming to London.'

Arne shook his head. 'Sorry, it's out of my hands now. My job's finished. And I've even been paid for it. Think of that. I write to the lady, sending her your name and address, and back comes a cheque by return of post. *And* a nice little letter, thanking me for my services. Not everyone does that, not by a long chalk. A lot of them don't appreciate what a lot of help one's been to them.'

'You say she kept you in the dark,' Luke said. 'Do you mean you really don't know what she wants with me?'

'She never told me a single thing about it. She just wanted me to find any living descendants of Georgina Goode, Maureen Gray, Edna Gleason and your grandmother, Lilian Garbury. That's all, I swear to you, that's absolutely all I know.'

'And you've no idea . . . ?'

'Oh, *ideas*!' Arne gave an abrupt laugh. 'I'm always full of ideas. But any ideas I've got cost money. You understand that, I'm sure. Ideas are what I live by. Now good-morning, Mr Latimer. Sorry I couldn't make you see things my way, but you can still change your mind.' He suddenly lifted his voice and shouted, 'Janie!'

The woman in the mustard-coloured tunic appeared in the doorway.

'Show Mr Latimer out, will you, pet?' he said.

Feeling uncomfortably conscious of the woman's bulging thighs and the deep fleshy wrinkles at the back of her knees, Luke followed her across the small outer office and emerged from it into the mysterious smells of the staircase.

CHAPTER III

AFTER A FEW lungfuls of them, even the tired air of Holborn smelled fresh and sweet. The late October day was mild, with a soft invitation in it to enjoy this last generous clemency of the weather before the chills and fogs of the winter.

Luke did not know exactly what he meant to do next. He had several friends who were solicitors and he had the time to visit one. But of course it would be an absurd thing to do. He had never had any real intention of going to the law for help in what he felt was a slightly ludicrous predicament. Yet he felt an urge to talk to someone about it.

In the end he decided on Mrs Doubtfire.

Walking all the way to the offices of Good Neighbours, Ltd, which were in Soho, he enjoyed the walk and arrived in a better temper and with a clearer head than when he had started out from his flat. He had even begun to wonder why he felt such an acute dislike of Gilbert Arne. The man had not actually been offensive, or more intrusive than he could help. His advice to Luke not to ignore Mrs Garvie-Brown's letters seemed to have been disinterested. If Luke stood to gain somehow by replying to the letters, Gilbert Arne did not. And after all, he had merely been doing the job on which he depended for a living. And oughtn't one always to be able to find some sort of charity in one for the conduct of people who have simply been doing their job?

The trouble was, however, that Arne completely baffled Luke's normally fairly acute perceptions. That was the source of a good deal of his dislike of the man. Arne had allowed him to see only the husk of his personality. That question of whether or not he had a wife, for instance, what was the answer? And did he sleep with that woman in the office? Was she by any chance his wife? To what sort of home, what squalid bed-sitting-room or ambitiously comfort-filled suburban villa, did he return when he was done with dogging the footsteps of evasive adulterers, planting microphones in bedrooms and taking photographs of the usual, drearily compromising scenes? For probably it was by doing that sort of thing that he made most of his income.

And had that, perhaps, made Mrs Garvie-Brown a nice change? Perhaps Arne had really enjoyed working for once for an old lady who happened merely to have an odd interest in the descendants of murdered women. Perhaps it was out of a sort of gratitude for the novelty of it that he had wanted Luke to respond to her.

Luke grinned at the idea. It was a pleasant one, but, of course, silly. That husk of a man, that hollow man with the brazen stare, would not expend his energies on anything from which he was not going to draw a solid benefit.

The offices of Good Neighbours, Ltd, were in a modern block with a doorman, two lifts and a slightly spurious air of prosperity. It was the sort of block in which people rented space for the sake of the address. Luke knew nothing about the finances of Good Neighbours, but suspected that Mrs Doubtfire often had more difficulty in making ends meet than she wanted anyone to know. It was her occasional moods of ingratiating sweetness to all her staff that made him uneasiest about this. He felt, when one of these moods was on, that she was a frightened woman, terrified that all these people, whom she had prudently organized to supply the services of the good neighbours that most people lack, would suddenly leave her and that she would be left helpless, with her efficiently managed, cosy little world collapsing all about her. When she was her more usual sardonic self, casually insensitive to the feelings of others, he knew that all was well with her. He had found that he liked her best when she was at her most offensive.

She was in good form today, greeting him with a stare and a harsh laugh before he had even told her why he wanted to see her.

'What's the matter with you?' she asked. 'Is it a hangover, 'flu coming on, or what? If it's 'flu, go away. I don't want to catch it from you. Or has that awful little girl you've taken up with kicked you in the teeth, as you deserve? I'm taking you off the job of finding her a room, Luke. You're too good-looking. As long as you're on it, she's going to make it drag out as long as she can.'

Mrs Doubtfire was at her desk, sitting very upright, as she always did because of the special corset which she had to wear to support her injured back. She admitted to being sixty. She was short and square-shouldered, with broad, sturdy hips, and muscular calves and ankles. She generally wore severe but expensive clothes, favouring tweed or grey flannel suits and white, tailored blouses of thick silk. Her hair was naturally pepper-and-salt, but she dyed it iron grey. In her small, square face, which had delicate features, a pink-and-white, surprisingly unwrinkled skin, and had probably been very pretty in her youth, her eyes were a faded blue and old and mocking.

There was a story that she had been on the stage when she was young, and another that she had worked for Intelligence during the war and done something heroic, and another that she had been married three times and had several children, and even some grandchildren somewhere. She liked to have stories circulating about her and never denied them, and it was Luke's opinion that most of them were true, though he could not remember that she had ever told him any of them herself.

'I'd like some advice, if you've the time to spare,' he said. 'I'd like you to read a letter I've had.'

'About another job?' she asked swiftly and apprehensively.

'Oh no, just something personal. At least, I suppose it is.' He sat down in the oddly shaped but comfortable chair that had come from Finland, which faced Mrs Doubtfire's across the desk. All her furniture was Scandinavian. The walls of the office were white, and being in central London, had to be frequently repainted. The curtains were buttercup yellow. There were always fresh flowers on the desk, and usually some knitting, to show that Mrs Doubtfire, appearances perhaps to the contrary, was as domesticated a woman as any of her clients, and capable, as a good neighbour should be, of understanding the difficulties which overwhelmed them and brought them to her.

"All right, show me,' she said, and Luke gave her Mrs Garvie-Brown's letter.

She read it and asked, 'What's your problem? D'you want us to find her a room? I should have thought you knew enough yourself by now to do that. Something near Russell Square, I should say. Central heating of a sort, preferably not too efficient. Private bathroom not an essential. Price, moderate. She's obviously a dignified, frugal type, who'll think there's moral virtue in a modest degree of discomfort.'

'Good God, no!' Luke exclaimed. 'Don't you see, I've got to stop her coming?'

'Why?'

'Well, there's some more to it, of course. She's written before.'

'So I gathered.'

'After sending a private detective to find me.'

'She did? Well, hadn't you better tell me the rest of it? I can hardly advise you if I don't know any more than that.' Mrs Doubtfire picked up her knitting and began to work on it smoothly. 'Did I ever tell you I was a private detective myself for a time? I might still be one if it hadn't been for my back. You can't go running around after people once you've got a bad back. Well, go on, Luke.'

He told her what he could remember of Mrs Garvie-Brown's first letter, and of Gilbert Arne's visit, and that he had just come from visiting Arne.

She said, 'You want to go, of course.'

'I've just explained that I don't,' Luke answered.

'You want to go,' she repeated. 'That's why you're so upset. You want to go, but it's all a little too bizarre for you. You're scared. You're a very conservative young man.'

'What, *me*?' Luke said, scandalized.

'Yes, you. That's why you've been going through such a bad time since your accident. It shook you up. And God knows, you must have been needing it badly to have reacted as violently as you did. But all the same, my guess is that in another few months you'll be safely back as a chartered accountant with a bowler and rolled umbrella.'

'I've never worn a bowler in my life,' he said.

'I can see you in a spiritual one, all the same, as some of my clients must be able to see the halo shining over my head, the way I look after the helpless creatures. Don't scowl at me, Luke. I'm only telling you what you know about yourself already. And now you've only come to me to have me tell you what you know, that you mean to go to Edinburgh to meet this Mrs Garvie-Brown. Of course you do. Who could possibly not want to, in the circumstances?'

'Me,' Luke said. 'I don't want to. I just want to be left alone.'

'You can have the time off, if that's what's worrying you,' she said. 'It sounds as if there just might be money in this for you, and I shouldn't like to think I'd stood in your way, if there is. You can always make it up to me some other time.'

This was not as generous as it sounded. Agreeing to make it up to Mrs Doubtfire, Luke had learnt by experience, meant mortgaging free Sundays, precious mornings and lunch-hours. She knew how to squeeze the last drop of value out of an obligation.

'But I don't want to go, Mrs Doubtfire,' he said. 'I keep telling you so.'

'But if there's money . . .?'

'I don't want it. Anyway, not when it's got strings tied to it by some crazy old woman. I've enough for my needs.'

'Your present needs,' she said. 'But what about the future—though of course you haven't started to think about the future yet, have you? Naturally the more there is of it, the less you think about it. Now me, I think about it most of the time. I see it like a thick fog in front of me and I know that at any moment I'm likely to blunder smack into some enormous obstacle and knock myself right out. Just death, no doubt. By the way, this business of all those murders, that's true, is it?"

'It's true that there were four murders, and they were all done in the same way by a man with the name of Duncan and a surname beginning with G. A journalist called Smithson dug it all up last spring and wrote several articles about it.'

'When did the murders happen?'

'In 1913, 1917, 1923 and 1928. My grandmother was number three.'

Mrs Doubtfire nodded. He had told her about his grandmother at their second meeting in one of his moods of boastfulness on the subject.

'Every four to five years,' she said thoughtfully. 'Was that the time it took him to get through the money he made out of each murder, or were there other, undiscovered murders in between? I'm rather intrigued by his success in disappearing between the murders. That may have meant that he'd another identity to slip into betweenwhiles. Perhaps in Edinburgh. Why not? You've noticed, of course, that the name Garvie-Brown begins with a G.'

'And that's one of the reasons I want to have nothing to do with that woman!' Luke cried explosively. 'I believe she read those articles Smithson wrote and somehow identified herself with all those dead women. Don't you think it must be something like that? Something quite repulsively morbid. And that man she sent to find me—Gilbert Arne —he's part of it. I don't know why, exactly, but I can't bear him. It's more than dislike. It's a sort of almost superstitious horror.'

'I know Gil Arne.' Mrs Doubtfire knew nearly everybody. 'He isn't a specially attractive little man, but I've never known him actually crooked, and you shouldn't let him rattle you. What's puzzling me is why you came to me if you really don't want to go to Edinburgh. I still think you do. And, as I said, you can take the time off if you do decide to go. But if you don't, then don't, and stop fussing.'

'But suppose she comes here.'

She grinned. 'Then go into hiding. Come and stay with me, if you like. I've a very nice spare room. You'd be welcome. You're quite good at carpentry, didn't you tell me? I've a table with a wobbly top and I can't get anyone to attend to it, except for an enormous sum. Why don't you come?'

The thought was so intimidating that Luke immediately lurched to his feet out of the comfortable Finnish chair, landing unsteadily on the carpet. That was the worst of that chair. It was very comfortable to sit in, but there was no way of getting out of it except by throwing your weight forward and trusting to luck that you would land on your feet.

'Thank you, that's very kind,' he said. 'Awfully kind. Thank you. But I suppose the fact is I'll just have to cope with the situation somehow myself. Thank you for letting me discuss it with you. That's really all I wanted—a talk, to help me get it into proportion. I've really been making an absurd fuss about it, haven't I? I see that now.'

As he swiftly left the room he was aware that Mrs Doubtfire's ironic grin had broadened.

That evening he took Stephanie Rackham out to dinner. She was the girl for whom he had tried to find a share in a flat. She was eighteen, had told him that both her parents were doctors in Brighton, and that she was still living at home and coming to London only for the day. Her reason for wanting to live in London, she had also told him, was to take some special coaching at a crammer's, having got only a Grade E in her A levels at school, yet hoping still to get into a university.

Luke did not honestly believe that she would ever get into a university. Her interest in the idea of going to one was obviously totally unacademic and based entirely on a picture in her mind of all the fun that she would have when she got there. But he thought her the loveliest thing that he had ever seen. Her hair was a heavy, gleaming curtain of gold, hanging about her shoulders. Her skin had the bloom of a child's. Her body was beautifully moulded and slender and flexible, and when she wore a dress that reached only halfway down her thighs, it somehow miraculously became her.

She had a way of sitting very still with her head slightly bent, not moving it at all when she wanted to look to the right or left, but only her eyes, which gave her a curious, passive, waiting, inviting look, as if she were expecting something important to happen to her. Luke kept hoping that he would turn out to be that thing. Her eyes were blue, wide-spaced and very gentle. They had never looked so gentle as when he told her the story of Gilbert Arne and Mrs Garvie-Brown and the two letters and she murmured in answer, 'Oh, darling, how marvellous for you, you must go, of course. There could be *money* in it . . .'

33

If this slightly put Luke off for the moment, it was not because he thought it showed up a mercenary streak in her. He thought it normal and sensible to be moderately mercenary, and that it was far better to show it than to pretend that you were not. But the day had given him the feeling that everyone was against him. No one, not even his darling Stephanie, who in a childish and fumbling way could occasionally be extraordinarily understanding, seemed able to grasp how important it was to him just then to be left alone. Just that. A small thing to want, surely. To be left alone. His kiss, when he saw her on to the Brighton train, was briefer than usual and a little absent-minded.

When he reached home a third letter in the small, spiky handwriting was waiting on the door-mat. It must have come by the second post, only a few hours after the one before. There was a cheque in the envelope for twenty pounds. The letter was the briefest of the three.

'Dear Mr Latimer,

It has only just occurred to me that perhaps I have been inconsiderate. Perhaps you have been put off visiting me by the expense of the journey. I therefore enclose a cheque to cover it, trusting that you will not be offended.

Yours sincerely,

Christina Garvie-Brown.'

It was the last straw.

Luke took the letter that he had received that morning out of his wallet, added it to the new one and the cheque and tore them all into small pieces.

But that was his mistake, the fatal turning-point.

For after he had torn up the cheque he realized that now he would be compelled to get in touch with Mrs Garvie-Brown. Otherwise she would think that he had accepted her cheque and spent it on himself instead of on the journey to Edinburgh. And even though she would

34

eventually find out that the cheque had never been cashed, for some days, weeks or even months, she might think of him as more or less a thief.

Of course, he could put the fragments in an envelope and post them straight back to her.

But supposing her to be a harmless sort of eccentric, wouldn't that be a very unkind thing to do? A real slap in the face of a well-meaning, trusting woman? He could not see himself doing it. Luke was very seldom consciously brutal.

So it happened that, two days later, at ten o'clock, he found himself at King's Cross, in a second class compartment of the Flying Scotsman, leaving for Edinburgh.

CHAPTER IV

THE TRAIN arrived in Edinburgh at four o'clock.

Luke's plan was to spend that night in a hotel, see Mrs Garvie-Brown in the morning and return to London by an afternoon train. He had booked a room by telephone the previous evening, picking the name of a hotel at random from among the cheaper ones listed in the AA book. Not knowing whereabouts in the town the hotel was, he took a taxi, which bore him up a ramp, out of the dark confusion of Waverley Station and into the street, through an opening which still, in the 1960s, was fantastically labelled, 'Carriage Exit'.

Ahead, the Castle, on its great prow of rock, looked like a huge ship dramatically becalmed in the centre of the city, under a sky turning rusty with the first faint reddening of the sunset. In the gardens in the deep cleft below the Castle, the lawns were scattered with yellow autumn leaves. Some of the trees had been stripped bare already, some were tawny or golden. On the far side of the gardens,

Princes Street, that muddle of dingy and pretentious buildings in a situation which cried out, if ever one did, for grandeur, was jammed with traffic.

The taxi, turning left, climbed a steep zig-zag of a street between tall, dark houses, into the old part of the town, then went on into Victorian suburbs. Luke's hotel was in a turning off Minto Street, one of the main arteries, leading south, out of Edinburgh. The hotel consisted of two houses which had been joined together and brightened up by a so-called sun-lounge and some coloured lighting. The bedrooms, however, were still much as they had been when the houses were built. Luke's had a remotely high ceiling, heavily decorated with plaster work, and an immense, much carved, mahogany wardrobe with a chest of drawers to match, which made the white basin with hot and cold taps in a corner of the room, and the very small electric heater with a shilling-in-the-slot meter, appear undignified anachronisms.

When he had settled in, Luke had a drink in the bar downstairs, then dinner in the dining-room, then went to bed early, meaning to read a few chapters of the paperback thriller that he had started on the journey. But soon, in the quiet of the room, in this town where he did not know a single soul, he found himself slipping into a mood of dreamy introspection.

It had always been one of Luke's problems, until recently, that he had never had enough time for free, disorganized dreaming. For most of his life there had always been someone or something pushing him on from behind to do things which he had accepted as important only for the reason that certain people whom he loved had thought them so. For instance, at school he had known that he must work hard because his parents had promised themselves that he should go to a university. At the university it had been important to do well to justify the sacrifices that they had made to get him there. Luke's father had been a newsagent in a small Midland town, a very hard-working man, far from prosperous, and the good grammar school had been more than he could really afford. The university, even though Luke had had a grant from the local authority, had put a further strain on his father's resources. And all that he had ever wanted from Luke in return had been that he should do better for himself than his father had before him. He had been the least demanding of men, the least tyrannical, the easiest in the world to love and to whom to feel an ungrudging gratitude. But only a year after Luke, by what steps he could hardly remember now, had found himself a fully fledged chartered accountant, Laurence Latimer had died of cancer. So Luke had had his mother to support.

He had not been unwilling to undertake it. He had loved both his parents, and since life had always run on tramlines, it had never seriously struck him as possible that it could do anything else. Even when his mother had died last year, very suddenly, of bronchial pneumonia, and he had been left at a loss for someone to work and strive for, it had not occurred to him to make any significant changes in his way of living. It had taken that drive home through the gale and the falling tree to shock him out of his old habits into something that was almost a new personality. A personality that continually surprised him, was insecure, unpredictable, often uncomfortable to live with, but endlessly interesting to him.

Tonight, lying in bed, he did not think much about Mrs Garvie-Brown or of why he had come to Edinburgh. He thought about the ever-present problem of what it was worth doing with a life which for one blinding moment he had accepted as lost, and then had found saved by a hair's breadth. For such a life surely must be treated as something peculiarly precious and not be senselessly, emptily squandered. And if that novel that he was trying to write turned out to be no damned good, as often seemed only too probable, what ought he to try his hand at next? Thinking rather vaguely and not very constructively about some of the problems in his novel, he at last fell asleep.

Next morning, after consulting the manageress of the hotel, he took a bus to Princes Street, from which, she had told him, he could easily walk to Heriot Row.

The morning was raw. Above the grey stone houses stretched a grey stone sky. But there were still roses in some of the gardens passed by the bus, and in one of them the grace of a birch tree with a slender, curving trunk and hanging tresses of pale gold made Luke think of Stephanie Rackham.

Heriot Row is a wide street of unpretentious dignity in the New Town of Edinburgh. It links the magnificence of Moray Place, at one end, with an unattractive muddle of buildings behind the bus station at the other. The houses are sober and plain, with handsome doorways and charming little wrought-iron balconies at their tall, first-floor windows. They look out over gardens densely filled with trees, holly and sycamore and ash and lime. Except when the street is jammed with parked cars, it has an air of amplitude and peace.

Luke walked along it slowly. The dead leaves on the pavement crackled under his feet, the nutty smell of their decay hanging with pleasant autumnal melancholy on the damp, still air. Now that he had got here, he wondered what he was going to say to Mrs Garvie-Brown.

'You wanted me to come. Well, here I am. I came because I wanted to explain about that cheque I tore up. That's all. Thank you—I'm sure you meant well. Good-bye.'

That was the sum of it. Only other people never gave you the chance to say no more and no less than was necessary. They involved you in explanations and complexities. They wanted to do a good deal of talking themselves.

They took up your time. It was never much use to plan in advance what you wanted to say to anyone.

Mrs Garvie-Brown lived near the Moray Place end of the street. Her name, on a small brass plate on the door, was almost worn away by years of polishing. Luke rang the door-bell, then saw that the door was ajar. After waiting a minute or two and hearing no approaching footsteps, he rang again, waited, then tentatively pushed the door further open.

Inside it was not at all as the distinguished appearance of the house had led him to expect. There was nothing there but a forbidding, steep, stone staircase. The steps were bare, their edges worn away by what, he supposed, must be nearly two centuries of footsteps. They looked grim and unwelcoming. And he found that they simply went up and up, between walls painted a dingy cream, with no doors opening on to them and looking as if they led to some dreary office, or perhaps were the emergency back-stairs of a public building.

He had climbed up two floors before he found any signs of domestication. Then, on a small landing, a few pot-plants were clustered on a bench under a window. Then, on the landing above that, there was a door, gaily painted a pale blue. The sudden brightness of it, after the starkness of the stairs, was as surprising as they had been after the fine façade of the house.

There was a bell beside the door. Luke had reached out to press it when he realized that this door too was open and that someone inside had been watching him climb.

As he paused, the door opened wider and he saw a girl.

She said, 'These stairs take it out of you, don't they? Are you from Mollison's? They said they'd send someone this morning about the books, but I'm afraid Mrs Garvie-Brown's gone out. I think I can tell you what she wants, though. Come in.'

She stood aside to let him enter.

Staying where he was, Luke said, 'I'm not from Mollison's. And I came to see Mrs Garvie-Brown herself. It's a personal matter. Perhaps I'd better come back later.'

'Oh, she won't be long. I'd come in, if I were you. No need to climb those stairs twice in a morning.'

She was about twenty-five, rather tall, rather bony, with an elongated, abrupt kind of elegance, in spite of the grimy jeans and man's shirt that she was wearing. Her hair was a gleaming shade of red and fell straight to her shoulders, curling up there in a soft, loose wave. She had grey eyes and a long, narrow face which perhaps would be craggy when she was older, but which for the present still looked smooth and appealing, in spite of the strong bones under the skin.

'Who are you, if you're not from Mollison's?' she asked.

'Who are Mollison's?'

'The bookshop.' Seeing that this conveyed nothing to him, she added, 'In South College Street. They're sending someone to go through my grandfather's books and advise Mrs Garvie-Brown about selling them.'

Luke's face told her that this still meant nothing to him.

'Don't you know Edinburgh?' she said.

'I arrived here for the first time in my life yesterday afternoon,' he said, 'and I haven't got around much so far.'

'Then who are you?'

'My name's Luke Latimer.'

He watched her face for any sign of recognition of his name, but saw only a faintly puzzled blankness.

She said, 'And you want to see Mrs Garvie-Brown about a personal matter?'

'Yes.'

'Well, you'd better come in, hadn't you?'

'Thank you.'

He walked forward into the hall and she closed the door behind him.

It was as if he had walked from one world into another.

Outside was that stonily bleak staircase. Inside was a lofty, beautifully proportioned hall, with tall doors opening off it and with another staircase, with a finely wrought-iron balustrade, mounting gracefully to the floor above. There was a complete house up here, not merely the flat that he had expected. And the tallboy in the hall and the little damask-covered sofa and the embroidered sampler on the wall and the fine, gilt-framed mirror all looked as if they might have been placed there by the first owners of the house, when Heriot Row had just been built as part of a New Town that was still truly new.

The girl led Luke into a big room that looked out over the brown and gold of the gardens below. The room, like the hall, was lofty, with the perfect proportions and the wonderful simplicity with which no building since that period has been able to compete. There was a marble fireplace, very finely carved with the lightest of flower-garlands. There was some delicate plasterwork along the cornice. The room was both grand and homely at the same time, beautiful to the eye and yet easy to live with.

Apart from that, it was chaos.

The carpet had been rolled up into a great sausage at one end of the room, leaving the floorboards bare. The curtains had apparently just been taken down from the windows and were in a crumpled pile on the floor. Sofas and armchairs had been stripped of their decent loose covers and stood revealed in their dismal, stained, patched and unmatched nakedness. A china cabinet, with its glass doors open, was empty. Pictures had been taken down from the walls, leaving unfaded oblongs on the wallpaper, and were stacked together, leaning against the legs of a table. A tall step-ladder, no doubt needed to take down the pictures and the curtains, stood gauntly in the middle of the room.

'I'm sorry about the mess,' the girl said. 'As you can see,

Mrs Garvie-Brown's flitting. I've just come in to help her pack and so on. Can you find anywhere to sit?'

She perched herself on the arm of a chair, the seat of which was occupied by a big crystal chandelier.

Luke remained standing, just inside the door.

'Is Mrs Garvie-Brown your grandmother?' he asked.

'No, she's my step-father's step-mother—one of them —so to speak,' she answered.

'*One* of them?' he said.

'The only one living, actually.'

'One of them,' he repeated. 'That means—let me think —it means that your step-father's father, or perhaps it was his mother, married twice and Mrs Garvie-Brown's the second wife—? Is that it?'

'That's very nearly right,' she said, 'except that my step-father's father—let's just call him my grandfather—was a very marrying man. He married four times. At first I think it rather shocked people, but by the time he died people had taken to calling him a wonderful old man. And my step-father is the son of his third wife. So I think of myself as having had three step-grandmothers, one of whom is the Mrs Garvie-Brown you want to see. She outlived him, like Catherine Parr. I've always had an admiration for Catherine Parr, haven't you? The only one of Henry's six wives to pull it off and outlive the old bastard. I admire Christina too.'

'*Four* wives!' Luke exclaimed with a chill prickle going up his spine. 'You did say four?'

'Yes, I know it's a rather liberal allowance, but not by any means unique. I suppose he was just very dependent on women.'

'And did they all die, or were there any divorces?'

'Oh, they all died.'

'What of?'

'This and that.' She looked at him curiously. 'What extraordinary questions you ask.'

42

'They didn't all die the same way?' he went on.

'No, one of them fell off a bicycle and cracked her skull on the kerb. And one committed suicide. She threw herself out of a window. And my grandmother, the one I think of as my real one, because she was the mother of my stepfather, who's the only father I can remember, died of gastro-enteritis."

'Gastro-enteritis! Oh God!" Luke pressed his hands to his temples. 'God help us!'

'Is something the matter?' the girl asked, a shade of worry appearing on her cool, fine-drawn face.

'But he's dead now, isn't he?' Luke said. 'There's no question of it, is there? He's safely dead and buried.'

'He's been dead for thirty years, Mr Latimer. I don't actually know about being buried. He left his body to the Infirmary for dissection. But I believe that when you do that they do have to put you more or less together in the end and give you Christian burial, so I expect it's all right to say he's buried. You do ask odd questions, you know. You aren't a detective, are you?'

Luke started. 'No, oh no. No, I'm not. What made you think of that?'

'Only that I know Christina's been in touch with one. None of us knows why, and it's very strange. It isn't in the least like her. We've all been wondering what she's up to.'

'All of you—you and the rest of your family?'

'Yes. You see, we're all very fond of her, and we've been rather worried about her recently. For one thing, she's got a bad heart and oughtn't to go on climbing all these awful stairs. That's why we persuaded her to move in the first place. She's coming to live in a bungalow next door to us at Blackhope. That's a village in East Lothian. And my father's a doctor, so it ought to work perfectly. And she seemed to want to come when we got it fixed up for her. She seemed awfully glad, and very grateful to my

43

mother for finding the bungalow for her. Sorry, of course, in a way, to be leaving this place, where she's lived for such ages, but even she admitted she couldn't cope with the stairs. And then—I don't know—something happened, and she got this detective. It's odd, isn't it? You're sure —I mean, you're really not the detective? It isn't just that you don't think you ought to tell me?'

He shook his head. 'I'm just what the detective found.'

He found himself wondering if she talked like this to every stranger who came to the house, the man who came to service the vacuum cleaner, the man who came to read the gas meter, the man who sold brushes. Or was there some special quality in himself that had evoked it? During these last few months of working for Mrs Doubtfire he had often wondered at the astonishing loquacity of clients and had not yet solved the problem of how much he brought it on himself.

The girl was staring at him now as if she had only just begun to see him. 'Why was he looking for you?'

'If I knew, I think it's quite probable I shouldn't be here,' he said. 'As it is—well, I don't think I ought to wait any longer. I'm sorry to have missed Mrs Garvie-Brown, but I think I'd better go.'

'Why?'

She had been fiddling with some of the crystals of the chandelier in the chair. They tinkled softly as she let them drop.

'Well, I—' The reason, of course, was all those step-grandmothers, who, like his own grandmother, might so easily have been murdered. For the accident to the first could have been brought about deliberately. The suicide of the second could have been caused by a smart push in the small of the back. And gastro-enteritis can be confused with poisoning by arsenic . . . 'I shouldn't have come here without an appointment,' he said. 'She isn't expecting me.

44

I'll telephone later and find out when it's convenient for me to come.'

'Only you won't,' the girl said. 'I don't know what it is, but something's put you off. Something I've said. You don't mean to telephone . . . Oh, there she is now, so you can't run away. That's a good thing, I'm sure, since she seems to have gone to a good deal of trouble to find you.'

Getting up quickly, the girl went past Luke into the hall, from which the sound had just come of the click of a key in the latch.

'There's someone here to see you, Christina,' she said. 'Mr Latimer.'

A slightly breathless voice responded, 'Mr Latimer—ah!' The breathlessness could have been caused by all those stairs, or else by a sudden excitement. A small, very erect woman advanced to meet Luke.

He guessed her age as about seventy. Her pointed face was finely wrinkled. Her hair was white. Her thinness, her narrow wrists and ankles and slender neck, made her look brittle. Yet there was a contradictory look of toughness about her as well, coming from some quality inside her. She wore a suit of a soft, chestnut-coloured tweed, a little out-dated but with a look about it which made even Luke able to recognize it as having been expensive. Her handbag and her high-heeled shoes, he thought, were real crocodile, not the plastic variety. She was carrying a string bag full of groceries.

'I'm so sorry I was out when you arrived, Mr Latimer,' she said. She held out a small hand to him, which felt in his like the fleshless claw of a bird. The heavy, old-fashioned rings on it bit into his palm. 'I've just been doing the messages.'

What messages, he wondered. Had she a habit of going out, sending mad letters to other people besides him? He had not yet learnt that doing the messages is simply Scots for doing the shopping.

There was a slight flush on her cheeks, but her blue eyes were calm and observant. Calm and surely very sane. Not that you can ever tell, he thought. So long as you feel normal to yourself, there is a good chance that you will seem so to other people until they get to know better.

'If I've come at a bad time . . .' he began.

'Not at all!' she interrupted crisply. 'But you must forgive this disorder. As you can see, I'm flitting in a few days' time, and in more than thirty years in one house it's terrible to discover how many useless articles one has accumulated. I've never been good at throwing things away. I always think the day will come when the most unlikely object will have its uses. But I'm moving into a small bungalow outwith the town and I really find myself compelled to get rid of a great many of my possessions. Vanessa —' she turned to the girl—'perhaps you would be so kind as to make us some coffee. I'm sure Mr Latimer would like some and I could certainly enjoy a cup myself.'

The girl gave a sardonic grin at being so abruptly got rid of, but answered, 'Yes, of course.'

As she went out Mrs Garvie-Brown went on, 'Vanessa has been very kind, coming in to help me with sorting through my rubbish and advising me how to get rid of it. I don't know how I should have managed without her. My late husband's books, for instance. He was Professor of Semeiotics at the University. Duncan Garvie-Brown. I don't suppose the name means anything to you, but he was considered a very distinguished man in his day.'

'*Duncan* Garvie-Brown?' Luke said, the shivery feeling returning.

'Oh, you've heard of him?' The look that she gave him was sharp and questioning. 'It's so unusual nowadays. Even the subject itself is out of date. It used to be in the Faculty of Medicine, but now it's actually an Arts subject, vaguely attached, I believe, to Linguistics. But all that sort of thing is over my head. I'm afraid I was never able to share my husband's intellectual interests, although I worked so closely with him for so long. I was his secretary for twenty years. Now please sit down. If you would move that chandelier, that chair is comfortable.' She sat down herself on a straight-backed chair which was islanded in the middle of the uncarpeted floor. 'Now let me say quickly, before Vanessa returns, that it was very kind of you to come. It was more than I expected. You do not understand, I imagine, why I set Mr Arne to find you. Nor do the rest of my family, and I do not wish them to do so. Not that any of them are actually my own family, except by marriage. Yet in a sense we belong together, like a clan. They are as good to me as if I were a blood relation. But I have not confided in them about my search for you and I do not wish to do so. You understand that? I should be very grateful if you would say nothing to any of them about having been found by Mr Arne.'

Luke moved the chandelier and sat down.

'I'm afraid I've already told your grand-daughter—your step-grand-daughter—that I was,' he said. 'But I don't think it mattered much. I discovered she already knew you'd employed a detective, and she told me the rest of your family did too.'

She clicked her tongue, 'Dear, dear, that's very unfortunate. I wonder how they could have found out. Well, never mind. What I want at the moment, Mr Latimer, is an opportunity to get to know you a little better. It's unfortunate that I can't ask you to stay here, as I would most gladly do in other circumstances, but as you can see for yourself, the house is barely habitable, even by me. If you would allow me, however, to take a room for you in a hotel—'

'Mrs Garvie-Brown,' Luke broke in with determination, 'please let me explain. I'm not staying. I'm going back to London this afternoon. I only came to see you because I wanted to tell you in person that I don't want to be drawn into anything that's got anything to do with my grandmother. I've had to live with that murder in the background all my life and I've had enough of it. It hasn't been pleasant. And it was somehow because of that murder that you wanted to see me, wasn't it? I haven't got that wrong?'

She hesitated, fiddling with her rings as she looked down at her hands.

'No, you are right,' she said quietly, 'there is a certain connection.'

'I also came because, having torn up the cheque you sent me—inadvertently,' he added hurriedly as she looked up swiftly with an expression of distress in her eyes, 'I wanted to explain to you that I hadn't cashed it and didn't intend to do so. And that's all, I think.'

'Please, Mr Latimer.' She had gone on looking at him, and the distress in her eyes had become a pain so intense that it made them brilliant. 'I haven't meant to cause you any worry. I've been foolish, I realize. I should have explained myself more fully in the first place. And now I can't, because Vanessa will be in with the coffee in a moment, and I don't want her to hear what I feel is so important to say to you. But if only you would stay for a day or two—out of kindness to me—for no other reason—please.'

Her voice trembled a little.

Luke was never much good at withstanding a direct appeal. To say 'No,' always seemed to leave an unpleasant after-taste behind it. He hesitated, and knew, as he did so that he was lost.

'Please,' she repeated.

'Well, just until tomorrow then,' he said.

'Good, then you'll stay.' Her voice was crisp again. 'And perhaps this afternoon—no, not this afternoon. Mollison's are sending someone about the books sometime today, and I said I'd be at home. But tomorrow morning I'm going out to the bungalow to check on what the plumber's supposed to have done, and I could call for you with the car and drive you out—not an interesting drive, but beautiful when you get there—and we could talk quite privately. And then perhaps we could call in on Frances—that's Vanessa's mother, who's my next-door neighbour out there—and get her to give us lunch. And I expect Kenneth, her husband, will be there, and as it's a Sunday, she might even get some of the others, just to oblige me.'

'Others?' Luke said, alarmed. He felt as if tentacles out of murky depths were wrapping themselves about him and beginning to suck him under the surface of reality.

'Yes, Charles—that's Lord Mooney—and Lucille and Casper. Lucille and Casper are the children of my husband's first wife, and Charles is Lucille's husband. Well, we'll see. Perhaps it would be better to leave all that till later. In any case, I'll call for you with the car and we'll drive out to Blackhope. Where are you staying?'

He told her and she said, 'About ten-thirty, then? And now here's Vanessa with the coffee, so we'll change the subject, shall we? Thank you, Vanessa, my dear, that coffee smells delicious. I don't know why it is that you make it so much better than I do. I'm sure I make it in exactly the same way as you. I'm quite ready for a cup of nice hot coffee myself. I thought there was quite a nip in the air and this house, in the state it's in, is as cold as charity.'

In no time at all they were all talking about the Edinburgh climate and whether or not Luke found it noticeably colder than London.

Vanessa smiled very slightly, but on the whole co-operated well in the pretence that there was nothing that needed explaining about his visit. A nice girl, he thought. She had a vivid, amused sort of face. She looked intelligent. If he had to stay on, he would not mind seeing more of her.

49

Afterwards he had a lunch of ham rolls and beer in a pub that he passed as he made his way back to Princes Street. In the way of Scottish pubs the place was under-heated and smelled of stale beer, and the beer was taste-less and gassy. But the stout, Irish barmaid was friendly and the rolls were crisp and fresh.

Sitting over them, Luke reflected that even now he could escape. He need not telephone. He need not write. He could, as he had intended earlier, simply fetch his suitcase from the hotel and catch the afternoon train back to London. And thereafter, whatever letters came, he could maintain unbroken silence. Surely then even Mrs Garvie-Brown, hell-bent as she was on drawing him into the web of her mysterious problems, would give up.

But the trouble was, he had said that he would stay. Besides, he had taken a liking to her.

Pushing his way out through the swing doors of the pub into the street, he went to a public telephone, rang up Good Neighbours, Ltd, and left a message for Mrs Doubt-fire that it might be two or three days before he re-turned.

After that he idled about the town, fascinated by the way that splendour so often stood next door to extreme shabbi-ness, and noble elegance to grimily provincial ugliness. He was fascinated too by the number of times he saw the words, 'No Popery', chalked up on walls. Conservative people, the Scots, he thought, still intent on fighting the sad old battles. But he admired the ingenuity and economy with which, here and there, some opponent of the scribbler had gone about rendering his message harmless simply by adding a curved line to each of the p's in 'Popery', which turned his statement into the innocuous and meaningless, 'No Bobery'.

Another white scribble on a smoke-blackened wall read, 'Gossip very unnerving—Who's a fool?—A man wants peace.'

What a bewildering, desperate cry!

Luke, reading it, felt more than a little unnerved. In a sense, it was what that novel that he had been trying to write during the last few months was really about, all five hundred pages of it. And here was a man who could say it in less than a dozen words. Was it time, perhaps, to tear the novel up?

Early in the afternoon, a fine drizzle started to fall, and he took refuge in a cinema and saw a very erotic film which effectively took his mind off Mrs Garvie-Brown and revived his feeling about Stephanie Rackham. But that night, in bed, he thought a great deal about the old woman and about her three predecessors and about his own grandmother, and those three other women who had been murdered, and a mood of such acute uneasiness grew in him that when, for no obvious reason and with a loud crack, the door of the huge wardrobe in his room suddenly opened, he almost hid his head under the bedclothes. It took an effort to make himself turn and look at it.

Of course it was empty, except for the one suit that he had brought with him and had hung up inside it before going to bed. The suit was stirring very gently in one of the mysterious draughts that haunted the room. Limp and headless, it looked like the broken-necked body of a hanged man, stirring in the wind on some wayside gallows.

As a man who had murdered seven women should have been hanged . . .

Luke jumped out of bed, closed the door of the wardrobe with a vicious snap, so that it could not play the same unpleasant trick on him again, returned to bed and soon fell asleep.

But his dreams were haunted by those seven women, and a frantic sense of inherited guilt. That was a feeling that had never troubled him before. It had something to do with the sense that for the first time in his life he was being drawn close to the murderer who was his grandfather, the man whose blood was in his own veins. In the dream it seemed that at any moment he would see the man's face and that it would be just like his own. It was terrifying.

CHAPTER V

NEXT MORNING Mrs Garvie-Brown arrived at Luke's hotel in a red mini, punctual to the minute. She was dressed as she had been the day before, except that, for driving, she wore a pair of worn, flat-heeled, suède shoes. Her high-heeled crocodile shoes protruded from the pocket on the inside of the door. In her crisp voice she said, 'I'm very glad to see you, Mr Latimer. I had half a mind to telephone before coming to make sure you had not left for London. But I see I was right to trust you.'

'I very nearly did go,' he admitted. 'I don't really like any of this, you know.'

'Nor do I, God knows,' she replied. 'But one has a duty to do.'

'Not to me,' he said.

She glanced at him sideways. They were driving along a wide street through a prosperous-looking suburb of the town, grey under a pale blue sky. The northern sun was still low enough in the sky for its glitter to dazzle them as they drove eastward.

'I haven't told you why I wanted to see you,' she said.

'No, but I've an idea I've worked it out,' he answered.

'Is that so? If you have . . .' She paused. 'If you have, it will save me a certain amount of painful explanation. At the same time . . .'

She paused for so long that Luke said, 'Yes?'

'At the same time I am very anxious that none of the family should know any more of this matter than can be helped until I have completely made up my mind as to a proper course of action. I'm upset that they know of my employing that detective. There is no virtue in causing useless uncertainty and distress. There have been so many things to consider. The future of the young people, for instance, Vanessa and Giles. For their sake, would it have been best to do nothing?'

'Who's Giles?' Luke asked.

'Vanessa's cousin. No, that's not right. They aren't related at all, which is fortunate, since they seem to be taking a considerable interest in one another, and I don't approve of marriage between first cousins. Vanessa is not a Garvie-Brown at all, though she has taken the name. She's her mother's child by a former marriage. Relationships in this family, you'll find, are very complicated. Anyway, Giles is a Mooney and the son of my husband's daughter by his first wife. He's thirty, an architect, and said to be very talented. I can't say I admire his style very much. The firm he works for produce those things that look like up-ended match-boxes, all glass and concrete. But people who I'm sure know far more than I about such things tell me they're excellent. And he's a very ambitious young man. To have his career blighted would destroy him. I believe he might never recover. And I suppose you could say the same of his father, Charles, Lord Mooney. The Mooneys live just round the corner from me, in India Street. Charles is one of the Lords of Session—a High Court Judge, in other words. For all I know, if this matter came to light, he might even have to resign. It would be terrible for him. And for Lucille too. She does so enjoy being Lady Mooney —though, of course, strictly speaking, she isn't Lady Mooney at all, she's Mrs Mooney, the other's just a courtesy title. But she does so enjoy being called by it.'

'But why should anything have to come to light?' Luke asked. 'I don't see any necessity.'

She drove for a moment in silence, then said, 'Mr

53

Latimer, you do know what I'm talking about, don't you? We aren't talking at cross purposes?'

'I think we're talking about what you ought to do if it turns out your husband was a murderer,' he said. 'A mass murderer. A Bluebeard. A Landru.'

'How extraordinary!' she exclaimed. 'It escapes me how you can have arrived at the fact so quickly. You must be a very astute young man.'

'Not really, when you remember that I started out knowing that that man Arne was employed to find all the descendants of four women who were murdered. And then there were the things I heard yesterday about your husband and all his wives.'

She clicked her tongue. 'Dear, dear, Mr Arne told you too much. He had no right to do so. The inquiry was supposed to be entirely confidential.'

'I should trust Mr Arne to be confidential, or anything else, rather less than half as far as I could see him.'

'Is that so? Yet he was very well recommended to me by an old friend,' she said. 'I knew nothing, as you may imagine, about how to go about employing a private detective, but I was most anxious not to employ a local firm, for reasons which you will not need to have explained. So I wrote to a friend in London, whose daughter had recently had a divorce, and she gave me the name of Mr Arne.'

'Mrs Garvie-Brown—' Luke hesitated, wondering how to approach tactfully the question that was most on his mind. 'I know that the Bluebeards and the Landrus must sometimes occur in quite ordinary families, but I do wish you'd tell me what's given you this—well, this rather bizarre idea about your husband.'

She answered promptly, 'No, Mr Latimer, that is something that I do not mean to tell you—or anyone else, if I can help it.'

'After all,' he said, 'to have the idea come to you after thirty years . . . Or have you known all the time?'

'Certainly not. What do you take me for?'

'I'm not sure. It's all so strange. What sort of man was he?'

'To me, the kindest, most considerate man imaginable. I was his secretary, I think I told you, for twenty years, so I should know. He was moody, of course, but so are most gifted people. He was subject to fits of acute depression. But they were more than made up for by his gaiety and warmth when he was in good spirits.'

'Then doesn't it seem probable that—well, that whatever's given you this idea about him—is completely misleading? That his wives all died natural deaths, and that there's no reason to connect him with those murders in London?'

As he said it, Luke was remembering that many murderers had been excellent husbands and friends, and sometimes kindness itself while they were in the very act of administering the cup of poison.

'No,' she said again. They were passing along a road of dreary little one-story miners' cottages, with slag-heaps in the background. In spite of the sunshine and the blue sky and the robust-looking children playing in the road, it was a mournful scene. 'I wish I were able to entertain even a suspicion of doubt. If I were, if the proof were not too conclusive to be ignored, I should probably have done nothing. But as it is . . . After all, I have a conscience, Mr Latimer, or I like to think I have, and if the truth is that I have been living in luxury all these years on what rightfully belongs to you, and which you were deprived of in a peculiarly atrocious manner, I don't believe I could rest until I had made amends.'

'But isn't there a time-limit to that sort of thing?' Luke said. 'Twenty years, or something like that? I'm sure there

55

is. I'm sure no one has any legal claim on you now.'

'A legal claim is not always the same as a moral claim. But as it happens, one of my problems at the moment is that I don't even know the legal position. And though of course we have the very best of legal knowledge in the family, Charles is the last person I would wish to consult. And to go to a lawyer myself and ask him a question of this sort, even if I called it a hypothetical question, might easily make him think some very strange things about me. Don't you think so? And because of my relationship to Charles and the others . . . Well, it would be a pity if unfortunate rumours were to circulate in Edinburgh.'

'Then don't you think, for everybody's sake, it would be best to let the whole thing drop?' Luke said. 'I can't see myself that there'd be anything immoral in doing that.'

'Not yet. I can't let it drop yet,' she said. 'Perhaps in the end I shall do so, but first I must make sure that I've done everything that must in decency be done. So I've been wondering since yesterday if you would help me. You impress me, if I may say so, as intelligent and trustworthy, and your advice to me to let the matter drop shows that you are not influenced overmuch by consideration of your own advantage. I think you are just the person I need.'

He shook his head discouragingly. 'You should watch it, Mrs Garvie-Brown. You thought Gilbert Arne was trustworthy.'

'On the advice of a trusted friend.' She was not to be easily shaken. She had a high opinion, he realized, of her own shrewdness. Through twenty years as a secretary and thirty as a widow, she had acquired the habit of making independent judgments and acting independently, and it was now a habit not to be broken. 'Now if you were to go to a lawyer for me,' she said, 'and put the position to him—'

'As a hypothetical question?'

'Yes, hypothetical, of course. You might say—oh, perhaps that you were writing a novel and needed the information for it.'

'I *am* writing a novel.'

'Splendid. Then you'd know just how to put it.?'

'Only it isn't that kind of novel.'

'I can't see that you'd be unjustified in concealing that fact.'

'Well, I've one or two friends in London who are solicitors. Perhaps if I put it to them as something to do with a novel they wouldn't be too annoyed with me for wasting their time.'

'Oh, a London lawyer would be no use at all,' she said decisively. 'The law of Scotland is totally different from that of England. So few of the English seem to know that. They've heard of our verdict of not proven, but that's about all they know about us. They don't realize that the basic principles of the law are different and that when it comes to such matters as property and inheritance it's particularly important to get your advice here on the spot. But there's no problem about that. I can give you the name of an excellent solicitor, who in fact handles all my business for me, and as you would be a stranger to him, you would simply have to take care not to mention that you came from me.'

'And what you want me to say is—let me see if I've got it straight. I'm to say, suppose a woman, a woman of high principles and tender conscience, somehow discovers that her husband, who was always regarded as a pillar of respectability and who's been dead a long time, was in fact a mass-murderer, killing off several wives as well as several other women he'd married bigamously, all for gain and becoming quite rich in the process, what legal obligation would there be on the one woman who'd managed to outlive him to return to the descendants of the others the wealth she'd inherited from him?'

'Perfect,' she said. 'Since no one has a right to money acquired as the result of a crime. You put it so well. Only it's a little more complicated than that.'

'*More* complicated?'

'I haven't inherited very much myself, you see,' she said. 'I am very well provided for, with an ample income, but the capital, on my death, will all go to my husband's children. So they are the ones who would suffer most if that money, as well as what they inherited from their father directly at the time of his death, turned out never to have been legally his.'

Luke crossed and uncrossed his long legs in the little car.

'Just who are they?' he asked. 'I'm not at all clear about that yet.'

'There's Lucille Mooney,' she said, 'whom I've been telling you about. And there's her brother Casper. He's the present Professor of Semeiotics at the University, like his father, and very like him in some other ways. And there's their half-brother, Kenneth, Vanessa's stepfather, who's a doctor out at Blackhope. And they're all accustomed to wealth, apart from the rewards their professions have brought them. You understand why I must move with caution.'

'And there are Giles and Vanessa,' Luke said. 'I suppose I shall get them sorted out in time.'

'You should,' she said, 'since in a sense they're all members of your own family. As a matter of fact, one has only to look at you to recognize that. There's the strongest family resemblance.'

They had left the mining district behind and entered Musselburgh, which advertises itself on a roadside sign, rather complacently, as 'The Honest Town'. Once it had an identity of its own, but now has been engulfed by the suburbs of Edinburgh. They drove up its wide main street, then alongside a race course, with a shimmering glimpse of the Firth of Forth beyond it, then turned at a roundabout on to a road running along the edge of the coast.

It was a dreary stretch of coast at this point, its beach blackened by cinders and drifts of mussel shells and with the looming bulk of a huge power station ahead. But across the Firth rose the hills of Fife, which today, in the clear, morning sunshine, were the softest of blues, with a dim shadowy line of higher hills behind them.

'The hills are nice, aren't they?' Mrs Garvie-Brown said after a little while. 'They're a different colour every time you look at them. Once I saw them a brilliant pink. It was winter and they were covered with hoar frost and the sunshine somehow turned them a wonderful rose-colour. The windows of my bungalow look straight out over the Firth. I've always wanted to live in a house with a view of the sea and now at last I've got one.'

'You don't mind moving, then,' Luke said. 'I'd have thought that leaving a house like the one you've got would be quite a wrench.'

'I can't wait to go! It's not just that the stairs are so dreadful, but it's always been far too grand for me. You've only seen it in a fearful mess, but I assure you, when everything was in order it was quite impressive. And I'm a simple person. I like simple things. Now we've talked enough about sordid matters for the moment. Shall we just enjoy the lovely morning? And tell me more about yourself. Tell me about your work.'

So Luke talked to her about Good Neighbours, Ltd, and Mrs Doubtfire. He talked about all the amusing experiences that he had had while he had been working for her. He even talked about his novel. He talked about anything that he could think of to keep the mind of Mrs Garvie-Brown off the subject that obsessed her, while the houses thinned out and came to an end, and the pebbled beach became clean, with low sand-dunes, covered with grey-green clumps of sea-buck-thorn, between it and the road, and herring-gulls balanced delicately on the ripples, or walked with cautious steps among the sea-wrack.

The tide was low and the waters of the Firth were almost still. Here and there a flat brown rock, protruding above the surface, looked like a seal lolling at the water's edge. They passed one or two villages. Then presently a signpost pointed to the village of Blackhope. Mrs Garvie-Brown turned the car inland along a narrow road that led into the village. Her bungalow was almost at the end of the road. The garden gate stood open and a straight drive ran down to a car-port, which had obviously only just been built on to the not very modern bungalow. It was a square box of a building, painted white, with a slate roof and a pale yellow front door and window-frames. The garden between the road and the bungalow was long and narrow and had little in it besides lawns and rose-beds. Plenty of the roses were still in bloom. Mrs Garvie-Brown exclaimed with pleasure when she saw them.

'Look—roses of my own to pick as soon as I move into the house! You don't know how I'm looking forward to the idea of having a garden—though of course looking after it is going to be a problem. But Frances says she thinks she can get hold of a man for me, and anyway, she and Kenneth have promised to help. And Vanessa too, when she's here. She's wonderfully kind, that girl. She's got a really nice nature. She's so straightforward and considerate and she'll always help anybody.'

'Doesn't she live out here, then?'

Luke had had a vague hope that the red-haired girl might appear at the bungalow today.

He could see her parents' home through the trees, standing in a large garden. It was a grey stone house, perhaps once a farmhouse, that looked much older than the others along this road, most of which looked as if they had been built in the between-wars period.

'No, she's got a flat of her own in Morningside, not far from your hotel,' Mrs Garvie-Brown said. She had driven the mini into the car-port and turned off the engine. 'She teaches art at Quinan's—that's a big girls' school there. She's just begun this term. I believe she enjoys her independence. I certainly did mine, when I was her age. But she comes home quite often.' Getting out of the car, she glanced at her watch. 'I've just time to show off my house to you, then we'll go next door. Did I mention that, as I hoped, Frances is giving us lunch. And all the others will be there.'

She led the way to the yellow door.

The bungalow had nothing remarkable about it, but it had all been pleasantly redecorated, had new central heating, the newest of kitchen and bathroom fittings, and smelled of fresh paint. She investigated some of the new plumbing, then said, 'And this is my sitting-room.' She had left it to the last and now threw the door open with a little gesture of pride. 'Don't you envy me?'

For the first time Luke realized why she was not too sad at giving up her home in Heriot Row. This room had a wide bay window, overlooking a strip of garden, all grass, except for a few trees, birches, hawthorns and wild cherries, which ended at a low stone wall, beyond which stretched the smooth, well-cared-for green of a golf-course. And beyond the golf-course was the sea. Not a house was in sight. The angle of the window was such that all the other houses along the road were invisible. Even the road along the shore was invisible, for it was sunk well below the level of the golf-course. You could dream, in this room, that the house stood by itself on a lonely island, with the mainland far off over there, where the dim blue hills of Fife, with the two blunt peaks of the Lomonds, rose out of the water.

If you enjoyed that sort of dream, which Luke, a very

61

urban type, honestly never had very much. All the same, the view was lovely. He said so and Mrs Garvie-Brown beamed at him.

'Now we'll go round to Frances,' she said. 'We could go through the garden, but we may as well take the car, as we shall want it for driving back into Edinburgh. Besides, I've left my shoes in it. I hope Frances has a drink waiting for us.'

She led the way out to the car.

'How have you explained me?' Luke asked as they drove up the drive, then a hundred yards along the road and down another drive to the grey stone house next door.

'I have not explained you at all,' she said, 'beyond saying that you are a young friend of mine from London. I very seldom find it necessary to explain my actions to other people. But perhaps I should explain Frances to you, in case she's in one of her moods. She is a very kind and charming woman, but she feels that in marrying a Garvie-Brown she has come down in the world. Her father was Governor of one of those African countries, and her first husband was in the Army with a very promising career ahead of him, but he was killed in a car-crash and left her quite without means. Nevertheless, in marrying a country doctor she felt definitely she was lowering her standards. Sometimes I think she is not very happy. And of course, it is hard on Kenneth, though some of it is his fault. He is a little on the mean side. Now I hope you will feel able to behave as if this were a perfectly ordinary visit.'

'But everyone will know that it isn't.'

'I think, for the moment, that is of secondary importance.'

She stopped the car, changed her shoes and got out.

As she and Luke walked towards the house, the door opened and a woman came out on to the steps, a woman of about forty-five, with the same reddish hair as Vanessa, the same tall, rangy build, and features sufficiently like hers that the two of them could hardly have been anything but mother and daughter. But the mother's face was taut and nervous. As she embraced Mrs Garvie-Brown, brushing her cheek against hers in that substitute for a kiss with which so many women greet one another, she looked straight at Luke. It was a hard, wary look, far from welcoming. A moment later, however, she was smiling at him and shaking his hand.

'I'm so glad you've had such a nice morning for the drive out here,' she said. 'Of course, autumn is quite the best time of the year in Scotland. The people who pour in here in August don't know what they're missing. But I do hope you aren't expecting anything much in the way of lunch, because there's only the usual dreary old Sunday joint and apple tart and some mousetrap. I'm never any good at whipping up exquisitely interesting little meals for people at short notice.' She had a high rattle of a voice, her words very clipped and rapid.

'My dear, you always do everything wonderfully,' Mrs Garvie-Brown answered. 'And I'm sorry about the short notice. It's very good of you to have collected the family for me. I did so want Mr Latimer to meet them while he was in Edinburgh.'

Offering no explanation of why she had wanted this, as she had said that she would not, she went into the house, followed by Luke and Mrs Kenneth Garvie-Brown, whose look, as soon as the elder woman's back was turned, lost all its welcome and again became hard with suspicion.

CHAPTER VI

THE JUDGE, the professor, the doctor, with wives and children, were all gathered in a drawing-room on the first floor, all with drinks in their hands.

For a startling moment, as Luke walked in on them, he had an astounding sensation of having walked into a room full of mirrors. It came from meeting his own greenish eyes looking back at him from so many different places, from seeing reflections of his own thin face and long bony limbs arrested there before him. But the feeling was gone in an instant. To see resemblances between the members of one's own family, or among people whom one knows well, is hard enough and to see a resemblance between anyone else and oneself is nearly impossible. After that one flash of recognition the Garvie-Browns and the Mooneys became simply a group of strangers to Luke.

If they resembled anyone or anything, he thought, it was a herd of deer, all with their heads held high on their slender necks, turned to look apprehensively in the direction of an approaching danger. The room was full of alarm and hostility.

It was not a room that appealed to him. Its high ceiling had been painted turquoise and the plaster cornice showily gilded. The wallpaper simulated crimson damask. The furniture was of the reproduction kind that uneasily hopes to be taken for Regency. The pictures were fashionably abstract. It was a somewhat shabby room too, without being comfortable, and did not speak of much wealth, although the doctor, like the other descendants of Duncan Garvie-Brown, Luke supposed, could not be without ample means.

But the windows, like Mrs Garvie-Brown's, looked straight over the green sweep of the golf-course at the sea and the distant hills. These were less clearly defined than they had been only a little while ago. A faint haziness that seemed to rise from the water made them appear both farther away and higher than they had before. Luke began to understand what she had meant when she said that they were different every time you looked at them.

She was responding brightly now to the greetings of her family, greetings that had been momentarily delayed by the long look that each of them had given Luke, a look of shock in which, no doubt, they too had been recognizing the family resemblance.

'Isn't this delightful?' Mrs Garvie-Brown was saying. 'It isn't often so many of us manage to meet like this. I expect the men will be golfing later. And now . . .'

She turned to Luke. The introductions began.

Lady Mooney.

Lucille Mooney was a slender, dignified woman of about sixty, thin-faced, sharp-featured, green-eyed, and if her hair was palest gold instead of dark like Luke's, it was not because she had been born with it that colour. She was unlike him, however, in having a singular lack of animation in her face. It looked set and empty. She was wearing a very plain, expensive-looking dress of lime-green jersey, a necklace of small pearls and a remarkable number of diamond rings on her long, thin hands. When she held one of them out to Luke, it felt as limp in his as a filleted fish. But, the thought crossed his mind, one of the more expensive sorts of fish, a Dover sole, for instance.

Lord Mooney.

Not a descendant, of course, of Duncan Garvie-Brown's but perhaps not wholly unlike him, except in his colouring, which was fair and florid. Perhaps it was a case of Lucille having been attracted by a man who reminded her of her father, for the judge was tall and lean, with strong, fine-drawn features that would look strikingly handsome under his judge's wig. Apart from that, he looked a friendly, cheer-

65

ful man, who probably enjoyed his own jokes and would easily be induced to drink more than he could quite carry. Luke was inclined to think that perhaps he had reached this stage already, for as he shook hands with Luke, Lord Mooney gave him a direct stare in the face, then laughed abruptly, without explaining the laughter, and went on chuckling while the introductions continued.

Professor Garvie-Brown.

Very like his sister, Lady Mooney, slender and pale, but without her elegance. A vague, lost-looking, untidy man, with fine skin, unusually sharply lined, drawn tightly over the bony structure of his face. The green eyes of the family looked oddly young and innocent behind his spectacles.

Dr Garvie-Brown.

He had been pouring out drinks for the new arrivals while Christina Garvie-Brown had been making the introductions. He was shorter and more broadly built than his half-brother and sister and he had very little of his dark hair left. There was a certain smoothness about him, too, which the others lacked, which came from plumper cheeks and an automatic sort of professional blandness. If he had been startled by Luke's Garvie-Brown features, he had masked it better than the others, perhaps as he would have masked his thoughts when a patient began to describe what were easily recognizable as mortal symptoms.

It was as Luke accepted a glass of gin and tonic from the doctor and met his reserved, diagnostic glance, that it occurred to him that no doubt it was as a sort of disease that this whole family regarded him, a strange and sudden growth that none of them could quite account for, and whether it would turn out to be benign or malignant, none of them yet knew.

And, of course, there was Vanessa. A very different Vanessa from the girl in jeans and a grimy shirt whom Luke had seen yesterday. She was wearing a well-cut, short, corduroy skirt of a burnt orange colour, with a

66

matching jersey and long jet ear-rings. She had rolled her hair high on her head and had a lot of greenish eye-shadow round her eyes, which made them look enormous.

There was also Giles Mooney, the member of the family who looked least like the others. A promising young architect, Luke remembered. Most obviously promising. If Giles had not been promising as an architect, Luke thought, then he would certainly have been very promising at something else. The look was there, the look of success in his grasp, held like an orb and sceptre. He was about Luke's own age, about the same height and also thin, but fair and high-coloured like his father, with very little Garvie-Brown in him except for that touch of the startled deer in his posture. He was standing by the window and was continuing to eye Luke with more suspicion than any of the others had allowed to remain on their well-bred faces.

Put all those faces together, it struck Luke suddenly, and you would have the face of Duncan Garbury . . .

They had never had any photograph of Duncan Garbury at home. There had been one of Luke's grandmother, looking vaguely pretty in a picture hat and tulle scarf, but the man who had killed her had left no likeness behind him. Not surprisingly. Luke, in imagination, had always endowed him with a high, starched collar and fluffy Victorian sidewhiskers. That had seemed appropriate wear for the domesticated kind of murderer that he had been. Actually it was absurd, since the murder had happened in 1924. Duncan Garbury had probably worn plus fours and a soft collar and been clean-shaven. At that time, if he had had any hair on his face, children would have shouted at him, 'Beaver!'

As soon as Christina Garvie-Brown and Luke had their drinks, everyone in the room began to talk about foreign travel, a better subject than the weather for people who do not know what else to talk about, for if it tends to be equally lifeless, it permits more variation. Lord and Lady

Mooney had been to Greece in the summer. They had liked the scenery and the people and the ruins, but not the food or wine. Their son had been to France and had liked the food and wine but remarked with casual arrogance that of course the French people were really the most insupportable in the world. Dr Garvie-Brown and his wife had been nowhere farther than Saint Andrews, because the doctor could not bear to be parted from a golf-course. Professor Garvie-Brown had been to Yugoslavia, had apparently liked nothing and been homesick all the time for his flat in Edinburgh and his evenings in the New Club. Christina Garvie-Brown had spent a month with a friend who had a cottage in Wester Ross and said that she had enjoyed every minute of it.

Luke had to admit that he had been nowhere. He had not had a holiday at all, he said, since he had only just started working in a new job.

'What job?' Vanessa asked.

'Yes, what's your line?' asked Lord Mooney.

For the first time since he had gone to work for Mrs Doubtfire, Luke felt a fearful temptation to say that he was a chartered accountant. It took him quite by surprise. He almost said it before he had had time to think. It would have put him on a level, more or less, with all these professional people. But something, a sense of loyalty to Mrs Doubtfire and to himself, stopped him in time.

'I work for an organization called Good Neighbours,' he said.

'Ah,' Lord Mooney said, looking as if he thought that he ought to appear impressed. 'The Church, of course. Splendid.'

Again, Luke was assailed by temptation, this time simply to leave it at that. But a vision of Mrs Doubtfire's sardonic old eyes dared him to do it.

'Well no,' he said. 'It's a private, strictly profit-making concern. I don't make out the bills myself, but I believe our prices come high. We supply a variety of services. We baby-sit, escort invalids on journeys, look after cats and dogs and canaries while their owners are away, find hotel-rooms, furnished flats and so on, fix you up with au-pair girls, do odd bits of research sometimes for authors who can't get up to London libraries—I rather enjoy that—and advise on almost anything.'

'But that sounds perfectly wonderful,' Lucille Mooney said in a sighing, expressionless voice. 'You aren't think-ing of opening up a branch in Edinburgh, are you? Is that why you've come here? I'll be your first client. I'll use all your services except the research. I shall never write a book. I have no brains.'

'You haven't a canary, either, so don't be an idiot, Lucille,' her sister-in-law Frances snapped at her. Her anxious, wary gaze searched Luke's face. 'That isn't what brought you, is it, Mr Latimer?'

The elder Mrs Garvie-Brown replied for him, 'Since when has one required a reason for coming to Edinburgh, other than to see the city itself?'

'Wise of you not to come in the Festival, anyway,' Pro-fessor Garvie-Brown said. 'People everywhere, all the people from all the foreign countries all over the world whom you least want to meet, turning up and expecting you to enter-tain them. And culture in great gobbets that stick in your throat. A loathsome ordeal. I always go away when it comes round.'

'My worthy Uncle Casper finds everything loathsome except food and drink,' Giles Mooney explained. 'Luckily he can give those all the attention he wants because he's been clever enough to become professor of a subject nobody wants to study. He's got no students, no responsibilities, no worries—except that they keep shifting his department round from one Faculty to another because they can't make up their minds where it'll be least in the way. He's the gifted member of the family, as you can surmise.' Giles had a light tenor voice which revealed education in an English public school, not in the city of his birth.

'You omitted to say that I work harder on more committees in the University than any other man in the place,' Casper Garvie-Brown said. 'Are you staying long, Mr Latimer?'

'I haven't any exact plans,' Luke answered.

'Yet you aren't here on holiday—you said one isn't due to you yet.' Lucille Mooney sounded, in her half-dreamy, distant way, rather as if she were taking part in a guessing game. She was looking out of the window at two golfers strolling past on the far side of the low garden wall. 'And you aren't here on business. How strange.'

'I am not aware that Mr Latimer said he was not here on business,' Christina said tartly. 'He merely said he was not here to open a branch of Good Neighbours, and he is too kind to say that his business, whatever it is, is no business of yours, Lucille.'

'Now don't be horrid to Lucille, Christina,' Lord Mooney said. 'You know she can't help that infernal inquisitiveness of hers. And you don't want to start a row with her and make Mr Latimer think you haven't brought him into a happy family.'

It could have been accidental, the way he had spoken of Luke having been 'brought into' the family.

But do judges, even over their third whisky on an empty stomach before lunch, say things like that accidentally?

Luke had never known a judge before, so he did not know. But he started to wonder how much this man with the slightly drunk, benign, highly intelligent smile, which revealed a most excellent set of dentures, actually knew about his wife's stepmother's reason for bringing Luke to see them. How much did they all know? How much had Gilbert Arne guessed, and how far had he betrayed her to them?

Then again, how much had they always known?

'If you don't like that drink, you haven't actually got to drink it, you know.' It was Vanessa, who had moved up close to Luke in such a way that she stood almost like a shield between him and the rest of the room. She had spoken softly, as if she had decided that it was time for the young people there to show that they had had enough of talking to their elders and now wanted to be left to themselves.

Luke realized that he had been glowering at his drink and had barely touched it.

'It isn't the drink,' he said and swallowed a good deal of it. 'Look, how much do you all know about why I'm really here?'

'Only what you told me—that you're what a detective found for Christina.'

'How do you know about the detective?'

'Christina's friend, Mrs Bayliss, who recommended him to her, told my mother about it.'

'I thought it must be something like that. But hadn't this friend been asked to say nothing?'

'Yes, but she was worried about Christina, you see. She couldn't think why a person like her should need a detective.'

'And so, being a really close and trusted friend, she promptly told everyone in sight what she'd been asked in the strictest confidence.'

'That's nasty,' Vanessa said.

'What she did was nasty.'

'It wasn't, it was to protect Christina. It was so utterly unlike her, don't you see, to employ a private detective to make some strange, secret inquiry for her? She's always been such an open, outspoken sort of person.'

'And you were all a bit afraid, weren't you, of what this inquiry might drag out into the daylight?'

Vanessa's eyes seemed to darken, as some people's do with anger. She took a moment to reply, then, looking down at her drink, she said softly, 'I liked you better when I thought you were the man who'd come from Mollison's about the books.'

'You didn't notice the family resemblance then?'

'Oh, vaguely. But it didn't occur to me that it meant anything. If you'll look around you, you'll see lots of your own sort of face in Edinburgh any day of the week. You aren't at all a remarkable type here.'

'But now you think it does mean something.'

'I suppose it must. Christina wouldn't have had you dug up and brought you here for no reason at all. She's a person who generally has very clear and definite reasons for everything she does.'

'Yet you don't know, you haven't any idea, what this reason is?'

She hesitated briefly. 'Do *you* know what it is?'

He did not answer.

'What is it?' she asked.

'I hope I can prevent you ever finding out,' he said. 'I promise you I'll try.'

'Tell me now.'

'No.'

Dr Garvie-Brown broke in on them then with an offer to top up Luke's drink and Vanessa drifted away to where Giles stood by himself, looking out of the window. They began to talk softly together. No doubt she was reporting the result of her questioning of Luke. He wondered if it had been agreed only by her and Giles that she should try it, or if it had been the whole family who had delegated her to do it.

'Do you golf?' the doctor asked.

'I'm afraid not,' Luke answered.

'Pity, we could have made up a foursome after lunch. A wonderful day for a round. Not that my game's what it should be any more. I get too little practice these days.

72

But I find there's a great deal of pleasure in it, all the same.'

'I thought the Scots were too Sabbatarian for games on Sunday,' Luke said.

'Another English misconception about our country,' said the doctor. 'There's only one day in the year when you really see no one out there on the course, and that's New Year's Day, when everyone's sleeping off the night before. Apart from that, rain or shine, frost or even snow, the game goes on. Of course, fog defeats us—the haar, as we call it here. You really don't play?'

Luke shook his head. 'In England it's a rich man's game.'

'Ah yes, of course. And you live in London, don't you? Are you married, by the way?'

Another inquisition starting, Luke thought.

'No,' he said.

'This job of yours—it's full of interest, I imagine. It must give you insight into the lives of all kinds of different people. But it isn't what you've always done, is it?'

The doctor's bland, amiable face was near to Luke's. Impersonal but searching, the medical gaze tried to diagnose Luke's case.

'No, not always,' Luke admitted.

'If I had to guess, I'd say you were a writer or something like that,' the doctor said.

Luke felt himself colouring at this prompt probing of his secret life. He felt driven at last to say, 'As a matter of fact, I'm a chartered accountant.'

'Really? Somehow, that surprises me. I thought a writer or a musician—I like to guess people's occupations.'

The doctor wandered off to top up someone else's drink, and Luke found himself taken over at once by the doctor's wife.

But Frances did not question him, she only poured out in her swift, crackling tones, her woes at having to live in Blackhope. It would be nice having Christina living next door, she said, because Christina was at least a human being, whereas almost everyone else in the place was practically subnormal, living on golf and coffee mornings and gossip and backbiting.

'And being the doctor's wife, I've got to be so bloody discreet and nice to everyone,' she complained, 'I hardly dare open my mouth. That sort of thing simply doesn't come naturally to me. Sometimes I think I've quite stopped being my real self. Which is an example of what I mean—saying a thing like that to a complete stranger. Do you understand?'

Luke thought that he did. He thought that she was an uncontrolled and unhappy woman, who was venting all the pent-up, irrational pain of living on the place and her neighbours, but who would be equally unhappy wherever else she might go.

He had a disturbing feeling, while she chattered on about herself, that she was making some sort of desperate appeal to him, but he also felt that this had nothing to do with fears concerning the problem of why Christina had brought him here. It was simply the appeal that some kinds of neurotics make hopefully to any stranger. In a few minutes she was disappointed in him and swept the whole party downstairs to lunch.

There the conversation returned to foreign travel. Upstairs they had talked of what they had done during the past summer. Now they talked of their plans for the next. Only Vanessa and Giles did not join in it. They sat side by side and were almost silent.

It was in a short silence which, for no special reason, suddenly fell on everyone, that there came the sound of a shot.

CHAPTER VII

LUKE COULD have sworn it was a shot and that it was in the house, yet no one moved or said anything until Frances abruptly began to swear.

'Damn them!' she shouted. 'Damn them to hell! They've done it again. That's the third this month. I don't know what's happened. And it's in the drawing-room again—I know the sound by now. I'll give them hell for it this time. I won't pretend to be nice about it any more.'

She had got up quickly from the table and made for the door.

'Do wait till after lunch, Frances,' her husband said irritably. 'There's nothing you can do about it now. Sit down. I'll ring up Gillespie presently. He'll send someone round.'

'But it isn't just the windowpane,' she cried. 'There'll be glass all over the room. And however much of it you brush up, there are always bits left behind and they get into the vacuum cleaner and cut the belt to ribbons, and one has to have it repaired again and again, and the golf-club doesn't pay for that, does it? They may pay for the window, but do they pay for my vacuum cleaner?'

She plunged out of the room.

Christina saw Luke looking puzzled.

'A golf ball through one of the windows,' she explained. 'It's the penalty one has to pay here for the beautiful view and I shall have to accustom myself to it too.'

'Does it happen often?' he asked.

Vanessa answered, 'We seem to have epidemics of it. Sometimes it's the wind that makes people hook their shots in here, or sometimes they move the tee to let the grass grow again, and some positions seem to be worse for us than others. I think they must have moved it recently, because we'd been over a year without any trouble, then suddenly it's happened three times in only four weeks.'

'What do you do if you're in the room when it happens?'

'Well, it's rather frightening, it startles one so. But unless one got a bit in one's eye, which hasn't ever happened to any of us, I don't suppose it would do one much damage. But it does make an astonishing mess.'

Frances returned from upstairs with a wild look on her face.

'Yes, it's the drawing-room, and there's glass everywhere!'

'Well, sit down, darling,' said Lucille in her mild monotone. 'We'll all help clear up afterwards. Now let me tell you about the Turkish driver we had on Rhodes, such an amusing man . . .'

Frances ignored her. 'I'm going to ring up that new secretary at the club straight away and I'm going to tell him that this has got to be put a stop to *now*! Not next month, not next year—now! My nerves won't stand much more of it. If it's the position of the tee, he's got to have it moved. And if it's someone doing it on purpose, he's got to find out who it is and make him resign from the club.'

'No one's doing it on purpose,' her husband said wearily. 'It's just bad luck. We'll probably go a couple of years now without it happening again.'

'How do you know? I think it could easily be malice,' she said. 'After all, *three* times! And there's so much destructiveness everywhere nowadays. Isn't there, Charles?' She turned to the judge.

He was sipping his wine and not looking too well pleased with it. 'Oh yes—yes, of course, Frances. But have you any enemies in Blackhope? Any of your coffee-party cronies, for instance, who've heard what you say about them when they aren't there, or some patient of Kenneth's whom he's trying to get off the booze?'

'I'm serious, Charles,' she said violently.

'So am I, my dear, so am I,' he said. 'I'd smash the windows of anyone who tried to get me off drink. Who sells you this stuff, Kenneth?'

'Comes from the village grocer, I believe,' the doctor replied. 'Is there something the matter with it?'

'There are the culprits now,' Giles remarked, as two adolescent boys walked past the garden on the far side of the wall. They did not look at the house, but kept their gaze turned carefully out to sea. 'Do you want me to go out and tackle them, Frances?'

'For God's sake, no!' the doctor said swiftly. 'I'll ring up Gillespie after lunch, and he'll get in touch with Henderson, the joiner, and he'll send a man down later today to repair the window. That's the normal procedure. There's never any difficulty about it.'

'But it's Sunday!' cried his wife. 'He'll never send anyone today, and we'll have to put up with the ghastly draught—'

'Stop it, stop it, everyone!' Casper Garvie-Brown suddenly roared. 'I'm enjoying my lunch. I refuse to have it spoiled by an absurd little incident like a golf ball coming through a window. Sit down, Frances. May I have a little more of that excellent Cheddar, please? One of the things I had against Yugoslavia was the cheese . . .'

Firmly he brought the conversation back to where it had been before the incident of the golf ball.

At first Frances resisted, muttering to herself, while patches of high colour stayed on her cheeks, but gradually she simmered down to normal, and after lunch, under her guidance, a working party was formed to sweep up the glass in the drawing-room. The glass had flown all over the room, mostly in tiny splinters. Yet the golf ball itself had apparently only bounced against the window, and fallen back into the garden. It lay on the lawn below, a few yards from the house, looking like a large, fresh mushroom in the grass.

The sweeping-up went on for some time, yet even when Frances at last conceded that no more could be done, small points of light still shone here and there in the carpet, showing where minute grains of glass were embedded.

'My vacuum cleaner!' she groaned. 'I wonder why we live here, I honestly do.'

'Because you love it, you know you do,' Lucille said.

'*Love* it?' Frances looked genuinely startled. 'God, how wrong one's family and friends can be about one! It's Kenneth who loves it. He can play golf, think golf, talk golf. That's all he's every wanted in life.'

'But you play yourself,' Christina said. 'You play exceptionally well.'

'Because I should drown if I didn't, I should go right under. I've got to be able to meet the people here on their own terms, or I'd blow my brains out. Mr Latimer, wouldn't you blow your brains out if you found yourself condemned for life to a golfing suburb?'

'Not Latimer,' Giles said. 'He would have too many other resources. I should say he's a very resourceful man. Aren't you, Latimer?'

It sounded innocent. Yet there was a gleam of malice in the young man's cool, inquisitive gaze, and he gave a quiet little laugh.

It was followed by silence.

Then the judge and the doctor began to talk of a round of golf. The professor, ignoring everyone, picked up a magazine and with it as ineffective camouflage, settled himself for a sleep in a chair by the fire. Vanessa and Giles decided to go for a walk along the shore, and Vanessa asked Luke to join them. But Christina Garvie-Brown said that it was time for her and Luke to return to Edinburgh, and took him away with her. As they left the house Luke wished that he could remain behind invisibly to hear what was being said about him.

On the drive back into Edinburgh, after a longish silence,

Christina said, 'Well, Mr Latimer, now you've met them. What shall I do?'

'About me?' he asked.

'Yes, and about telling them about the di—' She cut the word off, and Luke, glancing at her, saw horror on her face at what she had nearly said. 'About the evidence I recently discovered concerning my husband's past.'

'Couldn't you destroy the evidence, whatever it is?' Luke said.

'Destroying evidence of a crime is a very serious matter.'

'I should do it without hesitation.'

'Would you really?'

'Yes.'

'I wish I could feel as sure. Perhaps after consulting a lawyer—Well, you are going to see my solicitor for me, aren't you? That may be a great help.'

He stirred uncomfortably in his seat. He had hoped that she had forgotten her desire to consult a lawyer.

'I'm afraid I don't feel altogether happy about the idea,' he said. 'May I think it over?'

'How long would you have to go on thinking?'

'Oh, two or three hours,' he said vaguely. By that time he could be on a train to London, which would, he resolved, be far the best place to be.

'Will you ring me or shall I ring you?'

'I'll ring,' he answered dishonestly.

'Very well,' she said, but there was dissatisfaction in her voice. She did not quite trust him. Delivering him at his hotel, she said, 'You won't forget?'

He said, 'Of course not.'

As soon as she had driven off, he went to the reception desk and asked the clerk to get him a taxi as fast as possible, went up to his room, dumped his suitcase on to the bed, opened it and started packing.

It was not merely because he found the thought of approaching a lawyer with Christina Garvie-Brown's hypothetical question hair-raising. It was the sense he had of having been exposed, all the time that he had been out at Blackhope, to a hostility that he had done nothing to deserve. It was a sickening feeling, and he did not see that he had any obligation to endure any more of it. He tossed his belongings into his suitcase and slammed the lid down on them.

It was only then that he realized that he was not alone in the room. Someone had followed him in and was regarding him from just inside the doorway. A short, stocky figure in a creased grey suit and a tweed overcoat, with a little tweed hat perched high on his massive head.

'Well, well, what a hurry you're in,' Gilbert Arne said. 'They must have got you frightened.'

Fumbling with the catches of the suitcase, Luke said, 'Get out of my way. I'm leaving.'

'Why?' There was chilly amusement in Arne's grey eyes.

'That's my business. What are you doing here?'

'That's *my* business, to borrow a phrase.'

'Why have you been following me around?'

'Is there time to explain, if you're in such a hurry?' Arne advanced into the room, dropped into its one armchair and huddled his coat around him. 'Perhaps you'd tell me just why you're in such a hurry. Where do you think you're going?'

'I want to catch the four o'clock train back to London.'

'Not a chance, boy, not a chance. It doesn't run on Sundays.'

'Damn, I've got a taxi ordered.' All at once feeling futile, helpless and extraordinarily tired, Luke slumped down on the edge of the bed. 'All right, I'll wait till the evening. But I object to being followed around. How did you know where to find me?'

'I have my sources of information.'

'I don't like it.'

'No one ever does. Yet it does no one any harm. Could even do them good sometimes.' Arne brought a packet of cigarettes out of his pocket. 'Smoke?'

'No, thanks.'

'Mind if I do?'

'No, go on.'

'What's the matter anyway? Why are you in this state?'

The words that Luke had seen chalked on a wall the day before sprang to his mind. He raised his voice aggressively and almost shouted them. 'Who's a fool?—A man wants peace!'

'Eh?' The detective looked puzzled. He lit a cigarette, inhaled deeply and let the smoke come dribbling out of his nostrils. 'Say that again.'

'No, it doesn't matter. But I'm a fool. Yes, that's the simple truth. I'm a fool ever to have come here. I can't really remember why I did. Oh yes, I tore up that cheque —My taxi!' He shot up from the bed. 'I'll have to cancel it.'

He raced out of the room and down the stairs.

The taxi had just arrived at the door and Luke had to pay for having summoned it, of course, which made him think with dismay of the expensiveness of this futile visit to Edinburgh. Returning thoughtfully to his room, he lifted the suitcase off the bed, lay down on it, clasped his hands under his head and stared at the ceiling.

Arne waited for a minute or two, then when it appeared that Luke was not going to speak, said, 'I'm not offering any criticism, but in my opinion tearing up cheques is a habit to get out of.'

'Damn you, leave me alone,' Luke said.

'But you've got time now to listen to what I'm doing here,' said Arne. 'Don't you want to know?'

'Not particularly.'

'But I believe we could help each other.'

'I don't want help.'

81

'Oh, come now—'

'Listen!' Luke heaved himself up on to an elbow. 'The only help you've given me so far is to get me involved in an utterly ludicrous and humiliating situation, which I'm getting out of as fast as I can. You've got me involved with a group of people who are all scared sick that I'm a bastard grandson of their old man and that I'm going to exploit it somehow. Me—yes, me! They think I'd do that! They've been looking at me over their drinks and over their lunch with that in their eyes. If they don't think something even worse. I could see it. And I sat there, taking it and not shouting back at them that I didn't want anything to do with them, because I like the old woman who took me there. But I don't like you, and I'm not going to take anything from you, including help.'

' "There," being the house at Blackhope?' Arne said.

'Yes, of course. And they were all there, the judge, the professor, the doctor, the lot. Well, I let them look at me like that because, as I said, I like Mrs Garvie-Brown.'

'Just a minute, just a minute!' The cigarette wobbled between Arne's lips and some ash fell with a soft feathery splash on to his waistcoat. 'It's nothing nowadays having a few illegitimate relations. You'd never be able to put the bite on them for that.'

'Why not? This is Edinburgh, you know, not London.'

'Even in Edinburgh. I expect the illegitimacy rate here is as high as anywhere. A bastard or two would probably just add to the old man's credit.'

'But these are all very respectable citizens, high up in their professions.'

'It won't do. You can get away with anything these days, bastards, sodomy, drugs, everything, except—' A little smile twitched at Arne's tight lips. 'Except, just sometimes, murder.'

Luke swung his feet down to the floor, sitting up quickly and facing the other man squarely. He put his hands on his knees and thrust his chin forward. Speaking slowly, spacing the words far apart, he said, 'I'm tired of the subject of murder.'

'But Mrs Garvie-Brown isn't, is she?' Arne said. 'She thinks it's pretty interesting.'

Luke's face became mulish. 'It's nothing to do with me what she thinks.'

'She does think so, all the same.'

'All right,' Luke said. 'She does seem somehow to have made up her mind that her husband was a mass-murderer. And she thinks I'm the descendant of one of his victims and so she owes me compensation of some kind. Her reason may be collapsing, but her moral convictions aren't. She talked to me quite a bit about moral obligations and whatnot. She's a very upright, very honourable woman. She'd sooner die than not pay every penny she owed. And all the others thought I was going to work on that to screw blackmail out of them all.'

'But listen, boy,' Arne said patiently. 'Just give Mrs Garvie-Brown the benefit of the doubt for a moment, will you, and suppose she isn't insane. Well then, ask yourself next what's happened to her just lately to give her a wild idea like this one about her husband. After all, he's been dead thirty years, and she doesn't seem to have thought, all that time, there was any blemish on his memory.'

'I know, I know,' Luke said. 'I've been over all that myself.'

'She's kept up her connections with the University,' Arne went on. 'She belongs to a lunch-club for the professors' wives. When they moved his department to a new building, she was an honoured guest at the opening. And she'd known him pretty well, you know. The marriage itself only lasted two years—he married her when he was sixty-nine and he died at seventy-one—but she'd been his secretary for twenty years before that. In fact, he was the only job she ever had in life. She started working for him when she was twenty, and she's seventy now. So you've a record of fifty years of complete loyalty. And then suddenly, of all things, this! Well, why? What happened? And don't shout she's insane at me again, because we're assuming for the purpose of this argument that she isn't. So what happened? If you'll think for a moment, it stares you in the face.'

Luke shrugged his shoulders. 'I know you think you're talking sense, but it doesn't mean anything to me.'

Arne stubbed out his cigarette on the sole of his shoe, and flicked the stub at the hearth in front of the electric fire. The stub missed the hearth and fell on the carpet. He left it lying there.

'What happened to her lately is that she decided to move,' he said. 'To flit, as they say in these parts. She sold that house in Heriot Row where she'd lived with her husband, and for thirty years by herself, and she afterwards bought a bungalow out at Blackhope. And what's the first thing you have to do when you move?'

He seemed to expect an answer to the question, so Luke said, 'If you've any sense, you get in a reliable removal firm to do the whole thing for you.'

'No, before that. Think. You've been living in one place for thirty years. What have you been doing all that time? You've been collecting junk, that's what you've been doing. All the things you couldn't bear to throw away and have stuck at the back of a cupboard and forgotten the exisetence of. But when you move you decide you've got to go through it all and get rid of most of it, particularly if you're moving into a place that's only about half the size of the one you're leaving."

Luke nodded. 'That's right. When I arrived her step-grand-daughter, or some such person, thought I was someone from a bookshop who'd come to make an offer for her husband's books.'

'And before that there'll have been armfuls of clothes

and old curtains and so on sent off to those shops that sell stuff for charity. And there'll have been crates of old letters and papers of all sorts dumped for the dust-cart to take away. Papers!' Arne gave a tight-lipped smile that did not curve his lips, but only made a small rectangular gash in his face. 'Don't you understand yet, Mr Latimer? Somewhere down at the bottom of all those papers that had been piling up for thirty years, she found something that told her the truth about her husband. Something he'd left behind. Perhaps something he'd written. Proof that he was the man who'd murdered Georgina Goode and Maureen Gray and Edna Gleason and your grandmother, Lilian Garbury, and got away with their property. And perhaps, having been his secretary for so long, she could remember long absences of his which fitted with the dates of those murders. University people get leave of absence sometimes, don't they? Sabbatical years or something. They get away to pursue their studies elsewhere. Studies! There wasn't much he needed to study, that old man. He knew it all!'

Against his will, Luke had begun to feel himself gripped by an uneasy interest.

'You haven't said anything about the women he married legally,' he said. 'Did he murder them too?'

'I haven't made up my mind,' Arne answered. 'The modus operandi is different. Different in each case, whereas it was just the fact that it was the same with those other four women that gave your Mr Smithson the idea that they were all the work of the same man. But I'd guess the old professor murdered the lot. He was an educated man, after all, and education gives a man a sort of—well, vision and adaptability. He'd be able to see that he could hardly have four wives all dying in just the same way, though it may have been the way he liked best, and expect to go on being a professor in the University of Edinburgh. He'd have to think up a new method for each one. But that's just guesswork, mind you. It could be he was a man who was simply unfortunate in losing all the women he really loved, and that's why he took a sort of revenge on other women in his spare time.'

'Oh, for God's sake, spare me the psychology,' Luke said sourly. 'That's the last straw.'

'But you're beginning to think I'm right, aren't you?'

Of course, Luke was. In fact, he had thought most of it out already, since Mrs Garvie-Brown had begun a sentence in the car, then cut it short, breaking it off in the middle of a word which had sounded as if she had been about to say 'diary'.

'Well, even if you are, the man's been dead for years,' he said. 'There's nothing you can do about him. And I don't want to go upsetting all those people I saw today. They aren't specially my type, and they didn't like me, but I don't really hold that against them, in the circumstances. So what do you expect, trailing me around? What do you suppose is in it for you?'

Arne's eyes held Luke's in a hard, level stare. 'What's in it for you? That's what I'm really interested in at the moment,' he said. 'Just how much do you think is in it?'

CHAPTER VIII

LUKE NODDED. 'So you want to blackmail them through me. Put pressure on me to put pressure on them. I thought we'd get to something like that sooner or later.'

Arne appeared faintly surprised at his taking it so quietly. If he had known Luke better, he would have recognized it as a dangerous sign. Leaning forward, the short man massaged his little hands together. There was a look of hunger in the gesture.

'All you need is that incriminating something, isn't it?'

he said. 'That paper, that diary, whatever it is. You're the person who's in the best position to get it. All you have to do is go round and help the old lady with her move and keep your eyes open.'

'She's already got plenty of help,' Luke said.

'You can never have too much when it comes to moving, take it from me. I've had plenty of experience.'

'Moving? Why? Dodging your creditors?'

'Mr Latimer, that's insulting,' Arne said. 'You have no reason to think I don't pay my bills, the same as you.'

'Sorry, no, I haven't.' For the moment Luke's curiosity about the man before him had the upper hand of his other feelings. 'Where do you live now?' he asked. 'Are you married? Have you any children?'

'Please, my private life is my own affair,' Arne said. 'I keep it and my working life in two separate compartments. It's the only way to manage in a job like mine. Now about this—this thing you want—'

'Mr Arne, you seem to have misunderstood me,' Luke said. 'I don't want anything out of these people. Not anything at all. And I don't want you to get anything out of them either. Is that clear? I don't want to do them any harm whatever. And if you show any signs of trying to do them any harm, I'll go to them and tell them all about you. I'll tell them what your "confidential inquiries" really amount to. A toe-hold for blackmail. And with a judge in the family, I should think they'll know what to do about it. And now get out. Get out before I get on the telephone to Mrs Garvie-Brown and tell her just what you've been suggesting to me.'

Gilbert Arne did not move. With his hat perched perkily on the top of his head, and his tweed coat huddled around him, he looked like an old cock that has unaccountably gone broody.

After a moment he said, 'I'm sorry, I seem to have got you wrong.'

At his failure to rouse anger in response to his own anger, Luke felt deflated. He even had a feeling that he ought to apologize, in case he had somehow misunderstood the other man, attributing to him atrocious things which had not been in his mind at all. Only just managing to resist the impulse, he said, 'Oh, go away. Go away and don't come back. Don't come back for any reason whatever.'

'No need to quarrel, is there?' Arne's voice was flat and untroubled. 'Why don't we have dinner together? We're both stuck here for the evening.'

'No.'

'A drink then, just to show there are no hard feelings.'

'There are plenty of hard feelings.'

'Oh well, if that's how it is . . .' Arne got to his feet. His tone implied that Luke's attitude was both unreasonable and discourteous and that he himself was putting up with it very patiently. With a shrug of his shoulders, he walked out of the room.

Looking after him, wondering just what he ought to do if Arne went looking for the diary by himself, Luke sat down again on the edge of the bed, tugging at his lower lip. Then he got up abruptly, crossed the room and flung the window open, as if to rid the room of a sulphurous smell.

But the air of the October evening had a sharp nip in it and after a minute or two he closed the window again, lifted his suitcase back on to the bed, opened it and began to unpack it. He would stay on and see that lawyer of Christina Garvie-Brown's after all. And if he was the right sort of lawyer, a man to whom you could talk easily and freely, Luke would tell him about the goings on of Gilbert Arne, and explain that the Garvie-Browns might be in need of protection from him. So now the thing to do was to telephone Mrs Garvie-Brown and tell her that he would do as she had asked.

The hotel was not one of the kind that has telephones

in the bedrooms, but Luke had noticed a call-box in the lobby downstairs. Looking to see that he had some change in his pockets, he opened his door and came face to face with the chambermaid.

'There's a lady to see you, sir, waiting in the lounge,' she said.

So Mrs Garvie-Brown had not trusted him to telephone, but had come to make sure for herself that Luke would carry out his half-promise.

Only it was not Mrs. Garvie-Brown who was waiting downstairs. It was Vanessa who was sitting on one of the stiff little chairs in the lounge.

When she saw him she came swiftly to her feet in a fluid, almost fierce movement. Coming close to him, facing him, so tense that she might have been ready to spit abuse at him or reach for his face with her nails, she said in a surprisingly mild and matter-of-fact tone, 'It's too early for a drink.'

'Quite a bit too early,' he agreed.

'But I've got to talk to you.'

'About something that needs alcohol to wash it down?'

'It would make it easier. It's an embarrassing subject. I thought perhaps we could go to my flat. There are drinks there and it isn't far from here.'

Luke began to laugh a little wildly.

'What are you laughing at?' Vanessa asked suspiciously. 'It isn't far. It's in Morningside, just a few minutes' drive, and I've got my car outside.'

' "It isn't far from here."—that's what Don Giovanni kept saying to that girl he was trying to seduce,' Luke explained. 'He kept saying his castle wasn't far from there. It's always seemed to me one of the oddest inducements you could offer a girl.'

'Rather practical, I should have said, but this isn't a seduction,' she said austerely. 'It's business.'

'I knew it.'

'And I want to talk where nobody will overhear us.'
'All right,' he said. 'Let's go.'

He had forgotten that he had meant to make a telephone call to Christina Garvie-Brown. They went out together to Vanessa's car, which was a small Hillman, which looked as if it had seen almost as much of life as it could take. In the silence which fell on her and Luke as soon as they were inside the car he unconsciously began to hum the melody of the duet from Don Giovanni. After a moment Vanessa joined in. Neither of them knew more than a few of the words and Luke, at least, was a little off-key, yet it was a pleasant moment, although Vanessa spoiled it almost at once by saying, 'You know, of course, that I listened at the door.'

'Yesterday?' he said.

'Yes, while I was out making the coffee.'

'I rather wondered about that,' he said. 'I thought the temptation might be a bit much for anyone.'

He had wondered more than that about the girl beside him. Ever since yesterday morning her image had kept drifting in and out of his mind, usually coming uninvited, and without his fully understanding what it was doing there. It had occupied his thoughts for far longer than that of Stephanie, about whom he normally liked to day-dream.

Yet there was no question of comparing Vanessa with Stephanie. Vanessa was all angles. She lacked Stephanie's peach-bloom skin. She was quite without Stephanie's strange and exciting stillness, that air of waiting for the most wonderful thing in the world to happen to her. Vanessa, in fact, looked as if she expected to be the person who made things happen to other people.

At the same time, probably, a far more vulnerable character than Stephanie, Luke thought. His intuitions recognised the vulnerability in Vanessa because it was not unlike his own, whereas, as he was perfectly well aware, Stephanie, inside, was as tough as old boots.

He thought of Vanessa as she had been yesterday, free, friendly, talkative, then as she had been today out at Blackhope, mainly silent and suspicious, then as she had been just now in the hotel, both fierce and frightened, as if coming to talk to him were a desperate venture. What did she want? It would always be difficult to guess, he thought, because usually she would not know herself. Which was another thing that she had in common with him.

'I didn't sleep last night,' she said. 'I kept thinking of what I'd overheard. I didn't understand it. And then all of a sudden, I don't know why, a little while ago, it made sense. Of course, it isn't an altogether new idea to me. Giles and I have often talked about it.'

'You've talked about . . .?' Luke hesitated to finish the sentence in case he had misunderstood her.

But he had not. 'About our grandfather having murdered his wives,' she said. 'But of course, we were only joking about it.'

They were driving past the entrance to a park. Inside there was a pond with a lot of ducks on it and beyond the pond a low, craggy hillside with a dark sprawl of gorse bushes over it. Even now there was a faint sprinkling of gold on the gorse.

'Whatever put it into your head?' Luke asked.

'Don't you remember what you said yourself when I told you one of them was killed in an accident, and one threw herself out of a window, and my stepfather's mother died of gastro-enteritis? You looked quite frightened and wanted to make sure the old man was safely dead and buried now. Well, it was more or less like that with Giles and me. I don't remember which of us thought of it first, but if you ever read detective stories you always take for granted that deaths like that are really murders, don't you?

So we pretended they were, and that our enormously worthy and respectable grandfather had been a sort of Bluebeard. And if that sounds a bit gruesome to you, remember we never knew him, or any of his poor wives either —except Catherine Parr—Christina. But it was only pretending. And then this afternoon, suddenly, I realized it was all true. And he committed some other murders too, didn't he? When I was listening at the door I heard you speak about your own grandmother and three other murders. So it was all true.'

She had turned the car to the left, up a steep hill, then to the right, then to the left again. They were in a warren of demure-looking late-Victorian stone houses with trim front gardens in which some bronze foliage still clung to the trees and a few roses still bloomed. But dusk was coming quickly and a hint of fog with it. It made the quiet streets seem secretive, carefully keeping their own counsel until the intruders had gone by.

'It *is* true, isn't it?' Vanessa said.

'Suppose it is. Suppose every single word of it is true. What point is there in doing anything about it now? All the people concerned have been dead for years. You can only do harm if you rake it out into the open.'

'You really think that?'

'Of course I do.'

'Oh, I'm so glad! It's what I thought you'd say. I was sure you weren't a trouble-making sort of person.' Her tone changed completely. There was a ring of gaiety in it and she took her eyes off the road ahead to give him a wide smile, vivid and intimate, as if she felt that she knew him very well indeed. 'I'm so glad I was right about you. I hate being wrong about people.'

She stopped the car at the gate of a house in a curved terrace. The door of the house was open and a light was on in the small lobby. The light showed two doors, side by side, facing the front door, with a name-plate on each.

Vanessa pushed her key into the lock of the right-hand door, opened it and led the way in.

'I share this with a friend,' she said, 'but she's probably out.' She stood still in the hall and shouted, 'Connie!' There was no answer. 'Out,' she said. 'She's a research student at the University and she's got a special passion for working on Sundays because there's nobody much around to disturb her. Well, come in.' She opened another door, switched on lights, crossed the big room inside, drew the curtains, lit the gas fire, took off her coat, threw it down on a chair, went briskly to a cupboard and took out a bottle and glasses.

'I'm afraid I've only got sherry, and pretty bad sherry at that,' she said. 'I hope you can survive it. Sit down.'

She filled two glasses and brought them across the room.

Luke sat down in a chair on one side of the hissing fire, while Vanessa took the chair on the other. They both sipped their sherry. If it was not very good, it was not as bad as it might have been. No worse, in fact, than the sherry that was all that Luke could afford. Suddenly they were both silent, and an uncertain look appeared in Vanessa's eyes, as if she were not sure now why she had brought him here.

The room was sparsely furnished with what Luke thought were probably the odds and ends that her parents had not very generously decided that they could spare her when she set up house on her own. The chest of drawers, the table, the chairs, the bookshelves, looked the sort of things that the doctor and his wife would probably have bought for their servants in the 'thirties, in the days when servants were still to be had. But he was sure that the exotically patterned curtains at the big bay window were Vanessa's own choice, and so were the pictures. In fact, he guessed, giving them a second and more thoughtful look, they were probably her own work.

They were nearly all of the human figure, and whether

93

they were black and white line-drawings, or unfinished-looking water-colours, or laboriously painted oils, or of men or women, they all bore an elusive but unmistakable likeness to Vanessa herself.

She saw him looking at them and exclaimed shrilly, 'Don't look at them! I only hang them up so that I can think about them. I've got lots more and I keep changing them. And I know they all look like me. I try to make them not do it, but I can't help it. It's fearful narcissism, but it just creeps in. Have you noticed what narcissists the Scots all are? They're always talking about the Scottish character, what it's really like and what it ought to be. You don't do that in England. You just take that side of yourselves for granted.'

'Oh, I don't know,' Luke said. 'I'm writing a novel and when I began it I didn't mean the hero to be me, but now I realize he's even more like me than I am myself.'

'But that's personal, individual, not a national disease.' She smiled. 'There, you see, I am at it already myself. Tell me about being a writer.'

'I doubt if I am one. I thought I might be, but I'm fairly sure by now it was a rotten idea.'

'Was it why you took this job you're in? To have time, I mean.'

'No, it was time to sort myself out I needed,' he said. 'I got started in the wrong job and this is giving me a chance to find out what I really ought to be doing. Writing is just an incidental experiment.'

'What was the job you started in?'

'I was a chartered accountant.'

'And what was wrong with that?'

'It was I that was wrong. Besides, it's a profession that hasn't—oh, call it any philosophy. It's the one profession that hasn't. There's a philosophy of the law, isn't there, and medicine, and the church? And the army too, I suppose, if you've a military turn of mind. And the arts, the theatre . . . But I never heard of a philosophy of chartered accountancy.'

'I don't think that would worry me much,' Vanessa said. 'I don't much like philosophy. People who call themselves philosophers always seem to think they know things, and I don't think one ought to think one knows things. But I'm no good at figures, so I shouldn't want to be a chartered accountant either. But it must have taken tremendous courage for you to get out.' It could have been the almost automatic flattery that a woman doles out to a man whom she is trying to entertain, but if it was, Vanessa did it very well. 'What kind of woman is this Mrs Doubtfire you work for?'

He tried to tell her. But it was difficult to describe Mrs Doubtfire without making her sound a grasping and domineering old harridan, and she was something very different from that. 'I'm sorry,' he said after one or two false starts, 'I'm no good at describing people. She's got her faults. But she helped me a lot when I needed it.'

'You sound very fond of her,' Vanessa said, with more perception than he had expected. 'I wonder if she'd give me a job.'

When he smiled, she added, 'I'm serious. Do you think she would?'

'But I thought you'd just started in one here,' he said. 'Don't you like it?'

'I like it all right, but I'd like to get away from my family.'

'What's wrong with them?' He wondered if by any chance it was Giles that she wanted to get away from. Was the affair between them one of those begun in childhood, smiled on and encouraged by everyone around them, but, in fact, at least for her, a burden?

'Oh, they're all right,' she said. 'It's just that they're altogether too much for me. They crop up wherever I go. I can hardly go a walk in the town without meeting one of them. I ought never to have thought of taking a job here. But a few words were spoken by one of them into an obliging ear, and so I got this pretty good job at Quinan's. Very good for a complete beginner.'

She had been watching Luke all the time that they had been talking with a gaze that seemed to focus on a point two or three feet behind his head. It was as if she were absorbing him rather than looking at him. He wondered if some sort of portrait of him might not appear on a wall of the room soon after he left, a portrait in which his identity and hers had become mysteriously mingled.

'Actually, you're part of my family, aren't you?' she went on. 'We're some sort of cousin by marriage.'

'With some bigamy thrown in.'

'Oh yes. Could you stand some more of this sherry?'

'Thank you.' He held out his glass.

She refilled it and her own, then settled her distant gaze on the jets of flame in the gas fire.

If there had been anything in the least provocative in her attitude, if she had dragged in their obscure relationship as a means of drawing him closer to her, Luke would have known what to do next and would have been happy to do it. He was becoming more and more aware of her attractiveness, although it affected him in a way to which he was not accustomed. It made him feel unfamiliarly quiet and detached from himself. It was altogether different from anything that he had ever felt when he was with Stephanie, when he was always intensely aware of himself, and of her as a mystifying extension of himself, just possibly without any identity of her own.

After a moment, when the girl had not spoken, he asked her, 'Why did you really want me to come here, Vanessa?'

She did not reply at once, then she said, 'Oh, various reasons. To see if I'd guessed right about the sort of person you were. To see if I'd guessed right about all those murders. And to ask you something.'

'Yes?'

'You see, while I was thinking all this out last night when I couldn't sleep, and this afternoon, after seeing you again, I kept coming up against one problem. Why, after all these years, had Christina suddenly hired that detective? Why had she suddenly had you dug up, brought you here, introduced you to all the family and even dropped some mysterious remarks to my parents about the duty of the family "to right an old wrong", as she put it? Why after all these years? Why now?'

'And you found a simple answer, didn't you?' Luke drank some of his sherry. It was more vinegary than he had thought at first, or else some other thing had brought an unpleasant taste to his mouth. He began to quote Gilbert Arne. 'You thought, she's moving, she's been going through all the junk stored in her attics and throwing a lot of it away, she's been going through her husband's books and papers, and she's come on something, a diary, for instance, which proves he murdered a lot of women. And you want me to get round her somehow and persuade her to let me see this thing and then get it away from her.'

She looked up at him quickly. 'How did you know?'

'Because exactly the same proposition was put to me an hour or so ago by someone else,' he said.

CHAPTER IX

'Who?' she demanded.

'By Gilbert Arne, the detective who found me.'

'What did he want?'

'I think his object was blackmail. What's yours?'

He was sorry for his tone as soon as he had spoken. But Vanessa seemed not even to notice the offensiveness of the question. She gave a deep sigh and returned to contemplation of the gas fire.

'I'm not sure,' she said. 'I just feel, if there is such a thing as this diary, or whatever it is, it's an awfully dangerous sort of thing to have around, and it ought to be in safe hands.'

'Aren't Mrs Garvie-Brown's hands safe?'

'Oh no. She's shown that, hasn't she? I mean, what would you have done if you'd found a thing like that?'

'Burnt it on the spot.'

'So should I. But Christina's got much too much of a conscience to do a sensible thing like that. I believe she's really worried, you know, that she and the rest of us are living on money we haven't any right to.'

'I shouldn't think you could possibly sort out by now who's got a right to the money.'

'No, but if somebody started trying to do it, it would make wonderful headlines, wouldn't it?'

'So what you want me to do is to get this thing from Mrs Garvie-Brown and destroy it.'

'Yes.'

'With you watching the destruction?'

'Naturally.'

'I see.' At least the proposition was not repellent, as Arne's had been. 'Only why can't you do it yourself? You've been helping her clear out her junk. You've the run of her house, which I haven't. You'd be able to search the place much more easily than I could.'

'I've done all I can,' she said. 'And I don't think it's in the flat. I think she's got it in her bank, or at her lawyer's.'

'Then what can I do?'

'Simply persuade her to get it back to show it to you.

She's taken a liking to you. If you said you'd doubts about the whole thing and wanted to see her proof, I think there's just a chance she'd show it to you.'

'I don't,' he said. 'I did say something like that to her, and she told me she didn't intend to tell me or anyone any more than she had.'

'But you could at least try.'

And he could see the lawyer tomorrow, as he had promised Mrs Garvie-Brown, and please everyone. Alternatively he could catch the late train back to London, and please himself.

'Well?' Vanessa said after a short silence.

'All right, I'll try,' he said. 'But only once. I won't go on and on.'

She nodded as if she found that reasonable.

After that they began to talk about other things, including their politics, their childhoods, what gramophone records each possessed and the current wars in various parts of the world. Presently they went out together to dinner in a Chinese restaurant near by.

Vanessa's opinion, Luke discovered, on anything that she had thought about at all, tended to be on the simple and violent side. But if Luke, whose opinions always had qualifications and reservations attached to them, so that most of them were complicated and elusive and difficult to talk about, ever got them so far organized as to make him able to disagree with her, she listened courteously and attentively. In her way, she was an oddly grown-up person for her age, and he found himself wondering if this might not be partly due to belonging to the family from which she so much wanted to get away. She had probably listened from infancy to an unusual amount of intelligent discussion, conducted generally with tolerably good manners.

Thinking of this as he prodded at a prawn in his chow mein, he said, 'Vanessa, going back to what we were talking about earlier—this thing about those murders—have you really said nothing about it to any of the rest of your family?'

'Well, only to Giles,' she said.

'When did you do that?'

'After lunch, when he and I went for a walk along the shore. I hadn't really got it clear in my mind yet, and I hadn't really meant to say anything. I was meaning to keep it to myself till I'd done some more thinking and talking to you. But I've always talked most things over with Giles, and I just started doing it.'

'Did you tell him you were going to talk to me?'

'Yes, and he told me not to.'

'Why?'

'He said we knew so little about you. He said he thought you probably were distantly related to us, but now that Christina had picked you up, as lonely old women sometimes do, you were simply on the make. I said I didn't think it was like that at all. For one thing, Christina isn't that sort of old woman. She's very shrewd.'

'And will he have told the rest of the family your idea by now?'

'I shouldn't think so. Why? Does it matter?'

'It's just that if in fact they do know what we've been guessing, one of them, the judge, for instance, might be far better than me at getting the diary—let's call it a diary—out of Mrs Garvie-Brown.'

Vanessa shook her head. 'No, she hates being dominated. If she does it for you, it'll simply be because she likes you.'

'Which reminds me that I ought to have telephoned her before now,' Luke said. 'I promised I'd do it two or three hours after she dropped me at the hotel.'

'You can do it when you get back. An hour or two won't make much difference.'

But Vanessa was wrong. The hour or two made a great deal of difference. To begin with, Luke did not succeed in speaking to Mrs Garvie-Brown at all that evening. When he rang her number from his hotel at about nine o'clock, there was no reply, and when he tried again, half an hour later, there was still none. Thinking then that women of her age probably went to bed early and that he ought not to risk disturbing her, he did nothing again until after he had had breakfast next morning.

This time the telephone was lifted immediately and a voice said crisply, '22571780'.

Strings of numbers always tended to confuse Luke.

He said, 'Mrs. Garvie-Brown? This is Luke Latimer—'

'Mr Latimer!' Her tone of voice had changed amazingly since he had heard it last. There was not a trace of friendliness in it. 'I am astonished that you should telephone. After what you did last night, I thought, I hoped, I had heard the last of you.'

'I'm very sorry but I did try to telephone yesterday evening,' he said. 'I tried twice. But I was afraid of disturbing you in case you'd gone to bed.'

'I was having dinner with friends, as you must have known.'

'I didn't,' he said.

'Then if you telephoned, it was to make sure that I was out,' she said.

'But Mrs Garvie-Brown—'

She did not let him finish. 'Mr Latimer, listen to me! I only wished you well. I only wanted to do what would help you. I liked you and I trusted you. I now bitterly regret it. You came to my flat when I was out, you searched for—for proof of the matters we discussed—'

'Mrs Garvie-Brown, I did not, and I was only going to ask you now if you still wanted me to see that solicitor.'

'Is it likely, in the circumstances? No, and I do not want to hear anything of you again. I do not want you to trouble any of my relatives either. If, on the basis of any conversation that you and I have had together, any of us should hear anything further from you, I shall not hesitate to go straight to the police. You understand me?'

'I do not!' Luke heard his own voice begin to rise. He lowered it carefully. There is nothing more undignified and in the end less satisfying than a shouting match on the telephone. 'I agree I'd promised to telephone earlier than I did, and I apologize for that, but that's scarcely a police matter. And I'd like to remind you that it was you who troubled me, not I you, in the beginning. You even threatened to come to London to find me. And except that I like your step-grand-daughter, Vanessa, very much indeed —as a matter of fact, the reason I forgot to telephone you when I said I would was that I was spending a very pleasant evening with her—I have no wish to see or hear anything of any of your relatives again.'

There was a slight pause, then she said, 'You were with Vanessa yesterday evening?'

'Yes.'

'The whole evening?'

'No, until about nine o'clock.'

'I see.' The harshness came back into her voice. 'No, Mr Latimer, let me repeat what I have said. I hope to see and hear nothing more from you. But if I do, don't think for one moment that I shall shrink from going immediately to the police. It's the only way to deal with people like you.'

'But look here—oh, what the hell!'

Luke slammed the telephone down. Then he wished that he had done it quietly. Behind his momentary intense anger was a far deeper mood of sadness. The poor old thing, she was as mad as they come after all. Crazy, nutty, batty, round the bend. All those foolish, flippant words that people use to cover the worst tragedy of all.

And he had liked her and in spite of recurrent doubts to the contrary, had really believed in her good sense and warm heart. Well, at least he could go home today. There was nothing to stop him now.

There was also no particular hurry. He did not feel like hurrying. The unexpected row had left him in an odd state of lassitude. He decided to take the train at twelve o'clock. That would mean that he would be home in his flat by seven, could pick up a bottle of wine on the way, soak in a hot bath, make an omelette, a quantity of good coffee, and spend an evening with the sanities of television.

That was actually how the thought of television struck him for once. He had rented the set in the first place with some idea of studying how to write for it, then he had developed an addiction, attended by slight feelings of guilt, to its absurdities. But today it simply seemed to him the best friend a man could have.

He packed his bag, paid his bill and took a bus to Waverley Station.

That left him with an hour and a half to fill in before his train was due to leave.

Handing his bag in at the left-luggage office, he strolled out of the station into Princes Street and began to walk aimlessly along, passing on the left the recently cleaned bulk of the Scottish Royal Academy, which might have looked classically imposing if only it had not had a gigantic statue of Queen Victoria squatting on top of it like a broody hen, hoping to hatch out masterpieces.

Crossing the street beyond it, Luke stood still for a few minutes, charmed by the grace with which the statue of Allan Ramsay at the corner of the gardens there accepted the presence of the pigeons that perched on his turban and his shoulders. Smiling, confidently poised and charmingly casual about it, he made them look as welcome as they are to the little old men who go to Trafalgar Square with bags of stale bread or bird-seed, on purpose to tempt the birds into friendliness.

Luke turned to the left, then towards the Old Town, built along the spine of the hill stretching from the Castle to Holyrood. On the way he passed a domed building, the head offices of the Bank of Scotland, on top of which stands a large gilded lady with two golden circlets in her hands. Presumably these are laurel wreaths, with which some fortunate passer-by might find himself crowned, but as she is too far up in the air for this to be certain, she looks as if she were poised there for ever in the middle of a game of deck quoits.

Continuing past the bank, Luke crossed the High Street, where the ruggedly mediaeval and the tattily nineteenth century jostle each other with a rough but endearing familiarity, crossed it and wandered on along the wide street beyond. If he turned left soon, he calculated, and then left again, he would have walked along the four sides of a rectangle and ought to arrive back at Waverley Station.

He took the first turning to the left, walked along it and suddenly realized that the big building that loomed above him on the right was the University.

An odd thought came into his head then. He looked at his watch and saw that he still had plenty of time. Turning right instead of left at the end of the street, he passed through a tall archway, and into the noble Adam quadrangle of the Old College.

He wandered about in it for several minutes before he found the porters' lodge and went in to inquire where he would find the Department of Semeiotics. He was told that he had come to the wrong place altogether. He should have gone to George Square.

Was that far? No, just out into the street again, turn right, first right, first left, second right, second left, and there you were, you couldn't miss it.

Luke knew that he could miss anything, even when he had been given far simpler directions than those, but with the idea now firmly in his mind that he wanted to see the little world that had once been ruled by Duncan Garvie-Brown, he set off to find it.

But when in the end, after asking his way two or three times, he found the Department of Semeiotics, he realized that Duncan Garvie-Brown could never have entered its doors. For it was in a towering modern structure of concrete and glass which still had the raw appearance of a building that has been in use for only a year or two. Along one side of the square was a small remnant of Georgian Edinburgh, looking as if it were attempting to maintain a dignified ignorance of the revolution going on around it, but everywhere else modernity flourished.

Luke nearly went away. But having come so far he thought he might as well see what a Department of Semeiotics looked like, and whether or not it was likely to breed any more mass-murderers. Climbing some wide stone steps, he went in, asked another porter some more questions, cleared his way through a flood of students erupting from a lecture-hall, went up in a lift, and presently found himself in a narrow hall from one wall of which a portrait looked down at him. It was in a sombre gilt frame and about the face there was what had become a dreadful familiarity.

'An atrocious painting, isn't it?' said the voice of Casper Garvie-Brown behind Luke's shoulder. 'But we have to hang it somewhere.'

CHAPTER X

CASPER GARVIE-BROWN was in shapeless flannel trousers, a dark green pullover that had ridden up on his stomach, leaving a strip of shirt visible between the ribbing of the pullover and his belt, and a tweed jacket which had sagged so much at the pockets that it looked as if he must keep them weighted down with stones. His innocent, vague gaze through his spectacles gave him the look of someone who is trying to hide the fact that he has no idea of the identity of the person to whom he is talking, although he remembers just enough of him to know that there is something very wrong about having forgotten him.

Old humbug, Luke thought. The professor knew perfectly well who he was. He was probably the most on the spot of all those people whom Luke had seen out at Blackhope yesterday. That lost look of his was just worn for comfort and convenience, like his old clothes.

This was confirmed by the fact that the look remained even when Casper had revealed that he had not forgotten Luke. Saying, 'I'm very glad you came to see me, Mr Latimer,' he went on looking as if he were trying to mask a secret bewilderment. 'I'd actually thought of trying to get in touch with you myself. But I've had a fearful morning, one thing after another, people who come and talk and won't let one get on with one's own concerns—not that all mornings aren't fearful, and afternoons too. My father was a very fortunate man. He lived at a time when an academic career meant that a man could be a scholar. Now it means that he spends his time pursuing grants for research, and sitting on committees and chasing power—not because he wants it, but because someone else might get it if he doesn't, and could then make his life unbearable. One might just as well have gone into business.'

'But your father wasn't entirely satisfied with the rewards of scholarship, was he?' Luke said.

The remark brought no noticeably unusual reaction from Casper.

'Who ever is? We all want fame and money, don't we? It's true a good many of us have to reconcile ourselves to the fact that we're mediocrities or downright failures, and take up rose-growing, or carpentry, or Heaven help us, even an interest in the students, but never to have had dreams of something more is pathological.'

'At least he acquired the money, didn't he?' Luke said.

'By some rather advantageous marriages, yes. Not that I think he really concerned himself much about money. He just assumed it would be there when he needed it.'

'This portrait, is it like him?'

'Pretty like, in an uninformative, photographic sort of way. But he was very pleased with it himself. It makes him look a jolly, benign old fellow, doesn't it?'

It did. It gave the late Duncan Garvie-Brown a glowingly ruddy skin, arranged neatly and smoothly over the family bone-structure, skin that looked well-soaped and shaved and healthily wind-blown and that was gently folded into pleasant smile-lines at the corners of his lips and his eyes. Green Garvie-Brown eyes, that had a good-natured twinkle in them and a thick bristle of arching eyebrows above them. Although he looked at least sixty in the portrait, his hair was still dark, with distinguished-looking little wings of grey at the temples. He was wearing a scarlet gown that gave his spare form a touch of majesty.

'Wasn't he jolly and benign?' Luke asked.

'Anything but, anything but! Or to be more accurate, only sometimes,' Casper said. 'He had tremendous charm at times, a remarkable magnetism. But he was a man of uncontrolled moods. He could change between the extremes of gaiety and depression within minutes. He could be utterly ruthless when he was offended. He could be very generous too, suddenly and for no particular reason. A very frightening man, really. Perhaps that was why he was so venerated in the University. It was easier to venerate him than to oppose him. But my sister Lucille and I were quite simply terrified of him, particularly after my mother died. I think my first stepmother was frightened of him too. She was a gentle, timid sort of creature, and as scared of my father's high spirits as she was of his glooms . . . By the

107

way, am I boring you with this? Once I get started on my family, I'm rather inclined to run on.'

'I'm intensely interested,' Luke answered.

'Well then, why don't we go and have lunch in the Staff Club? I was on my way there when I happened to catch sight of you. And as I said, I'd been thinking of trying to get hold of you this morning to talk over something I've got in mind. Do come, won't you?'

'Well, I . . .' But after all the trains that Luke had already missed, what did it matter if he missed another?

'Thank you very much,' he said. 'I should be delighted.'

'Good. My car's in the square.' Casper took Luke by the elbow and steered him back towards the lift. As it took them downwards, he went on, 'I've only just realized I haven't asked you why you came looking for me.'

'I didn't really,' Luke said. 'I came because I wanted to see something of where Duncan Garvie-Brown worked.'

'Ah. Oh. Indeed?' Casper explored Luke's face with a swift glance that was neither lost nor innocent. 'Disappointing for you then, finding us in this new place?'

'In a way. But it was interesting to see his portrait.'

'Was it? For any special reason?'

'About as special as your reason for wanting to talk to me, I expect.'

'I see. Then that's going to simplify things, isn't it? We shan't have to beat about the bush. I'm glad of that. I'm not a subtle fellow. I like to go straight to the point when I can.' It was said with a friendly smile and was about as complete a misstatement, Luke felt sure, as anything that he had heard for a long time.

They emerged into the square. During the short time that he had been in the building it had started to rain and there was a gusty wind with it, which clutched at the few leaves left on the trees in the big gardens in the square and sent them damply fluttering over the lawns.

'And I thought it was going to be fine today,' the professor said disgustedly as he unlocked his car. 'Tell me, have you ever seen such a moody city as Edinburgh? On some days she's a queen. She's regal. She's immensely proud. The days when there's a fine blue sky and a glitter in the air and everything's sharp and clear and her greyness has a magnificent dignity. And sometimes on autumn evenings, just around this time of year, when there's a sort of rusty copper light in the sky, and there are wonderful cloud patterns over the Castle, mystery takes over and you feel yourself slipping away into the remote past. History nudges you familiarly in the ribs. And on days like today she's just a dingy and bedraggled slut. Then again, there are innumerable days when she's a worthy, stolid matron, tramping along bravely with her rubber-tipped walking-stick. Incidentally, have you ever seen as many rubber-tipped walking-sticks as you see in Edinburgh?'

'I don't think I've noticed,' Luke replied.

'Ah, you should never stop noticing,' Casper said. 'Not here. You can see almost anything at any time. Once I went into a tobacconist and there were three boys there. None of them could have been more than fifteen years old and they were all wearing leather jackets and jeans and talking with accents that even I could hardly follow, though I've lived here all my life. And they were buying a cigar apiece. But when they'd got them they didn't know how to light them, so the kind old lady who kept the shop showed them how and they started puffing away at them in a self-conscious way. Then all of a sudden they popped tarbooshes on to their heads—I swear it, tarbooshes, the tall, narrow, Persian kind—which they'd all been holding out of sight behind their backs till then, and off they went along George IV Bridge, smoking those cigars and wearing the tarbooshes. Who knows what they had in their minds? That problem keeps coming back to haunt me. What were they after? But anyway, the minds of the young are a mystery, aren't they? The only real guide we've got to them are our memories of our own minds when we were young, and by now one's got a bit forgetful. I'm dealing with the young all the time and I only get more and more bewildered. Here we are.'

He turned the car into a car-park down the centre of one of the streets along which Luke had walked a little while earlier.

'Now I warn you,' Casper went on as they walked towards a doorway in a building all of smoke-darkened stone, except for some panels of wood which had obviously been let into it recently, together with some large windows, which gave warning that, as in George Square, modernity had crashed its way in, 'I've no objection to talking business over meals. I don't hold with the view that it's uncivilized. What's uncivilized is keeping people on tenterhooks when they might be enjoying their steaks. We'll have a drink, shall we, and get down to the matter in hand immediately?'

'Business?' Luke said dubiously. 'Have we any business to talk about?'

'Why, my dear chap, what else?' Casper was guiding him towards the bar at the far end of a long room. 'Now what will you have to drink? Gin and French—good, so will I.' Waving Luke to a chair, he dived into the crowd round the bar, emerging presently with the drinks and sitting down beside Luke at a small round table.

'You did come to talk money, didn't you?' he said.

'No,' said Luke.

'But I assure you, there's no need to beat about the bush with me. I told you so. I think there's more pernicious false delicacy in talk about money than about anything else nowadays. It goes far beyond sex. I'm very strongly opposed to reticence on the subject. If I want to talk money, I do, and in plain figures.'

'But why should we?' Luke asked. 'Talk about murder

if you want to—I'm getting used to that. But money seems rather irrelevant at the moment.'

'Murder?' Casper looked particularly vague. 'You're interested in murder? We've had some outstanding ones in Edinburgh, of course, some of them even involving the University. There was that Burke and Hare business, for instance. I'm not sure if we've ever quite lived that down. And a part of the Old College is built on the site of the Kirk o' Field, where they blew up Darnley. But that isn't what you meant.' He cocked his head a little on one side, studying Luke.

'No,' Luke said.

'Then what do you mean?'

'What do you mean by talking about money?'

'But that's simple. I just don't like the thought that you may have been misled by Christina into believing things and hoping things which are almost certainly going to lead to disappointment. If she's been leading you on with promises, because she believes you're somehow related to us, it's very wrong of her. I admit it isn't like her. She's always been a hard-headed, straightforward woman. But I suppose there's a first time for everything. Perhaps in a sense she hasn't had a very satisfactory life, marrying too late to have children of her own and so on, and she was bound to break out in some way sooner or later. But although, for her lifetime, she's a fairly wealthy woman, her money's all tied up, you see. When she dies, the capital gets divided between my sister Lucille and my step-brother Kenneth and me. So perhaps Christina could help you out in some relatively minor way at the moment, and I don't see why she shouldn't, if she wants to, but there's nothing to look forward to. I did just feel you ought to know that. And I thought that if this visit has run you into expense, I'd like to make it up to you.'

Luke said nothing. He was leaning back in his chair with

his legs stretched out before him and was holding his glass up, gazing dreamily at the faintly coloured fluid. He was experimenting with a variety of feelings, trying to decide which was the dominant one. Anger? Insult? A mischievous desire to frighten this fluent and probably devious but somehow rather charming character with some mysterious hints and half-revelations? Yes, that feeling was strong. But curiosity was strongest of all.

'To return to murder . . .' he said thoughtfully.

Casper Garvie-Brown finished his drink at a gulp and spluttered over it, 'For God's sake, why?'

'It isn't on your mind at all? When you talk of money, the thought of murder isn't lurking anywhere in the background?'

If the bewilderment on Casper's face were not genuine, he was a very fine actor. But perhaps he was a fine actor. He was a man, Luke thought, who acted nearly all the time. It might have begun as a defence against his father, if his father had been the kind of man whom he had described, a man whose moods had irresponsibly dominated the life of his family. Against such a man defences are always needed, and subtle ones at that. A whole personality can be built up on the need for them.

'I think we've got our lines crossed,' Casper said. 'Could we just stick to money for the moment?'

'There's really no need to,' Luke said. 'Do believe me that I honestly didn't come here to get any out of Mrs Garvie-Brown or any of the rest of you. So now can't we change the subject?'

'Just a minute. Will you tell me why you did come here?'

'No, I don't think I will. You can try asking her, if you like, but I don't think you'll get much out of her either.'

'But you came because she asked you to, didn't you?'

'Yes. But there was a certain amount of misunderstanding involved. And we haven't exactly hit it off either. When

112

I last spoke to her, which was on the telephone this morning, she told me that if she or any of you heard any more of me, she was going straight to the police.'

'But good lord—no, I can't believe you. That doesn't sound at all like Christina.'

'I didn't think she sounded quite like herself,' Luke said. 'Something happened last night that seems to have upset her rather. Perhaps it would be a good idea if you went to see her.'

Casper frowned into a vacuum in front of him. He said thoughtfully, 'She's been behaving rather oddly lately.'

'That's how it seems to me.'

'And you really weren't expecting anything from her? She hasn't misled you? You don't feel she owes you anything?'

'What I'm hoping is that she's going to leave me alone now,' Luke said.

'But then, my dear chap, I don't know how to apologize!' Casper exclaimed. 'I've been talking to you as if you'd been all but demanding money with menaces. Anyway, I was trying to buy you off, thinking Christina had got herself into some sort of mess that you were exploiting. I can't say how sorry I am. I've behaved abominably. Will you still have lunch with me, or have I gone too far?'

'I'm pretty hungry,' Luke said.

'Good, good. But another drink first, don't you think? And we'll talk about something else, anything you like, even murder. Though why you should want to . . . Are you a journalist or something?'

'Let's drop that subject too.' Luke felt fairly sure by now that if Christina Garvie-Brown's suspicions of her husband had ever occurred to his son, they had long ago been buried deep, perhaps even out of his own reach, in the convenient bogs of self-deception in which a man's whole spirit may drown with almost no discomfort to him.

Over lunch they talked about travel, just as they had

yesterday at Blackhope, except that today Casper concentrated on the Highlands and went so far in friendliness as to suggest that if ever Luke returned to Edinburgh, he should let Casper know in advance and he would then drive him over to the West coast and up to Glencoe.

'Where,' he said, 'they'd have had to invent a massacre, if there hadn't really been one. Not that it would rate as a massacre nowadays. The numbers would be dwarfed any bank-holiday weekend by the road deaths. And not that it's as sinister as it used to be, with people selling ice-cream and picture postcards and a ski-lift and so on. Still, there's an atmosphere . . .'

There was an atmosphere about the lunch too. Both of them worked hard to make it normal, but each had too many thoughts in his mind which he was keeping to himself. Both hid their relief when it was over in strenuous over-friendliness. Walking back to Waverley after it, Luke at last caught a train to London.

That night he forgot to set his alarm clock and next morning he slept late. Not that it mattered. Mrs Doubtfire would not be expecting to hear from him at any particular time, and when he woke he found that the long sleep had given him a comfortable feeling of having got the whole absurd Garvie-Brown episode out of his system.

Drowsing on in bed for a time, he thought that later on today he would telephone Stephanie and see if she would have dinner with him. Come to think of it, though, he was a little short of money. Being high-minded had come expensive. The journey to Edinburgh and back and the three nights that he had spent in the hotel meant that he might have to borrow from Mrs Doubtfire on his next month's salary. This being high-minded, what a pity it was to have been born that way. Why shouldn't he at least have got his expenses out of Casper? What would have been wrong about that?

Getting up at last, he went to his front door to fetch

in his milk. It was only as he reached the door that he remembered that there would be no milk. He had stopped the deliveries before leaving for Edinburgh and of course had not yet had the chance to telephone the dairy to ask them to resume them.

But some post had been pushed in at the letter-box and lay scattered on the rug before it. There were one or two obvious bills and a somewhat bulky package, which the postman must have had some difficulty in pushing in through the slit in the door. Luke gathered them up and took them into the kitchen, where he put the water on to boil for his coffee.

He did not bother to look at the bills, but he turned the package over, examining it curiously before he opened it. It was in a thick envelope which had been sealed with several lengths of Sellotape and had his name and address written large on it in childish-looking capital letters. It had an Edinburgh postmark. It felt as if it might have a small book inside it, a notebook, perhaps, or a diary . . .

His hands suddenly beginning to shake, Luke slit the envelope open.

There was money inside it. Nothing else. No letter. Only one hundred pounds in old one pound notes.

CHAPTER XI

THE ANGER that Luke had been unable to feel against Casper Garvie-Brown while he was drinking with him exploded inside him now. The crumpled notes littering the draining-board beside his sink seemed to him by far the dirtiest things that he had ever seen there. And he was capable of letting dirty dishes pile up for two or three days at a time. Keeping abreast of the washing-up had never been one of his strong points.

Making coffee and toast and taking them into the sitting-room, he lit the gas fire and sat down before it.

With his gaze on its brightening glow, he started to make up in his head the letter that would accompany the money back to Casper. He made up several, all with a lofty bitterness of tone, but what he finally settled for, when he had finished his breakfast, was a note of mild dignity.

'Dear Professor Garvie-Brown,
    I return herewith the one hundred pounds you sent me. I meant what I said to you. I do not want it, or anything else from any member of your family.
                      Yours sincerely,
                              Luke Latimer.'

Then he gathered up the notes from the draining-board, wrapped his letter round them, fastened them together with a rubber band, wrapped up the package in the sheet of slightly crumpled brown paper in which his last week's laundry had been returned, tied it with string and sealed the knots with sealing-wax.

Realizing that he did not know Casper's home address, he wrote on it, 'Professor Casper Garvie-Brown, Department of Semeiotics, George Square, Edinburgh,' and, on second thoughts, added, 'Private and Confidential'. Then he got dressed, took his small parcel to the post office, had it registered, and with that done, set off for the offices of Good Neighbours, Ltd.

He did not see Mrs Doubtfire that morning. She was out conducting a very confidential deal for a secondhand fur coat for a titled and wealthy but thriftily-minded client, who often made use of Mrs Doubtfire's services and for whom she never trusted anyone in the agency to act but herself. The woman, she said, might be rude, crafty and slow in paying her bills, but her recommendation was invaluable.

Mrs Doubtfire's secretary sent Luke off to the British Museum to gather some information on smuggling in the seventeenth century for an author who lived in Cornwall. Luke was also given baby-sitting assignments for that evening and the next, which put paid to his hope of seeing Stephanie. Before setting off for the British Museum, however, he looked through her file to see how her search for a room had been getting along and saw that during his absence one had been found for her. It was in St John's Wood and had a telephone. He made a note of the number and when he got home that evening he rang it.

She was in and sounded glad to hear his voice. Or perhaps it was just any voice. He sensed an unfamiliar forlornness about her. Perhaps having got settled in London at last had brought on an attack of homesickness. She told him that she was not sure that she liked the flat. She was not sure that she was going to get on with the other two girls who shared it. She was not sure that it had been fair on her parents to leave them to themselves. She put on a little air of uncertainty about being free on Thursday, but then agreed to have dinner with him.

She arrived at the restaurant looking as lovely as ever, wearing a short black leather coat over a thigh-length, jade green corduroy tunic, with a high-necked, long-sleeved black sweater under it, and some complicated pieces of copper jewellery attached to her here and there. Her wonderful hair hung about her shoulders and so nearly hid her face that her eyes looked like those of a strange little animal, peering out of its burrow.

Luke's heart warmed at the sight of her. He had not meant to talk about the trip to Edinburgh, but in a few minutes he was pouring it all out. But she was in a querulous mood. She seemed not to want to listen to what had been happening to him, but only to talk about the two girls with whom she was sharing the flat, about their clothes, their boy-friends and about the way in which they were both trying to impose on her, she being the newcomer, when it came to tidying up and cleaning. She complained in a soft, gentle voice, looking at Luke as if somehow, she knew, he could put this injustice right for her.

He was hotly on her side at first. Then he began to feel irritated. If the girls really were bitches, he said to her, why couldn't she kick them in the teeth?

She hung her head, so that her face was quite concealed by her hair, and murmured something almost inaudible about his unkindness and lack of understanding. It occurred to Luke suddenly that if you went on seeing much of a girl like this, you might discover one day that you had a reputation amongst your best friends for such a lack of understanding that it amounted to monstrous cruelty. And you might even have become cruel too, for while she was playing her little game of victim, she might easily evoke the victimiser, the brute, that lurks in the heart of most of us.

He knew that no one arouses one's antipathy more than the person who evokes the evil in one, and he had spent most of the last few days meditating on a man who had had a great deal of evil in him, a man who happened to be his own grandfather and whose legacy to his grandson was a load of guilt, utterly irrational, but of which he had been becoming more and more sickeningly aware.

Delivering Stephanie back to her flat in St John's Wood and arranging to meet her again in two days' time, Luke retreated into the night with the feeling of escaping from something strangely dangerous.

And that, he knew, was very unfair to Stephanie, for wasn't all the danger in himself? And that mostly imaginary. Had he ever wished serious harm to anyone? He could not remember that he had. For the odd small revenge, yes, the minor humiliation, the failure when success had been anticipated, the trivial loss. In shameful moments of inadequacy, he had certainly had such desires. But anything to make him seem irremediably scarred by his heritage? No. So why distress himself?

Next morning he received a letter from Casper Garvie-Brown. It was accompanied by the hundred one-pound notes that Luke had thought he was rid of.

'Dear Mr Latimer,

There has been a misunderstanding of some sort. I did not send you the enclosed hundred pounds. I took you at your word when you said that you had no wish to have the expenses of your journey to Edinburgh re-imbursed, and that you did not wish to make any other claim on any member of my family. In the circumstances I do not know what else to do with the money but return it to you. I am sorry not to be more helpful. I can only suggest that the money was posted to you in error and that your wisest course might be to take it to the police —that is, if you are really sure that you do not know where it comes from, as is suggested by your attributing it to me. But after our talk it would really not have occurred to me to be so gross as to send it.

I meant what I said about that trip to the Highlands. Let me know if you are returning.

Yours sincerely,
Casper Garvie-Brown.'

The notes had spilled out of the envelope on to the carpet. Luke made a stack of them on the table, and sat looking at them, thinking. After a little while he made them up into a package again and put them into his pocket. Then he telephoned Mrs Doubtfire. He said that he would like to talk to her about a personal matter. Had she any time to spare that day? She replied that if he would come into the office at five o'clock, when the rest of the staff would be leaving, they could talk there.

He spent a futile day in the British Museum, trying to

work up some interest in the habits of seventeenth-century smugglers, but found himself unable to keep his mind on what he was supposed to be doing. He kept putting his hand into his pocket to feel the bundle of notes there. He left the Reading Room early, and arrived at the offices of Good Neighbours, Ltd at twenty minutes to five, only to be told that Mrs Doubtfire had gone out a few minutes ago and had not told anyone when she expected to be back.

However, she was a woman who tended to keep her promises, so although she had not returned by five o'clock, Luke stayed on when her secretary and the receptionist went home, and at a quarter past five she appeared.

She said, 'Oh, you waited—good. Come on in.'

She was in one of her severe grey suits, with a short ocelot jacket over it, and a slightly crazy-looking purple hat tilted far forward over her eyes. All her hats, and she had a great many, were a little mad, yet in a grotesque way always stylish.

With the unnaturally upright walk that she owed to her steel-boned corset, she went ahead of Luke into her office, lowered herself cautiously into the chair at her big desk, propped the small of her back against a small, hard cushion and gave a groan.

'My back's been giving me hell all day,' she said, 'and I found I'd run out of my tablets, so I went out to get some. I could have sent one of the girls, but I thought a short walk might limber things up a bit. It's only made the damned thing worse, of course. What I really want is some gin. It's the only thing that really works, even if it's not for very long. Get me a drink, will you, Luke? A big one. It's over in that cupboard there. And help yourself too while you're at it.'

Luke did not need to be told where Mrs Doubtfire kept her gin. All the office knew that in her opinion it was the only thing that did her back any good. He went to the cupboard, poured out two generous drinks, tinted them faintly with vermouth, handed one to her, put his own on the edge of the desk opposite to her and brought the bundle of notes out of his pocket.

'Will you look at that?' he said, pushing it towards her.

'I don't need to,' she said. 'Even without my glasses I can see it's money.' She took a long swallow of the gin, gave a little shudder and a sigh. 'God, I wish I was at home in bed on my hot blanket. It's all from worrying. I've had an attack of worrying about the future, about what I'll do when Neighbours packs up, as of course it will. I can't keep going for ever and who is there I can delegate all the management to? People like you don't stay. I give you another three months at the outside. And that girl Marilyn who's been so useful lately, she gave me notice today. Said she was going to get married. "All right, get married," I said, "why not, but why stop working? You'll soon get bored, sitting at home, listening to the clank of the dishwasher. And you can use the money, can't you?" So she told me she found she was going to have a baby and thought it was time she settled down. So my back's bad. Psychosomatic, of course.' She drank some more gin and gave a harsh little titter. 'I wonder who made up that word. He must have laughed himself sick when he thought of it.'

'If you really want to go home,' Luke said, 'we could talk some other time.'

'No, go on, tell me about this money,' she said. 'It's always cheering to talk about other people's money troubles. What's the matter with it? Is it forged?'

'No, but it's a longish story.'

'You got it in Edinburgh, did you? So it was worth going. I told you it would be. But get me another drink first. I'm beginning to feel a bit better.' The look of pain had begun to fade from the aged eyes in her pink, youthfully unwrinkled face. 'Well, go ahead.'

Luke refilled her glass, picked up his own and sank back

into the Finnish chair facing her. The chair's odd shape always made him think of the upper set of a pair of false teeth, and he half-expected it to swallow him down when he sat in it, but in fact it was very restful after a disquieting day.

Starting with his visit to Christina Garvie-Brown in Heriot Row and his meeting with Vanessa, he told Mrs Doubtfire everything that had happened to him since then. He told her of Christina's imminent move, of his visit to her bungalow at Blackhope and the talk that he had had with her on the way to his meeting with the other Garvie-Browns in the house next door, of his further meetings with Gilbert Arne, Vanessa and Professor Garvie-Brown, and of his return home and the arrival of the money.

When he mentioned the unexpected appearance of Arne in Edinburgh, Mrs Doubtfire gave a grunt and muttered, 'I don't like the sound of that.' But the rest of the time she kept silent, nodding her purple hat from time to time and at one point suddenly taking it off, dropping it on the floor beside her and combing her hair with her fingers.

When Luke stopped, she went on looking at him expectantly, as if she thought that there must be more to come.

He pointed at the money again. 'Well, what do I do with that?'

'That's going to take some thinking out,' she said. 'Old, soiled one-pound notes, not in series . . .'

'Shall I take it to the police?'

'And tell them you're being paid blackmail for you aren't sure what, by you don't know whom? Is that your idea?'

'Yes, more or less.'

'They'd laugh in your face.'

'Wouldn't they do anything about it? Wouldn't they stop it?'

'They'd just talk to you nicely and send you home again.'

'But if I told them the rest . . .'

She shook her head. 'One of your troubles, Luke, is

you look a crank. Not seriously eccentric, I'm not suggesting anything like that, but even if you'd go and have your hair cut, which I wish you would, you still wouldn't look as if you'd got both your feet on the ground. If you tried to tell the police the story you've just told me, there'd be some covert grins, and then a bit of impatience, and then you'd find yourself ushered politely out, hundred pounds and all. And you know that, or you wouldn't have come to discuss the affair with me instead of going straight to them. No, what we need to do now is think rather carefully, because, although I don't want to alarm you, I've a feeling this is only the beginning of something not very nice.'

'I've got that feeling myself.' Mrs Doubtfire's gin was quieting Luke's nerves by making his anxieties seem sensible and normal. 'I'm so glad you don't just think I'm a fool.'

'I've never thought that.' She tapped her teeth with a pencil that she had picked up from the desk. 'I hope you kept the letter that came with the money this morning.'

'Yes, it's in the flat.'

'Well, put it in a safe place, because you just might need evidence you'd tried to return the money to the person you thought it came from. But now let's go over this story of yours and see what it amounts to.' Mrs Doubtfire's stiffly upright position had relaxed a little. The combination of her favourite medicine and Luke's story seemed to have taken her mind off her pain. 'I believe Arne's right, you know. He's an acute little bastard. Mrs Garvie-Brown decides to move, she starts to sort out the accumulation of years, goes through trunks, cupboards and all the rest of it, and she comes on the diary you both think she's got, and it's explicit enough to convince this reasonable and highly practical Scotswoman that her husband murdered all the wives he'd had before her, as well as four other women, to whom he'd been bigamously married when he was supposed to be on leave of absence, for one reason or another, from the University. A total of seven. Seven Sleepers. By the way, who were the Seven Sleepers, Luke? I just seem to remember them in some poem of Donne's. Do you know who they were?'

'They were seven Christian youths of Ephesus, who bolted to a cave somewhere or other to escape from persecution and went to sleep there for over a hundred years. Then something woke them up, but they died pretty quickly afterwards.'

'I don't blame them,' she said. 'When I get woken up out of a nice sound sleep, I often wish I could just die. Don't you? Well, something's woken up those seven poor women, hasn't it? Made their influence active. And someone's hoping very much they'll die off again soon. But let's stick to Mrs Garvie-Brown for the present. What does she do? She hires Arne, and she sets him to trace the descendants of those four wives, and he finds you. She wants to meet you. She probably hasn't really made up her mind what she wants to do about you, because she hasn't discussed anything with the rest of her family yet. They know she's hired a detective, because the friend who recommended Arne has kindly passed the fact on to them, and they're suspicious of you, but they don't yet know how or why she's taken you up. But your resemblance to them makes them think it's something to do with your being an illegitimate offspring of their father's.'

'Except that Vanessa listened at the door, and did some guessing about the murders, and told her cousin, Giles Mooney, and he may have told his parents. In fact, the whole lot of them may know all about it by now.'

'But they didn't when you arrived.'

'I don't think so.'

'So I'd guess Mrs Garvie-Brown was still just fumbling around in her own mind, feeling you'd had a very peculiar wrong done to you, and wanting to put it right somehow, but not having decided yet just what to do. And she wanted you to go to her solicitor for her to find out what the legal position about the family money was. Meanwhile, what does she do with this thing she's found, this diary? A diary telling all, and which he probably had a wonderful time writing, hoping it would be found some day, so that people would know at last what a clever fellow he'd been. Anyway, let's suppose that's how it was. Well, what did she do with it?'

'Vanessa thought she'd have deposited it in her bank or with her lawyer.'

'I don't.'

'Why not?'

Mrs Doubtfire leant forward and put her elbows on the desk. But the movement reminded her of the pain in her back. She winced and sat upright again, propped up by her hard cushion.

'Those tablets ought to have started to work by now,' she said, 'but they don't do a thing. I don't know why I take them.' She drank some more gin. 'Well, if I were in her position, the way I'd think would be this. I'm old and I'm ill, I may drop dead at any time, and if I put this bomb I've found in a bank or at my lawyer's, and I do drop dead, my executors will have to see it, and then what? The cat will be out of the bag, quite uncontrollable by me.'

'Couldn't she write on it something like, "To be destroyed in the event of my death"?'

'I'm not sure if that would have any legal standing. Suppose what was inside a package of that sort were valuable —as, my God, this is! Think what you could get for serialization of it in the Sunday papers! Well, wouldn't it be part of the estate, and subject to tax, even if it were to be destroyed?'

'I don't know. Would it?'

'It's a very interesting speculation. How little most of us actually know about the law we live under. I wonder how it would be assessed as a concealed asset. It's possible past death duties ought to have been paid on it already and that the interest on them has been piling up for years and years. Of course, I don't know. But neither does Mrs Garvie-Brown. That's the point. So what she'd do, I think—anyway, it's what I'd do myself—is hide the thing for the time being among my other possessions, meaning to do something more definite about it later.'

'What *you'd* do,' Luke said, 'is destroy it, as I should too.'

She gave a grin. 'I don't think I should, you know. I'd know it was what I ought to do. But I'd keep wanting to have another look at it. I'd get sort of fascinated by it. And I'd keep putting off doing anything definite. The older you get, the more inclined you are to postpone things. If it's disturbing to think about a thing, you just switch your mind off on to something else. What difference is it going to make in the end anyway? So let's suppose I've hidden this thing somewhere in my flat, and I've persuaded a young man to go to my solicitor to ask him all the questions I'm afraid of asking him, and say it was information he needed for a novel—'

'Yes, and then you turn on the young man and tell him to go to hell and that you're going to the police if he doesn't!'

'And she told you what? That she'd been out to dinner, wasn't that it? That was why she didn't answer when you telephoned, it wasn't because she'd gone to bed early, but because she was out. So her flat was empty. And someone got in and searched for the diary.'

'And found it?'

'Who knows?'

'But who really did that? Arne?'

'He seems the likeliest. But it could have been the girl, Vanessa, or the Mooney young man, or any of the others, even his lordship. In fact, I rather like the idea of its being the judge. Who can think faster and be more decisive and more ruthless than a judge? All the same, I suppose it was probably Arne.'

'And now he's going to milk the family of everything they've got.'

'That would seem to follow.' She gave a quite mellow smile, pleased with the logic that had led her to this conclusion. 'Now just a little more gin—not a big one this time—and then if you'd be a dear, Luke, and go and nobble a taxi for me before the effect begins to wear off . . .'

'Just a minute,' Luke said. 'What about this money? If Mrs Garvie-Brown thinks I took the diary or whatever it is, did she send me this money?'

'She or someone,' said Mrs Doubtfire, not very helpfully. Her gaze which she turned now on the pile of notes, had just that moment changed from clear and lucid to fixed and glassy. 'To get you to keep quiet about the whole affair. In the circumstances, it seems a pitifully small amount, doesn't it? Scottish thrift, perhaps. If I were you I'd hold out for more. Lots more. Luke dear, please get me that drink, or I shall start getting drunk.'

He took her glass to the cupboard and filled it about half as full as he had before. She sipped it slowly and nodded her head. 'That's better.'

'But what am I going to *do* with the money?' Luke demanded.

'You're much too high-principled just to take it and spend it, I suppose?' she said.

'Too scared,' he answered.

'Well then, would you like to leave it in the office safe? I'll give you a receipt for it, and if ever an occasion arises when you're questioned about how you came by it, I'll back up your story of coming to me with it for my advice, and say I recommended you to put it in the safe here and wait and see what happened next. That *is* my advice, on the whole.'

'Yes, that's excellent,' Luke said gratefully. 'Just to get rid of it somehow, to dump it somewhere . . . Thank you so much, Mrs Doubtfire. You're a tremendous help.'

'All right. Now you be getting me that taxi and I'll put the stuff away.' She got slowly and stiffly to her feet, grimacing, picked up the bundle of notes and made her way towards the safe in a corner of her office while Luke went out to find a taxi for her.

Being without the money gave Luke a wonderfully lightened, carefree feeling. He walked most of the way home, enjoying his aloofness from the crowds swirling down into the Underground stations and the patient queues at the bus stops. He always enjoyed walking in London, particularly at twilight.

Stopping at the shop near his flat which his landlady called 'the delly', he bought half a cold chicken, a carton of Russian salad, some Gorgonzola and a bottle of Yugoslavian Riesling. He had his evening planned. He would have a bath, get into pyjamas and dressing-gown, eat his supper peacefully by the gas fire, and then, in a relaxed and comfortable mood, with the remainder of the wine at his elbow, start reading his novel from the beginning and find out what he really thought of it.

And he would forget the money and the problem of who had sent it and everything that had happened during the last few days.

It went almost as planned. The only thing that went wrong was that when he started reading his novel, he found it so appallingly bad that the peace of the evening, which he had been cultivating so carefully, evaporated completely. He became extremely agitated, started talking to himself, walking about the room and from time to time assaulting the manuscript with a ball-point pen as if he were trying to penetrate the armour of his worst enemy. What triteness, what immaturity, what limitless dullness! Had he really been capable of this? If there had happened to be an open fireplace in his room instead of a gas fire, he would have torn the pages into little pieces and burnt them there and then.

What he did with them in the end was to put them into a box-file which he put away in a cupboard. Then he put the cover on to his typewriter, closing it with a little click of finality. That was that for the present. No more novel. But he would not destroy the thing, because, who knew, perhaps next week, or next month, or next year, he would be able to nerve himself to take another look at it and might find that at least some of it was not as bad as he felt tonight. Perhaps he might even feel better about it tomorrow. He ought never to have tried reading it this evening. His nerves were far more on edge than he had realized. He ought to have stuck to watching television.

He slept restlessly and woke up with an unpleasant headache, wondering drowsily if perhaps he was getting 'flu. That would really be a rather pleasant thing to have happen just now, he thought. His landlady was always very good to him when he was ill, and there is nothing like a good dose of 'flu for cutting one off from the outer world, making its most dreadful problems negligible.

But he had no sore throat, no catarrh, no pains in his joints. He got out of bed and wandered, yawning, to his front door, to fetch his bottle of milk and the morning paper.

An object of horrible familiarity lay on the rug inside the door.

It was a package in a thick envelope, sealed with several lengths of Sellotape and addressed to him in large, childish-looking capital letters. The postmark was Edinburgh.

With fingers clumsy with anger, he tore the package open. Inside were more soiled, crumpled pound notes. One hundred of them.

CHAPTER XII

THE SIGHT startled him less this time, and made him less
excited. He knew where the money belonged. It belonged
in Mrs Doubtfire's safe, along with the other hundred
pounds. Or did the arrival of this second donation alter
the situation somehow?

Shaving and getting dressed, he pondered the question.
Someone, he thought, the person who believed that he had
whatever it was that could bring scandal, perhaps tragedy,
to the Garvie-Browns, had been thinking about the rise
in the cost of living. He, or she, had realized that a
hundred pounds didn't go very far these days. So he,
or she, had doubled it. That was all. The basic situation
was unaltered. Someone was trying to buy his silence.

Or was someone trying to frame him as a blackmailer?

He was shaving when he thought of this. His hand
jerked and he cut himself. Was someone trying deliberately
to make him appear that most despicable kind of criminal?

But who was there who had anything to gain by doing
such a thing?

The only answer to that question that he could think
of was that it was some member of the Garvie-Brown
family who wanted to put Christina Garvie-Brown off
doing anything for him financially. Someone who did not
know how violently she had already turned against him.

Far-fetched?

Wasn't it much more likely that he was simply being
paid for his silence by someone who believed that he had
the diary? And anyhow, the money was not going to be
found in his possession. It would be in Mrs Doubtfire's safe
and he would have her receipt and her assurance that,

if it became necessary, she would back up his story of how and why he had brought it to her.

With the money in his briefcase, he set off for the office. He was told that Mrs Doubtfire was not coming in that morning. She had telephoned, her secretary said, to say that her back was too bad for her to leave home. Her secretary could have opened the safe, but she would not have understood why Luke wanted to deposit a package there, or the importance of giving him a receipt, and he did not want to take her into his confidence. Wandering disconsolately out of the office, he got on to a bus to take him to the British Museum.

The thought of those seventeenth-century smugglers sickened him this morning. They had been a disgusting lot, dishonest, dangerous, murderous, their so-called glamour coming only from the satisfaction that the normally law-abiding person feels when he manages to slip an unde-cleared bottle of spirits or scent through the Customs. How-ever, Luke had a job to do. He owed that much to Mrs Doubtfire. So he did a hard morning's work, reading and making notes for this writer character in Cornwall, and hoping malevolently that when the man eventually came to write his book, and to read what he had written, it would give him as nasty a shock as Luke's book had given him the evening before. Then at one o'clock he went out for lunch at his usual snack-bar.

It was while he was eating his ham sandwich that all of a sudden he made up his mind that this hundred pounds that he was carrying around with him was not going into Mrs Doubtfire's safe after all. It was going back to Edin-burgh, where it had come from. And he was going with it, to make a few things plain to the whole clan of Garvie-Browns.

He finished his work on the smugglers that afternoon, re-membered to telephone Stephanie to tell her that he was returning to Edinburgh and so could not take her out that evening, took the notes that he had made on the smugglers back to his flat, and packed a bag, putting the notes, as well as bank notes, into it. At King's Cross, he was lucky enough to be able to book a sleeper on one of the late trains, then had fish and chips in a seedy little café near the station, after which he had a longish wait in the station, but at last got on to the train.

When it started he did not try to sleep, but sat on the edge of his bunk, making a précis of his notes on the smugglers, which he then put into a stamped envelope that he had brought with him, addressed it to Good Neighbours, Ltd, where it would be typed before being sent to Cornwall, put it back into his bag, undressed and got into bed. He was sustained all the time by a sense of confidence and self-sufficiency. He was glad that he had not put the money into Mrs Doubtfire's safe. He had been becoming far too dependant on her, he saw. It was kind of her to allow it, but it was going to be very bad for him if it went on much longer. It was time for him to start standing on his own feet, even if, as she had told him, they did not look as if they were ever quite on the ground.

He knew exactly what he was going to do when he got to Edinburgh. He was going to insist on seeing all the Garvie-Browns at the same time. He was going to slam the hundred pounds down in front of them all, and tell them to sort out amongst themselves to whom it belonged and to leave him alone. Goodbye. And that would be that.

He did not think that he owed it to Mrs Garvie-Brown to keep her counsel any more, since she had turned so unjustly against him. Let her manage her own problems and leave him out of them.

Some time in pondering this course of action he fell asleep and did not wake until the train, in the twilight of the early morning, was slipping past some stark stone houses, rising like cliffs above the railway, near the approach to Waverley Station.

He remembered to post his letter to the office in the station, then he had a breakfast of bacon and eggs and tea in the station buffet. Then he telephoned the hotel in which he had stayed before and made sure that there was a room available. But naturally they would not dream of letting him occupy the room until twelve o'clock, unless he paid for the night that he had not spent there. Faced with the predicament of all travellers in Britain who have travelled through the night but are refused admittance to their hotels until noon, Luke strolled up the ramp past the notice that said 'Carriage Exit', and on into Princes Street.

It was almost empty of traffic. He could see from end to end of the broad, straight mile, and he could think that since the nobler past of the street was irrevocably lost, it could still be one of the finest in Europe if only they would tear down all the buildings along it and start again from scratch. Provided, of course, that they used a few better ideas than the last lot of builders had cooked up in some decidedly off moments.

But what was he to do for the next hour or so? It was still only eight o'clock, and he could hardly appear at Christina Garvie-Brown's door as early as that. He guessed that she was the sort of woman who would be an early riser, but to call on her at eight o'clock would be overdoing things.

The twilight had gone and a pale blue sky arched over the grey roofs of the city. The air was wind-still, with a frosty tingle in it. Luke wandered on along the street. He saw that his old friend, the wall-scribbler, had been at it again. This time he had committed himself to a more extended statement than before. He had written, 'No Popery!—Capitalism Out!—Rangers!'

The message might have puzzled Luke, who had not much interest in sport, if he had not possessed a television set, through which he had learnt that Rangers was a football team, whose supporters for the main part also supported the Church of Scotland, and were in deadly rivalry with Celtic, a team whose supporters were mostly Catholic. He knew too that this rivalry had often led to shocking destructiveness and mild bloodshed. So this was a package declaration of faith, relating to the three most passionate feelings in the soul of the scribbler, religion, politics, football. Luke turned away from reading it, and as he did so happened to see a bus go by to Morningside.

It gave him an idea. If it was still too early to call on Mrs Garvie-Brown, why shouldn't he drop in on Vanessa? She would probably give him house-room for an hour or two. He chased the bus, caught it at the next stop and sprang on to it.

It was harder for him to find Vanessa's flat than he had expected. He had gone there before by car, from a different direction. However, after leaving the bus and taking one or two wrong turnings, he recognized a slightly curved terrace of stone-fronted houses, one of which had its front door open and two doors inside, and Vanessa's name-plate on one of the doors. He rang her bell and at once heard quick steps coming to answer it.

But it was not Vanessa who opened the door. It was, Luke supposed, the research student with whom she shared the flat. The girl was small and dumpy, with dark curly hair, a round, clean-looking face and a wide, inviting smile.

'Vanessa?' she said. 'I'm sorry, she's spending the week-end at Blackhope.' Her voice had the melody of the West Highlands. It made Luke think of soft mists, and islands in the sea, and peat bogs and heather-covered hillsides. She wore an old sheepskin coat, a short tweed skirt, scarlet stockings and stout, flat-heeled shoes. 'And I have to go out myself in a few minutes. Is there anything I can do for you?'

'No, don't worry,' he said. 'I just hoped Vanessa would let me stay here for an hour or two. I've just got in from

London, and I want to see Mrs Garvie-Brown as soon as I can. But it seems a bit early to call in on her now, so I thought of coming here. My name's Luke Latimer. I don't know if Vanessa's spoken of me.'

'Oh, that's who you are—yes, of course she has. She said you're a second cousin or something, aren't you?' The girl smiled at him happily. 'Come in. I'm sorry I'll have to leave you alone, but I've got an experiment going at the lab and I just can't leave it. Do you think you can manage alone? There's lots of hot water, if you'd like a bath after your journey, and there are clean towels in the cupboard in the bathroom, and if you poke about in the kitchen, you'll find coffee and milk and everything. Do help yourself to anything you want. But Vanessa won't be home till fairly late this evening. Perhaps you should telephone her. The number's in the book. Will you be coming back after you've seen Mrs Garvie-Brown? Anyway, in case you can't, I'll tell Vanessa you came. I *am* sorry I can't stay. I know it seems horribly inhospitable, but I really can't help it. Goodbye.'

Luke found himself alone in the flat as she darted out, cheerfully slamming the door behind her.

A second cousin or something.

Luke grinned.

But the thought of a bath was extraordinarily attractive. It was more than he had hoped for. He was glad that he had brought his bag with him instead of depositing it in the left-luggage office. It meant that he could shave and put on a clean shirt, which would add to his moral courage when he tackled Christina Garvie-Brown. He was glad too that he had come in his best suit, a sober brown worsted, well cut, which he had scarcely worn since he had stopped working as a chartered accountant. It would give him more authority than the flannels, sweater and corduroy jacket in which she had seen him before.

But catching sight of himself, as he went looking for the

bathroom, in a mirror that hung in the hall, it struck him that what he really needed to make him look a responsible member of the human race was a hair-cut. Very well, when he had had a bath and some coffee, he would look for a barber and have the hair-cut that he had been promising himself for the last month.

But of course it was Sunday. No barber's shop would be open. His hair would have to stay as it was. He turned a door-handle. Was this the bathroom? He opened the door and found himself in Vanessa's bedroom.

He knew that it was hers and not the research student's, because of the smell of paint in it, the untidy assembly of brushes and canvases, and because of a half-finished portrait of Giles Mooney which looked straight at Luke from an easel. At least, he supposed that it was half-finished. It was like a note, a mere jotting down of Giles's features, made, Luke thought, with a felt-tipped pen. But casual as it was, it had caught Giles's calm arrogance. The faint smile of the lightly drawn lips had all his self-confidence.

Luke felt no inclination to return the smile. Its effect on him was to depress him suddenly and cruelly. The pain of it told him something very important about himself. He was falling in love with Vanessa, that was what it was. Perhaps had already fallen. Perhaps it was already too late to draw back. But also too late to advance. Too late all round. He looked at the portrait of Giles with deep resentment, and retreating from the room, shut the door behind him with far more of a bang that was necessary.

He tried the next door and this time it was the bathroom. The water was steaming hot. He undressed while the bath was filling, had a long, relaxing wallow in it, shaved, dressed again and did his best to comb his damp hair smoothly back from his ears. He felt pleased with the tie that he had chosen for the occasion. It was of dark brown silk, faintly shot with dusky red. If he could find out now where the girls kept their shoe-cleaning apparatus, he could go forth to meet Mrs Garvie-Brown, and as many of her family as she cared to have present, without any uneasy feeling of inferiority.

He found shoe-polish and brushes in the kitchen, also coffee, milk and sugar. The kitchen was a minute place, which had probably been made out of the old scullery when the house had been converted into flats. The two girls must be very good friends, he thought, to be able to share it without quarrelling. Not that Vanessa was a quarrelsome type, of that he felt certain. She might be opinionated and strong-minded, but would not be petty or inclined to go looking for trouble. And the other girl had seemed charming. How sad, how very sad, even if it was for his own ultimate good, that he was not going to be able to see any more of Vanessa, would be very well advised never to try to see her again . . .

Feeling all the more melancholy, however, because of the misleading sense of intimacy with her which having been left alone in her flat was giving him, to have a bath and shave and cook and be at ease, he cleaned his shoes, made coffee, helped himself to some biscuits from a tin in a cupboard and took them into the sitting-room.

He supposed that the two girls shared this room as they did the kitchen. Besides the armchairs and the dining-table with four chairs round it, there were two writing-tables and a clear division of interest in the long bookcase along one wall. At one end there were nothing but scientific text books and a few books of verse. At the other end was a mixture of novels, old and new, and some books on painting, pictures, antique furniture, china and glass, history and travel. There was the same contrast in the two writing-tables. One was used for serious work. There were orderly heaps of notes on it, and piles of foolscap and graph-paper. The other was littered with letters and bills, had a cheque-book sticking out of a pigeon hole, and some envelopes, stamps and a roll of Sellotape scattered over it.

It was the Sellotape that suddenly caught Luke's attention.

Not that there was any good reason why it should. It is to be found in most households. But this happened to be of the same width as the Sellotape with which those two packages of money that he had received had been fastened. As if helplessly drawn across the room by a magnet, Luke walked to the desk. He knew what else he would find before he got there. And there they were, beside the roll of Sellotape, the remains of a packet of thick white envelopes of just the same and type as those in which the money had arrived.

Oh, Vanessa! Oh God, the poor fool!

To his own surprise, Luke felt no anger, but only an astonished pity that with all her intelligence, she could have been so unperceptive and so simple. Yet he had half-known it all along, because who else in the Garvie-Brown clan would ever have imagined that if he were the sort of man who had to be bought off, two hundred pounds would do it? Two hundred that it had been a little difficult to scrape up, or how else explain the money being sent in two instalments? All the older members of the family, accustomed to handling daily far larger sums than Vanessa probably did in a month, would have had more sense of proportion. There seemed to Luke to be a fearful pathos in her ignorance.

But that did not make him hesitate in what he did next. He reached out for her cheque-book, opened it and looked at the stubs. There it was, 'Self, one hundred pounds.' But not a cheque for the second hundred pounds. Yet this was all the proof that he could possibly want. But just where did that land him? Was there any point now in going to see Mrs Garvie-Brown? Wasn't it Vanessa herself whom he had to see?

At that moment the telephone rang.

At first he ignored it, but it went on ringing, and after a moment he picked it up, thinking that he might at least take a message for whichever of the girls the call was for, in return for the bath and the shoe-polish and the coffee and biscuits. Reading the number on the dial, he spoke it into the instrument.

A man's voice said, 'Mr Latimer?'

He started and said, 'Yes.'

'Arne here,' the voice went on. 'I've got to speak to you, Mr Latimer. Now, as quickly as possible.'

'Arne?' Luke said incredulously. 'How on earth did you know where I was?'

'I have my methods,' Gilbert Arne replied, as he had once before. 'Wouldn't be much good in my job if I didn't, would I? Now how soon can you meet me?'

'I don't want to meet you at all,' Luke said.

'Oh, come now, this is important.'

'Where are you? In Edinburgh?'

'Yes, of course in Edinburgh. I'm in Waverley. We could meet in the lounge of the North British—'

'No,' Luke interrupted firmly. 'I've other things to do. I came here for a reason.'

'Of course you did. So did I.' There was an undercurrent of anger in the flat, inexpressive voice that Luke had not heard in it before. 'So let me advise you to meet me before you take any steps on your own.'

'I don't know what you're talking about,' Luke said, 'and I don't want to know, and I don't want to meet you. Goodbye.'

'Wait!' Arne barked at him fiercely. 'I tell you, if you try anything, you'll be in trouble. I'm a peaceable man, but there are things I won't stand for and you can easily guess what they are. Now when will you meet me?'

'I won't,' Luke said. 'Anyway, not if you won't tell me how you knew where I was. Have you been following me?'

'Where d'you think I'd find the time for that?'

'That's what I was wondering. Well, as I said before, I've things to do. Goodbye.' Luke put the telephone down.

Almost immediately it started ringing again.

He let it ring. Picking up his coffee-tray, he took it out to the kitchen and meticulously washed up everything that he had used, made sure that he had left the bathroom tidy, closed his bag, returned to the sitting-room, and while the telephone continued to ring with manic persistence, pocketed Vanessa's cheque-book and let himself out of the flat.

CHAPTER XIII

To KEEP his mind off Vanessa, in the bus back to Princes Street, Luke tried to think out how Gilbert Arne had known where to find him that morning.

Could it have been by sheer chance? Had Arne just happened to be in Waverley Station when Luke's train arrived, caught sight of him there and followed him out to Morningside? He had said that he was telephoning from Waverley Station, but it could just as easily have been from a call-box near the flat.

Luke dismissed the possibility that Arne had been following him around in London for the last few days and so could have known when he left for Edinburgh. For one thing, Luke would have seen him. And even supposing that Arne had the incriminating diary of Duncan Garvie-Brown in his possession, as Mrs. Doubtfire had suggested, why should he have bothered with trailing after Luke, who had too little money, too little social status, and too little feeling for the Garvie-Browns, to be worth blackmailing? No, Luke thought, Arne must have stayed on here in Edinburgh when Luke returned to London, must have started to get his teeth into the Garvie-Browns and had rung Luke up that morning because he was afraid that Luke was somehow intending to horn in on his project.

Yes, but how had Arne known where to find him?

It had to be by chance. In a town the size of Edinburgh you would always be seeing people you knew by chance.

Luke got off the bus in Princes Street and took the turning that would lead him uphill, then down, to Heriot Row.

Being a Sunday morning, the wide streets had remained almost empty of traffic. For once they had the air of serenity that they had been meant to have. It was possible to enjoy their spaciousness and dignity. The sky was a brighter blue than it had been when Luke arrived, with a sparkle of sunshine in the frosty air, which took the sombreness from the stone buildings. Luke wished that he had something pleasanter to do with such a morning than what he had in hand.

The gardens in Heriot Row were barer than when he had been here last. There must have been some strong winds while he had been away, for many of the trees had been stripped and the drifts of dead leaves on the lawns and pavement were thick and already growing treacherously slippery with decay. Luke tramped up the depressing staircase to Christina Garvie-Brown's flat in a mood to get his business with her over as fast as possible.

There was a possibility, of course, that she would refuse to speak to him. If she was still in the mood that she had been in when they had spoken last on the telephone, she might slam the door in his face. If she did, he was going to push money, cheque-book and an IOU for the hundred pounds in Mrs Doubtfire's safe through the letterbox, and go away. The one thing that he would not do was dither, listen to arguments, become involved again.

But what had become of the potted plants that he remembered under the landing window? They were gone.

Or had he still another flight of stairs to climb? No, there was the cheerful, light blue door, with the name Garvie-Brown on it. The door happened to be standing wide open. Reaching the doorway, Luke looked in and saw that, like the potted plants, all the furniture had gone. Inside there were only bare floors, bare walls, bare stairs. Mrs Garvie-Brown had flitted. She had gone to Blackhope.

He cursed quietly at not having thought before that that might have happened. He had wasted time coming here. He ought to have been inquiring how to get to Blackhope by bus. He turned to go downstairs again.

Just then he heard a voice inside the flat, a child's voice, high and clear.

It said, 'And if we say something like—oh, like, "I hate you, I wish you were dead!"—we pay threepence. But if we say something *bad* we pay sixpence.'

A small girl appeared in the doorway of what had been Christina's drawing-room. The child was backing out of it, talking to someone inside the room. A sound from Luke made her turn round and stare at him. She was about ten and was dressed in scarlet woollen tights and a dark blue quilted anorak. Her dark hair was cut very short. Her eyes were dark and large and innocent.

'Hallo,' she said.

'Hallo,' said Luke.

'Do you want something?' she asked politely.

'I'd like to know what's worse than wishing a person dead,' he said.

'Oh, *you* know,' she answered.

Of course he did, even if he thought the sense of values curious.

'And whom do you pay the money to?' he asked.

'Oxfam,' she said. 'We decided to sort of fine ourselves, to collect money for them.'

'Who's we?' he asked.

'The girls at school.'

'And who decided the scale of the fines?'

'The what?'

'I mean, who decided that wanting to do murder should only cost threepence and that these other awful things should cost double?'

'We decided ourselves,' she said. 'And the mistresses pay sixpence too if they do something like forgetting our right names. Why?'

'Oh, it's interesting. The milder the crime, it seems, the more you have to pay. Citizens of tomorrow. You may be even more frightening than what we've got around today.'

'It isn't that it's *milder*, it's just that it isn't real, you see.'

'Isn't it real sometimes?'

She looked puzzled. 'You do say awfully funny things. Don't you think we ought to collect for Oxfam?'

'Oh, yes, yes, good luck to you.'

'We've got twenty-seven shillings already.'

'Splendid.'

'But you didn't come here just to ask about that, did you?'

'No, I was looking for Mrs Garvie-Brown.'

'She's gone. This is our house now.' She turned her head and called over her shoulder, 'Mummy, there's a man here who wants Mrs Garvie-Brown.'

A young, pleasant-looking woman in a tweed coat and head-scarf appeared in the doorway through which the child had come.

'Mrs Garvie-Brown? She moved out on Friday,' she said. She hesitated, obviously uncertain as to whether or not she should give Mrs Garvie-Brown's new address to a stranger.

Luke helped her out. 'To the bungalow at Blackhope?' he said.

'Yes.'

'I knew she was moving shortly,' he said, 'but I wasn't sure when. I wonder if you can tell me how to get to Blackhope. I'm a stranger in Edinburgh. Are there buses, or trains, or what?'

'There'll be buses from the bus-station in St Andrew's Square,' she replied. 'It's quite near. You walk straight along Heriot Row and Abercrombie Place, and turn right up Duke Street and there it is ahead of you. The buses go quite often, I think about a quarter past and quarter to the hour. I sometimes play golf there, that's why I know.' She glanced at her watch. 'It's eleven o'clock now. You can probably catch the eleven-fifteen if you hurry.'

'Mummy,' the child said, tweaking her mother's sleeve, 'the man thinks we ought to pay more than threepence for saying we wish someone was dead.'

Luke smiled at her. 'Don't take any notice of the man.'

He thanked the young woman for her help, turned and went running down the stairs.

He found his way to the bus station without difficulty. He had more difficulty, when he got there, in finding out from which part of it the buses left for Blackhope. When he found the right platform, a queue of passengers was already moving into a bus that was waiting there. But the queue was not very long and there was plenty of room inside. Luke went to a seat near the back and sat down next to the window.

He thought that he was going to have the seat to himself until just before the bus moved off a man leapt on board and came quickly down the aisle and sat down next to Luke.

' "Brother," ' said Gilbert Arne with a smug smile, ' "are you going my way?" '

For a moment Luke was so angry that he did not trust himself to speak. Sitting beside the window, with Arne

144

between him and the aisle, he felt hemmed in and helpless. The bus began to move.

'So you *have* been following me,' Luke said.

'Only in my thoughts,' Arne replied as the bus emerged from the station and began to circle the big square outside. 'If they tend to run in the same direction as yours, you can't blame me, can you?'

'Don't talk such bloody nonsense!'

'It isn't nonsense. It's just that I seem to know, kind of intuitively, what you're likely to do next.'

Luke answered more rudely.

'No, no, I mean it,' Arne said earnestly. 'When my mind's working very hard on the same thing as another person's, I sometimes find I'm sort of in contact with them. I can't explain it, but I've learnt to trust it. Not that I expected to find you on this bus. I just had this feeling it would be a good idea to go out to Blackhope on my own, since you wouldn't meet me, and I came up here from Waverley and there you were in the queue and I ran for it, because, as I was saying earlier, I think we ought to talk.'

'All right, you don't mean to tell me how you've been keeping track of me,' Luke said. 'There's no need to make up a lot of guff. But we've still got nothing to talk about.'

He did not recognize the route that the bus was taking. Mrs Garvie-Brown had driven him out to Blackhope by a different road.

'We've the diary to talk about,' Arne said.

Behind them a woman had started to tell her companion how she intended never to have anything more to do with one of her oldest and dearest friends because the friend had failed to ask her to her wedding until a week before the day, and had only done it then for the sake of the wedding-present. The companion said, 'Aye,' at intervals in a tone of cynical agreement.

What a lot of aggressive people there were in the world,

Luke thought absently, people ready to give offence, to take offence, to look hopefully for further opportunities to give and take still more offence.

'You don't think I've got the diary, do you?' he said quietly.

Arne nodded. With his coat-collar turned up round his short neck against the frosty chill of the morning, his large head looked more than ever as if it had been put down on his shoulders by chance and might roll off at any moment.

'That's what I do think,' he said.

'And I think you've got it.'

The large head was shaken. 'No, I won't say I hold it against you, the way you're trying to doublecross everyone, but of course I know you've got it.'

'Everyone? Who?' As Arne did not answer, Luke added, 'More intuition!'

'Call it reasoning this time,' Arne said. 'What's brought you back to Edinburgh, what's taking you out to Blackhope, if you haven't got it?'

'What's brought you?'

'You have. If I can see it's natural to try on what you're doing, I still don't like it. No hard feelings, but I don't let a person get away with anything like that if I can help it.'

'You know, you're still talking the most incredible nonsense,' Luke said, still mildly. 'There's never been any kind of agreement between us, so how can there be any doublecross?'

'Did I say it was me you're doublecrossing?'

'It's yourself you're worried about.'

The conductor, who had been coming along the bus, taking fares, stopped beside them then, and before Luke could speak, Arne, who was next to the aisle, asked for two tickets to Blackhope and paid for them with a ten-shilling note.

'How much was it?' Luke asked as the conductor moved on.

'You can pay on the way back,' Arne replied.

'What makes you think we'll be coming back together?'

'I'm going to see that we do.'

'Well, you still haven't answered my other question,' Luke said. 'What makes you think I want to doublecross you in any way?'

Arne looked impatient, as if Luke's stubborn lack of understanding were beginning to annoy him.

'Look, you've got the diary, haven't you?' he said. 'You're going out to see the old lady. You're going out to see if you can make some sort of deal with her. Well, if it wasn't for me, you wouldn't even know there was a diary. You wouldn't be making deals with anyone. I found you, I put you in the picture, I did all the spadework for you. Isn't that the truth? So if you're thinking of leaving me out, that's a doublecross, isn't it?'

'But I haven't got the diary,' Luke said. 'You've got it.'

Behind them the woman who had not been asked to her friend's wedding in time was reciting the subtle revenges that she intended to take for the horrible slight. With maddening monotony, her companion in the bus kept responding with an approving, flat and extraordinarily penetrating, 'Aye.'

Luke began to feel that if she said it just once more, he would turn round and hit her.

'Aye,' she said again. 'Aye, I'd do the same mesel'.'

He clenched his hands on his knees and turned to look at Arne. 'You *have* got the diary, haven't you?'

'No,' Arne said.

'I don't believe you.'

'I don't believe *you*.'

'I could quite easily prove to you I haven't got it,' Luke said. 'Could you prove to me you haven't?'

147

'How can you prove it?' Arne asked.

'Because I'm not going to see Mrs Garvie-Brown to get money out of her, but to pay her some,' Luke said.

Arne's head swivelled on his heavy shoulders. 'How's that?'

'I've got a hundred pounds with me which I'm going to hand over to Mrs Garvie-Brown,' Luke said. 'Someone else has been making the same mistake about me as you seem to have been making. They think I've got the diary and they've tried to pay me for my silence. I—I don't know who it is, so I'm handing the money over to Mrs Garvie-Brown for safe-keeping till she can find out where it came from.'

He could hear Arne breathing heavily beside him.

'How do I know any of this is true?' Arne asked.

'You can be there, if you like, when I give her the money,' said Luke. 'There are some things I want to say to her in private, but you can see me give her the money.'

The private things that Luke wanted to say to Christina Garvie-Brown concerned Vanessa's cheque-book. He did not want to see Vanessa again, but he felt a certain protectiveness towards her, and did not want anyone else to be there when he showed the cheque-book to Christina and explained what it meant and how he had come by it.

'All right,' Arne said. 'Fair enough. But who *has* got the diary then?'

'I think you have.'

'Look,' Arne said, as if explaining something to the mentally retarded, 'if I had it, why should I worry about what you're up to with the old lady? Why should I be here at all?'

'To pick up your blackmail, of course.'

'Listen, if I were thinking of blackmail, I'd be keeping as clear of the place as I could. I'd have fixed up some way of being paid off that didn't mean I'd even got to show my face in this town. Can't you see that?'

'Yes,' Luke said reluctantly. 'But you could say the same of me.'

'Only you're an amateur. You might not know much about how to go about the operation.'

'What makes you think the thing's been taken, anyway?'

'I rang up Mrs Garvie-Brown when I was here before,' Arne said. 'I'll be straight with you, I was going to warn her you were a dangerous character. I hadn't liked the way you treated me when I came to see you in your hotel. If it comes to that, I hadn't liked the way you treated me from the start, as if I was something crawling in the slime. So I was going to tell her you weren't to be trusted and she ought to take care in any dealings she had with you. And before I could get a word in, she started saying all that herself. And without her actually saying you'd taken anything, it was what I worked out.'

'Just a minute,' Luke said. 'You say she didn't actually tell you I'd stolen the thing?'

'Not in so many words.'

'She didn't employ you to get it back?'

'She didn't employ me—no. But there are sometimes things one feels one owes to a client—'

Luke interrupted, 'Yet you *have* been trailing me around to get it back for yourself. You've been keeping an eye on me in London. You followed me to Edinburgh. You followed me to Morningside. You followed me to the bus station.'

'I tell you, I did not.'

'You must have.'

'And you never once saw me? You know me quite well by sight, yet you never had a glimpse of me. Man, you must think I'm a genius at my job.'

'You'd some operative of yours on the job then.'

Arne gave a sigh. 'I'm a one-man show, not counting Janie. My secretary, d'you remember? I expect you do. Those legs of hers, once seen never forgotten. I've tried

149

to persuade her to wear longer skirts. She won't listen. She doesn't know what she looks like from behind.'

'Are you trying to change the subject?'

Arne did not answer. He stared before him, frowning in thought and hunching his shoulders, so that his head looked as if for once it were lodged safely in a nest.

The bus, by the route that Luke had not travelled before, entered 'The Honest Toun' of Musselburgh and he found himself recognizing the scene, the wide main street, the race course, the Firth beyond it. But this morning the Firth had no blueness or sparkle. A dense, fluffy quilt of fog hung over it. It completely obscured the water and the distant hills, and as the bus moved on, came rolling inland towards it. It came almost as suddenly as snow might come. At one moment the bus was driving through bright, frosty sunshine, at the next was lost in a wet whiteness.

'The haar,' the woman behind Luke said, her thought momentarily distracted from the iniquities of that dearest of her friends. 'I thought it was too fine the morn. I thought, we'll pay for it.'

'Aye,' said her companion, the rightness of having to pay for all that gave pleasure filling her with sombre satisfaction.

The bus had to slacken its pace. The fog was patchy, sometimes not as dense as it had appeared at first, with water and sky shining hazily through, but at others muffling the landscape in a cloud so thick that the edges of the road were hardly to be seen. Soon Luke found that he no longer knew where he was. He recognized the dim outlines of the power station, but he saw nothing of the dunes with their spiny clumps of sea-buckthorn and he might have missed the notice board with Blackhope on it and gone on right past the turning into the village if Arne had not suddenly dug his elbow into his ribs, said, 'Here we are,' and gone lurching along the bus to the door.

'You've been out here before then,' Luke said as the bus went on and he and Arne set off walking through the chill of the fog.

'Aye,' Arne answered in a flat-voiced imitation of the woman who had sat behind him and they both laughed. It was the nearest that they had come, since their first meeting, to anything approaching friendliness.

The fog was not so thick that they had any difficulty in finding their way to the bungalow, but as Luke and Arne approached it down its straight drive, Luke found that the place seemed eerily different from his memory of it. With the sea and the golf course and the neighbouring houses all obliterated, the little building looked as alone as if it were on an empty moor. There was a strange silence too, no chirruping of birds, no distant sound of traffic. Only at intervals, faintly and far away, a foghorn hooted.

The red mini was in the car-port, which suggested that they would find Christina at home. But when Arne rang the doorbell, no one came to the door. Impatiently he rang again, keeping his thumb aggressively on the bell. They could both hear the shrill sound of it inside.

Still no one answered it.

'She must have gone next door to see the other Garvie-Browns,' Luke said.

'Looks like it.' Arne put his hand on the door-knob and gently turned it.

'Here, what are you doing?' Luke exclaimed. 'You can't do that.'

'Just a try,' Arne said. 'It's locked, anyway.'

'You mean, if it weren't, you'd go in?'

'Just thought I'd take a quick look round while I had the chance,' Arne said. 'No harm in that, is there? She'd never have known anything about it. In my job it's always a sensible thing to find out what you can when you get the chance, just on general principles. I think I'll take a look round at the back while I'm at it.'

Luke felt deeply shocked. He thought of privacy as one of the most sacred things in life.

'What are you looking for?'

'Well, for one thing, to see if there are any signs she's living here yet. Bed made, food in the kitchen, that sort of thing. We know she moved out of the other place only a day or two ago, so this'll still be in a mess and she might easily be staying with the people next door till she's got it straightened out a bit. And if she isn't staying here, we've got to decide whether we're going round to see her next door, which means meeting the rest of the gang, or should we telephone, or what?'

He set off round the bungalow.

Against the grain, feeling that he was putting himself utterly and unforgivably in the wrong by doing it, Luke followed him.

Christina Garvie-Brown was not living in the bungalow. It took them only a moment to discover it. She was not living anywhere any more. Even from the garden, looking in through the wide bay window of the sitting-room, they could see that the woman sprawled on the floor in a far corner of the room was dead. She was on her back. Her eyes stared sightlessly at the ceiling. There was a fogginess inside the room, for although the window was closed, one of its big panes had been shattered, and the fog had seeped in through the gash. White and new, a golf ball lay on the carpet, within a few inches of one of her outflung hands.

CHAPTER XIV

ARNE AND LUKE had both moved up close to the window, with their faces almost against the gash in the glass. Neither spoke. Then Arne pushed an arm gingerly through the ragged edges of the hole and reached for the latch of the window.

'What are you doing?' Luke asked in an unnecessary whisper. 'You can't go in there.'

'Don't you want to know if she's dead? Don't you want to know if there's anything we can do for her?' Arne's voice was matter-of-fact.

'You can see she's dead,' Luke answered.

Arne's hand grasped the latch and moved it. 'But you wouldn't like just to make off, would you, leaving her like that, without making absolutely sure?'

'I wasn't suggesting making off. I was suggesting getting a doctor and the police, without disturbing anything.'

'Well, the nearest telephone's over there.'

It was on the floor of the room, in which the furniture still stood about where the removal men had left it. It looked as if no one had get done much about helping Christina to settle into her new home, except that curtains had been hung and the carpet laid.

'And why d'you want the police? A doctor, yes,' Arne went on. 'She'd a bad heart. Obviously she had a heart attack, perhaps brought on by being shot at with golf-balls. Come on.'

He had levered the window open and climbed in.

Wondering why in fact he had felt that the police must be called, Luke followed him.

Arne crossed the room to where the dead woman lay. He walked delicately, with his usual neat little steps, which made him look as if he were a floor-walker, advancing obsequiously to greet a favoured customer. He stooped and touched her cheek with the back of his hand, then lifted one of her hands an inch or two from the floor and let it drop again.

'Pretty cold but no stiffening yet,' he said. 'You're right, though, we'll have to get the police.'

'Why?'

'Well, look at that.'

Feeling numb, but trying to act as if death were not the terrible shock to him that it was, Luke came nearer to the body on the floor. On the side of the dead face, at the temple, which had been invisible from the window, he saw that there was a discoloured mark and a slight grazing of the skin. A few drops of blood had oozed from the small break.

'Well, get on with it,' Arne said.

'With what?'

'Calling the police. Dial 999.'

Obediently Luke went towards the telephone.

But before he had picked it up, Arne exclaimed, 'No, stop! Don't touch it. Use your handkerchief to hold it.'

'Fingerprints?' Luke said. 'You don't suppose he—the —the murderer—did any telephoning from here?'

'You never know. Suppose she was telephoning and dropped the thing when she was attacked and the murderer put it back on the stand. We've just got to be very careful about everything we do in here. The police don't like having evidence mucked about.'

Luke took his handkerchief out of his pocket. 'Won't this smudge any prints there are?'

'A bit, of course. Just handle it as little as you can. And then keep your hands in your pockets. Don't touch anything you can help.'

Luke spread his handkerchief over the telephone, picked

it up cautiously between two fingers and put it to his ear. There was no dialling tone.

'No good,' he said after a moment, replacing the instrument on its stand. 'I suppose it was disconnected when the last people moved out and she hadn't had it connected up yet. One of us had better go next door and tell them what's happened and get them to telephone.'

'All right, go along,' Arne said. He had straightened up but was still looking down thoughtfully at Christina. 'Notice something interesting about her?'

Luke had not really begun to notice anything much yet, but at the question he tried to concentrate and made himself look at the dead old woman, not with one quick, evasive glance, but with deliberation.

With the tensions of living wiped from her face, it looked younger than usual, but apart from that the interesting thing to him was that she looked so much the same as she had when he had seen her last. Her white hair was not disarranged. She was in the same chestnut brown tweed suit, which might, for all he knew, be the only garment she possessed, since he had never seen her in anything else.

He wondered what Arne meant.

'Do you mean her shoes?' he asked. They were the worn, low-heeled, suède shoes that she used for driving and generally kept in the car, not the costly, high-heeled, crocodile pair that she wore at other times. 'Or her hat?'

A hat of olive-green felt, which matched the cashmere jersey that she was wearing with her tweed suit, lay on the floor near her.

'The glass,' Arne said.

Luke noticed it then and wondered why it had not been the first thing that he had thought of when he climbed into the room. There was glass everywhere, mostly in tiny fragments as he had seen it in the drawing-room of the house next door when the golf ball had broken the window.

There were minute glittering splinters sprinkled over the newly laid carpet. They shone in the chestnut brown tweed and in Christina's white hair and one lay like a tear on her smooth, pallid cheek.

And there was the golf ball, of course.

'You see what it means,' Arne said. 'She was killed before the fog came rolling in from the sea. If she'd been killed before it, the glass would be under her, not over her. Because no one goes on playing golf in a fog like this. And that gives you and me a nice alibi, in case we should happen to need it. We were in the bus together when it ran into the fog. What time was that, would you say? The bus left St Andrew's Square at eleven-fifteen, so I suppose it was eleven-forty or thereabouts when we got through Musselburgh. Well, it's always comfortable to have an absolutely unbreakable alibi when it's a case of murder. Now why don't you get off next door?'

'No,' Luke said.

'One of us has got to go.'

'Yes, you go.'

'Oh, I see,' Arne said. 'The old distrust. You don't want to leave me alone here.'

'That's exactly it.'

'What d'you suppose I'd get up to?'

'I don't know. You might start hunting around for the diary.'

'I thought I was supposed to have it already.'

'Well, you might mess about with the evidence for some peculiar reasons of your own.'

'So might you,' Arne said. 'But I don't mind, I'll go. But there's just one thing we'd better decide on first, because we may not get a chance to talk later. Do we tell the police —do we tell anyone—about the diary?'

Luke took a long time to reply. He wished that he could think clearly, but the foggy chill in the room seemed to paralyse his mind. Arne, as if he recognized this, watched him sardonically.

After a pause that was probably not as long as it felt, Luke said, 'Actually we don't know any diary exists.'

'Dead right.' The small, crooked smile on Arne's face widened. 'It may not. It isn't evidence.'

'All the same,' Luke said reluctantly, 'I'd say it's certain we'll have to tell the whole story.'

'Which no one is going to believe.'

'But if it's the motive, if someone came here, looking for it . . .'

Arne nodded. 'I'm afraid you're right, but they still aren't going to believe you. Well, I don't expect I'll be long.'

He went to the door and Luke heard his footsteps crossing the hall, then the opening and shutting of the front door of the bungalow.

At first, when he was alone, Luke had a feeling of being nailed to the spot where he stood, about a yard away from Christina's body. It felt as if movement of any kind, in any direction, would turn out to be impossible. When at last he did move, it was with a sense of extreme lethargy. He went to the window, which he had left open behind him when he had climbed into the room after Arne, and closed it, but the fog and the cold still poured in through the hole in the glass.

Luke stared out through it. He could see the misty shape of the low wall that separated the garden from the golf-course, but not far beyond. The fog there looked as solid as the wall, and except for the intermittent, hoarse, throat-clearing sound of the foghorn, the silence was complete. His own footsteps, as he moved away from the window towards the door, sounded abnormally loud.

He went out into the little hall. It had a more furnished look than the sitting-room, because there had been fewer things to arrange in it. There was a Persian rug on the floor, a semi-circular table against one wall, a rosewood chair with a red damask seat beside the table, and on the wall above it the gilt-framed mirror, which, Luke remembered, had hung in the hall of the flat in Heriot Row. On the table were a pair of gloves and a handbag. Luke's attention clung to them for a moment without his knowing why, then he realized that it was because they made him think of her hat, and of the fact that he had never seen Christina in a hat. When he had first seen her, when she had just come in from 'doing the messages' in the New Town, and next day, when she had called for him in her car at his hotel, she had been bareheaded. So why a hat today?

For church, of course. A woman of her generation would never dream of going to church without a hat.

He turned the thought over in his mind, with the feeling that turning it was like trying to beat up some thick, gluey substance in a bowl, a substance that clung stickily to the sides of the bowl and the spoon. Yet it seemed important to go on.

She had been about to leave for church, then something had stopped her. No, she *had* left for church. She had got at least as far as her car, for she had changed her shoes. Her good shoes must be in the pocket on its door.

In a moment he would go out and check that. Assuming for the present, however, that they were there, it meant that she had put on her hat, taken her gloves and handbag and had gone out to the car, got in, changed her shoes and then had either started out and for some reason turned back later, or else had been interrupted before she started by the occurrence of something unexpected. Perhaps the arrival of someone. Or perhaps she had remembered something that should have been attended to in the house before she left, an electric fire to be switched off, or a window closed. In any case, since she had not changed out of her driving shoes, she had not expected it to detain her long.

But there was the fog to consider, the haar. Had she driven off, then been overtaken by it when she had driven only a little way, lost her nerve and turned back?

No, wait a minute, that wouldn't do. It could not have been because of the fog that she had turned back. The splinters of glass glittering in her clothing indicated that she had been killed before the fog came in. And hadn't he and Arne agreed that their bus had run into the fog at about eleven-forty? Rather late to be going to church. So Luke's reconstruction of Christina's movements just before her death was cock-eyed. That sort of thing, plainly, was over his head. He had better leave it to the experts, whom he hoped to God would arrive soon.

But while he was still alone here, he thought that he would just nip outside and see if her good shoes were in fact in the car. Forgetting Arne's instructions that he should touch as little as possible, he opened the front door, fastened the latch so that he would not find himself accidentally locked out, and went to the car in the car-port.

The shoes were there. He could see them sticking up from the pocket on the door. Also the key was still in the ignition, additional evidence that she had not meant to stay long in the house. And a Bible and prayer book were on the seat beside the driver's. Luke returned to the bungalow, let the latch go so that the door locked itself again, and went back into the sitting-room.

The fog was beginning to recede a little. He could see halfway across the golf-course now. But the chill of it in the room felt even worse than it had outside the moment before. He wondered how long it would be before someone came. The time since Arne had gone away was beginning to feel very long. For the first time Luke wondered if there was any risk that Arne did not intend to return. And if he did not, if he had simply vanished quietly away into the fog while he had the chance, would anyone believe Luke that the other man had ever been there? Arne had been careful, if Luke had not, not to leave fingerprints anywhere. And wasn't there something in the law of Scotland about two witnesses always being necessary before evidence of any kind could be accepted?

A chill that did not come from the fog turned Luke's skin clammy. How long should he wait, he wondered, before taking some action himself?

He was still asking himself this, and looking down at the dead woman in a cloudy and bewildered mood of pity, because even if she had turned against him and believed unspeakable things of him, he had liked her and was sure that she had only believed those things because she had somehow been skilfully misled, when he heard the click of a key in the latch and quick footsteps crossing the hall. Then Frances Garvie-Brown came in.

She had on an anorak over slacks and a jersey. So had Vanessa, who followed her. Beads of moisture silvered their red hair. Giles came in quietly after them. They all stood just inside the door of the room, with shock draining the colour and blotting the expression from their faces. For a moment Luke was not sure that Arne had returned with them. But then he sidled out from behind them and into the room.

'Mrs Garvie-Brown's telephoned the police, who are getting in touch with her husband, who was called out to an accident,' he said. It took Luke an instant to realize that he was referring to Frances Garvie-Brown and not to the woman on the floor. 'They'll soon be here.'

'But I don't understand what you're doing here, Mr Latimer,' Frances said in her high, rattling voice, which to Luke, in the overwrought state that he was in, sounded almost as if she were shrieking at him. 'Why did you come? Did Christina invite you? She told me she'd done with you, didn't want to see any more of you. So what are you doing here?'

'And what's Mr Arne doing here?' Giles Mooney asked. 'That's a puzzle too.'

He walked forward till he stood near Christina's feet. He was dressed in flannels and a waterproof golfing jacket. His fair hair had been crinkled into untidy waves by the damp outside. After the glance that he had given Arne as he asked his question he looked sombrely down at Christina. There was not much grief in the look, Luke thought. Perhaps Giles had had too many step-grandmothers to feel much about any of them. Or perhaps it was simply not in him to feel much about anyone.

'Well?' Giles barked at Arne, as the detective had not answered.

'Not that it's strictly your business,' Arne said, 'and in a sense it's even confidential—I'm not sure I shouldn't save it for the police—but I don't suppose it'll matter if I tell you that I came here simply to interview my client.'

It was untrue, of course. Luke knew that. But he did not feel inclined to challenge it just then.

'And Mr Latimer!' Frances exclaimed again. 'What are you doing here?'

Luke looked at Vanessa as he answered. She did not meet the look. In fact, she had somehow avoided looking at him since she had come into the room. Her face was very white and had a strained, staring look as if it might crumple into tears at any moment.

'I came to return some money to Mrs Garvie-Brown, which seems to have been sent to me under some sort of misapprehension,' he said.

'She sent you some money?' Giles asked, looking up swiftly.

'I didn't say that.'

'I thought you did.'

'Perhaps I shouldn't have talked of *returning* it to her,' Luke said. 'That wasn't quite accurate. Actually I wanted to give it to her to return to the person who sent it to me, because I didn't know who that person was.'

Vanessa drew her breath in sharply. 'I don't believe you.'

'It's an absurd story,' Frances said. 'Some unknown person's been sending you money and you wanted to return it and you thought Christina might know who it was?'

'That's exactly right,' Luke said.

'It's nonsense,' said Vanessa's mother.

'Here's the money, all the same,' Luke drew the packet of notes out of his pocket. With it he drew out Vanessa's cheque-book, but as soon as he was sure that she had seen it, he pushed it back out of sight, then he returned the notes to his pocket too. 'One hundred pounds,' he said, 'and there's another hundred pounds, which came a few days earlier, in my employer's safe. Those will be returned too, unless I have to hand over both lots to the police.'

'I suppose there's something in this story,' Giles said, 'or you wouldn't have the nerve to tell it. And I'd guess myself the money came from Christina. She was a wonderfully generous person. Even if she'd no more use for you, which is what she told us all, it would have been just like her to feel she owed you compensation.'

'Compensation, what the hell for?' Luke had not been listening very carefully, for he had been watching Vanessa. A tear or two had slithered over her lashes on to her pale cheeks and she had brushed them away with the back of her hand. Her eyes had reddened. Besides the sorrow in them, there was a deep bewilderment.

'I think he only came to tell Christina the hundred pounds wasn't enough,' Frances said. 'He thought he had some hold over her and he came here to get more. And he's only told us this story now because he knows the police will want to know what he was doing here and might even search him.'

'*Search him?*' Arne broke in violently. 'Mrs Garvie-

Brown, do you understand what you are insinuating? You are insinuating that my friend, Mr Latimer, had something to do with this poor lady's death. But it happens that at the time when she died he and I were either still in Edinburgh, or else together in the bus coming out here. So any attempt to involve either of us in this tragedy I take as offensive in the extreme. Yes, indeed, in the extreme! You are all much more likely to be searched yourselves than either of us.'

There was something very interesting to Luke in this explosion of outrage. He thought it was wholly false. Arne was not angry, but for some reason, with shrewdness and calculation, had decided to pretend that he was.

'The time when she died?' Giles said curiously. 'Just how do you know when she died, Mr Arne?'

'She died before the fog came in, didn't she?' Arne said. 'You can see the bits of glass all over her. And golfers can't play in a fog. So she was already lying here dead when that golf ball was hit into the room. So she died before approximately eleven-forty.'

'Why eleven-forty?' Giles asked.

'Because that's when the bus ran into the fog. It came rolling in from the sea very quickly. It was like being suddenly smothered in a blanket.'

Giles shook his head. 'Not here, Mr Arne. There was thick fog here already by ten-thirty. I know because I drove out from Edinburgh myself to have a round of golf, and had to give up the idea when I got here because it was so foggy. It's often like that along this bit of coast—very patchy. Not that I suppose it makes any difference to you. If you and Mr Latimer can show you were in Edinburgh all this morning, then you certainly can't be involved in whatever happened here.'

That made sense to Luke. Eleven-forty, ten-forty, or even nine-forty, what difference did it make to either Arne or himself at what time the Blackhope golf-course had been smothered in fog?

But the strange thing was that all colour had drained out of Gilbert Arne's long, smooth cheeks. For the first time since Luke had known him, he looked frightened.

CHAPTER XV

THE DOORBELL rang.

Vanessa went to answer it. It was Dr Garvie-Brown.

As he came in Luke made a mental note of the fact that when Frances had arrived from next door she had not had to ring the bell. She had had a key with which to let herself in. Christina must have been one of the people who always leave a spare key with their neighbours, as a precaution against locking herself out, fires in their absence, and other possible difficulties.

The doctor looked all round the room at each face. As he met Luke's gaze, his features immediately contracted. It was as if he felt that in Luke's presence he must guard against showing any expression. Without speaking, he went to his stepmother and knelt down beside her. Just then the doorbell rang again.

This time it was the police. They had come from the county town of Haddington. There was a superintendent, a sergeant and a constable. There was also a constable from the little police station in Blackhope. The bungalow seemed suddenly to be impossibly full of people and of their heavy footsteps on the floors where carpets had not yet been laid, and of their voices, raised one against the other, as if a house-warming party were being held there. Only their hostess was silent. In their different ways they all came and paid court to her, but she was without response, deep in her silent indifference to them all.

The superintendent and Dr Garvie-Brown knew one another. After a short, low-voiced talk which they held standing one on each side of the old woman's body, the doctor told his wife that the superintendent would like her, with Giles, Vanessa, Mr Arne and Mr Latimer to go home and wait for him there.

Frances tightened her lips, as if she very much objected to having Luke and Arne foisted upon her, but with a brief nod of agreement she led the way out of the bungalow and through the garden to a gate in the fence which separated the garden from that of the house next door.

'I suppose this is going to take all day,' she said as they entered the house. 'Perhaps I'd better get lunch of some sort, though God knows, I don't feel like eating anything. But one only feels worse if one gets too hungry.'

'Leave it,' Vanessa said. 'I'll see to it presently.'

'Drinks, then,' her mother said. 'Giles, will you look after that?'

She dropped her anorak on a chair in the hall and led the way upstairs to the drawing-room. 'Mr Latimer, I've been horrid to you,' she went on. 'And Mr Arne too. For no real reason. I'm sorry. It's my rotten nerves. I'm always horrid to everyone around when I'm upset, and you can't say that what's happened this morning isn't upsetting.'

It was as if, on finding herself hostess to the two men, even if it was against her will, she felt a compulsion to go through the motions of making them welcome.

Luke and Arne both muttered acknowledgments as they accepted the drinks that Giles brought them. Luke stood looking out of the window. He could see hazily across the golf-course now and even some shadowy shapes beyond it, which he thought were the clumps of the buckthorn that grew on the dunes. There was a faintly dazzling white light in what was left of the mist as sunshine began to penetrate it.

'Sit down, for heaven's sake, sit down!' Frances went on,

as if the sight of them all standing about the room had suddenly become profoundly irritating to her. 'You'll see, we'll be here all day. But d'you know, it seems funny to me, the way we all jumped to the conclusion it's murder? I can't understand why we did, except that Mr Arne came here, saying Christina had been killed and would we get the police and a doctor immediately, and so of course I did—it took me a few minutes to track Kenneth down, because he'd been called out to an accident in the fog. And then seeing you, Mr Latimer, all I could think of was Christina telling me she didn't want to have any more to do with you, and yet there you were, with her dead and the window broken . . .' She gave a deep sigh. '*Is* it murder?' she demanded.

No one answered, but they all made their ways to chairs and sat down.

They sat in different attitudes of tension, Vanessa too upright, Luke too near the edge of his chair, Giles with one foot tapping, and Arne, square and stolid, looking almost at ease, except that he seemed to have forgotten how to blink his eyes.

As if silence were the one thing that could make things even worse than they were, Frances rushed into speech again. 'We got her to come and live here because we wanted to help her—think of that! We worried about her living alone and having to climb those stairs and we persuaded her to move. And the first day she's in that bungalow, she dies. But why should we all be acting as if it's murder? Why didn't we just think the move was too much for her? Then that golf ball coming through the window, hitting her on the face and frightening the life out of her. Or perhaps she got that bruise on her temple by falling against something . . . Anyway, you know what I'm like about the golf balls, even if I'm not in the room when it happens. They terrify me. So why shouldn't she simply have had a heart attack when it crashed in? Why not? Mr Arne, I believe you've made us all make fools of ourselves, calling in the police like that. What I ought to have done was get hold of my husband and leave it to him whether or not to call in the police.'

'Well, it's done now,' Giles said. 'The rest is up to the forensic boys.'

'But who could possibly want to kill Christina?' Frances chattered on. 'A tramp, or hooligans, or someone like that? I know Kenneth, Casper and Lucille stand to gain a certain amount of money now she's dead, but we aren't any of us exactly in straitened circumstances. We'd all like more than we've got, of course, but not to the point of murdering poor Christina to get it—'

'Oh, Mother, please!' Vanessa broke in violently. 'Have we got to go on talking about it?'

'Then talk about something else, if you can, but I'll be surprised if you get very far with it,' her mother said. 'And sitting here like mummies won't help much. I know what'll happen to me if we don't talk. I'll begin to think it must have been one of us. Or Mr Latimer, or Mr Arne, or both of them together, and I'll begin to feel frightened of having them here, with Giles the only other man in the house.'

Vanessa stood up abruptly, upsetting her glass as she did so. A wet stain darkened the front of her jersey. Without showing that she had noticed it, she ran out of the room.

Luke got up from his perch on the edge of his chair, put his glass down on a table and left the room too.

He heard her run downstairs, followed her and found her in the large, bright kitchen, which had been made, very expensively, as old-fashioned as possible, with the old tiled floor of the farmhouse left uncovered, blue and white china on a dresser and copper utensils on the walls. Vanessa had gone to the sink and was starting to shred up some lettuce. But tears were streaming down her cheeks and sometimes they splashed into the sink and when that happened she started washing the lettuce all over again. She did not hear Luke come in.

When he had watched her for a moment from the doorway, he went up close behind her and said, 'I shouldn't worry too much about the tears, they'll probably salt the salad dressing nicely.'

She started violently and turned. They looked at one another without speaking, then she found a handkerchief, mopped her eyes and blew her nose.

'I shouldn't worry about the salad either,' he went on. 'Nobody's hungry.'

'I had to do something,' she said.

'I know.'

'I couldn't sit there a moment longer and listen to my mother talk on and on and on. She'll go on, you know, until the police get here and she'll probably try to talk them down as well. She always does.'

'Yes, well, I can imagine that.' Luke pulled a ladder-backed chair out from the new, white, wooden kitchen table and gently pushed Vanessa down on to it. He propped himself against the edge of the table. 'About that money, Vanessa . . .'

She interrupted him with a hiccupping sob.

'That money! Luke, I don't know what happened. I don't know how I could ever have believed . . . Oh, I'm such a fool.'

'It *is* yours, isn't it?'

She nodded dumbly.

He produced the packet of notes and put it down on the table before her and added the cheque-book to them.

'Some time when you're feeling better I'd like to find out what made you think of sending it,' he said, 'but there's no need to go into it now.'

'I don't understand what you're doing with my cheque-book,' she said. 'How did you get it?'

'I went to your flat to see you,' he said, 'and the girl you share it with let me in and gave me the freedom of the place, and then went away, and I had a bath and made some coffee, and then I saw some Sellotape on your writing-table, which made me think of the way the package with the money in it had been done up, and then I saw your cheque-book in a pigeon-hole . . . Vanessa, do you think this thing that's been causing all the trouble, this diary we've talked about, could possibly be simply a piece of fiction that Mrs Garvie-Brown thought was true? A sort of murder story?'

She thought it over. 'I don't see how it could have been. She couldn't have thought it was true if it didn't come pretty close to the facts, and could old Duncan possibly have sat down and cheerfully written a murder story about the deaths of his own three wives unless—well, unless they *were* murders?'

'Yes, I'm afraid that makes sense,' Luke agreed.

'But why did you come to see me?' Vanessa asked. 'How did you know I'd sent the money?'

'I didn't,' Luke said. 'I hadn't an idea who'd sent it. At first I thought, for certain reasons, it was Professor Garvie-Brown, but when I sent it back to him, he returned it to me, saying he didn't know anything about it. So I'd decided to give it back to Mrs Garvie-Brown and ask her to spread the news around her family that I didn't want it. But when my train got into Edinburgh it was too early to go and see her, so I thought I'd drop in on you, and see if you'd let me stick around till a more reasonable hour. Of course, if I'd known she'd moved already, I could have come straight out here. It wouldn't have been too early to visit her by the time I got here. But I wasted time going to your flat and then to Heriot Row.'

'And found the flat there shut up.'

'No, the new owner was there. A woman with a child.'

She said quickly, 'Did you speak to them?'

'Yes, just a few words. Why?'

'Do you think she'll remember you?'

He thought of his conversation with the child and smiled slightly. 'I should think so. Why? . . . Oh, of course, an alibi. You still don't trust me very far, Vanessa.'

'It isn't how far I trust you, it's how far the police will trust you,' she said. 'Nobody would think of trusting that man Arne, and if Christina's death was really murder and his word that you and he were in the bus together was all they had to go on, I think they might make a lot of trouble for you.'

'There were other people on the bus, the conductor, several passengers. Someone would remember us.'

'Except that in that suit you look exactly the same as everybody else,' she said. 'Besides, don't you understand, being on that bus isn't any sort of alibi at all?'

'It isn't? I don't understand.'

She put an elbow on the table and propped her head on her hand. Her tears had dried but her eyes were red, and her face was very pale, except for harsh little patches of colour on the cheekbones.

'No. I started working it out while we were still over in the bungalow,' she said. 'We think Christina was killed before the haar came in, don't we? And that was about half past ten. I remember it because my mother said something about hoping Christina wasn't driving into Edinburgh to church—we'd been playing golf and had to give it up because of the fog—and I looked at the clock as we got in and realized she'd probably have left already.'

'Just a minute,' Luke said, 'why should she have been driving into Edinburgh to church? Isn't there a church out here?'

'Yes, of course. But Christina's been going to the same church nearly all her life. She wouldn't change a habit like that.'

'I see. Go on.'

'Well, about the bus. What time did it leave the bus station?'

'I think about eleven-fifteen.'

'That's what I thought. And it would have taken just around forty-five minutes to get here. But it would also have taken forty-five minutes *to get to the bus station from Blackhope.* Don't you understand? The same bus goes in and out. And the time that bus leaves Blackhope is ten-thirty. So if you couldn't show that you were in Edinburgh well before the time you caught the bus at eleven-fifteen, you just could have been out here, and you could have caught the ten-thirty into Edinburgh and then very cunningly come straight out again.'

'Yes, I see. Very, very cunning that would have been,' Luke said soberly.

Vanessa misunderstood the reason why he sounded and looked so thoughtful. Flushing, she said, 'I know I'm a fool. Even if you hadn't an alibi, it still couldn't have been you, because you . . . Oh, I'm all mixed up about everything. I'm a fool, that's all.'

Luke shook his head. 'You've done some very clear thinking. Now suppose you get back to the salad. And can't I do something to help, open tins or whatever you were going to do?'

He did not tell her that she had shown him why Gilbert Arne had suddenly looked so frightened when he had learnt that Mrs Garvie-Brown must have died at least an hour earlier than he had believed, or had pretended to believe. For it had been in the bus station in St Andrew's Square that he had seen Luke and had followed him on to the bus that left at eleven-fifteen. A bus which had just come from Blackhope and which Arne might have left only a minute or two before Luke got on to it.

But had he?

Luke wanted to think it over before he talked to anyone else about it.

'I'm a fool,' Vanessa repeated, getting up and turning back to the sink under the window. 'Even now I don't . . .' She paused, jerking the cold tap on so sharply that the water gushed out with a loud hiss and marked her clothes with some new splashes.

'Don't what?' Luke asked.

'Don't altogether believe in that diary. I keep on feeling as if Giles and I must have made the whole thing up as a joke. But it must be real, or Christina wouldn't have gone looking for you, would she? But where is it now? Who's got it? That's a terribly important thing to find out, isn't it? For all of us. Who's got it now?'

She stopped because just then several people appeared, walking past the window.

They had come from the bungalow. Her father came first, then two men whom Luke had not seen before, then the superintendent from Haddington and finally Professor Garvie-Brown. He was some paces behind the rest, caught sight of Vanessa and Luke at the window, stood still, and while the others went on to the front door, turned back swiftly and with an air of furtiveness disappeared from sight.

A moment later he reappeared at the back door which opened straight into the garden.

'The poor woman,' he said as he came in. 'Of course, I've seen it coming. Anyone could. I ought to have warned her.'

'Then it was a heart attack after all,' Vanessa said eagerly. 'It wasn't murder.'

'No, no, no, it was murder,' he said. 'And she was asking for it, wasn't she? Waving a deadly weapon about and saying that her conscience told her to, even if it went bang. Oh, the poor, poor, silly woman.'

'You mean, you *knew* about it?' Vanessa exclaimed.

He looked puzzled. 'Of course I did. We all did.'

'About the diary?' she said.

'Diary? Who's talking about a diary? I'm talking about this young man here, to whom she felt we all had some obligation, on account of some lapse of my father's, and who seems to have repaid it—'

'Uncle Casper,' she interrupted, 'Luke has an alibi.'

Casper stopped himself with obvious difficulty. 'An alibi?'

'Impregnable,' she said.

His innocent, wild gaze settled on Luke's face. 'You have?'

'I have,' Luke said.

'Then I'm sorry. I'm sorry all over again. I keep having to say I'm sorry to you, don't I? I'm sorry, very sorry, for it. I hope you'll forgive me. I'm a person it's best not to take too much notice of.' Casper caught sight of the bundle of pound notes on the table. 'Ah, the money—the same lot as before?'

'Similar, not the same,' Luke answered.

'Is that what brought you here?'

'More or less.'

'I'm sure you wish it hadn't. Well, I'll see you both presently, no doubt. Is that some lunch you're providing us with, Vanessa?'

'Of a sort,' she said.

'Good, I'm hungry. When I'm upset, I always develop an awful nervous hunger. I'm really terribly upset, do you know that? If there weren't so many damned police about, I'd sit down and cry. I've known Christina nearly all my life, do you realize that? One didn't notice her much, but she was always there, and always good and sensible and reliable. Poor, poor Christina, to have been so sensible all her life and then to have got into such a stupid mess at the end of it.'

He went out.

There was silence for a moment, then Vanessa said, 'It's

a pity for him he can't cry. I cry horribly easily, I don't know why. I hate myself for it.' She put up a hand to her eyes and brushed away some new tears.

Without knowing that he was going to do it, Luke moved closer to her and put his arms round her.

'Don't hate yourself,' he said. 'You aren't at all hateable.'

He felt her give an abrupt shudder, then she relaxed against him.

'Luke, about that money.'

'Don't worry.'

'But I want to say something about it. Listen, when they ask you about it, tell them the truth.'

'That you sent it?'

'Yes.'

'Are you sure you want me to do that?'

'It's the only thing to do. Too many people know about it not to, and somebody's going to talk about it all. So tell them the truth straight away. About the diary too. Otherwise we'll all start contradicting one another and we'll get into a real mess and the police will begin to think the money may be very important.'

'And it isn't?'

'It's you who knows if it is or it isn't. Only you.' She started shaking the water out of the lettuce and heaping the shredded-up leaves in a wooden bowl.

CHAPTER XVI

THE TWO MEN who had followed Dr Garvie-Brown into the house turned out to be members of the Edinburgh CID. One was short, animated and running to fat. The other was tall, cadaverous and spoke with care, always in completed sentences, putting in the punctuation. They established themselves in a small downstairs sitting-room, a bare room with straight-backed chairs against the walls and a table down the middle of it, with some ancient magazines on it. A waiting-room for the doctor's patients, obviously.

Luke had a long session there presently with the two men, a very difficult session, for he tried to tell them everything that had happened from the time that Gilbert Arne had first appeared at his door, and he had to admit to himself, as he worked his way on, step by step, that the events of the last three weeks made a very peculiar story indeed. He did not blame the two men for disbelieving him, which he knew that they did.

In the end they concentrated on how he had spent that morning. That was plain sailing. It was easy to tell that part of the story. He had arrived in Edinburgh at seven o'clock, he said, had gone to Miss Garvie-Brown's flat in Morningside, a fact which could be corroborated by the friend with whom she shared it, had presently gone to Mrs Garvie-Brown's former flat in Heriot Row, a fact which could be corroborated by the new owner and her daughter, and then he had gone to the bus station, where he had caught a bus to Blackhope at about eleven-fifteen.

The perfection of his alibi gave him a feeling of virtue. While he had been telling the rest of his story he had suffered irrationally from a feeling of guilt, as if the strangeness of the things that had happened to him was somehow blameworthy, and as if he was bound sooner or later to be tripped up in his description of them and be shown up as a fraud and a trickster, if nothing worse. But his alibi made him feel safely entrenched in respectability and for once in his life he found it an entirely agreeable feeling.

It appeared that the police believed, on the basis of what medical evidence was so far available to them, that Christina Garvie-Brown had been killed between approximately ten and eleven o'clock, and that the weapon that had killed her, it had been deduced from a trace of blood on it, had almost certainly been the telephone receiver.

After the murder it must have been wiped clean of finger-prints, for there were none upon it, not even Christina's own. Luke remembered Arne's caution to him not to leave his on the telephone, and for once felt grateful to him.

'You can see how it was,' the shorter of the two detectives said chattily, almost as if he found entertainment of sorts in the story. 'She's there in the room with her murderer. She picks up the telephone to make a call he doesn't want her to make. He snatches the instrument from her and in his rage he strikes her with it. Perhaps he was not even intending murder, and the blow need not have been violent. It just happens the lady has a weak heart and falls dead at his feet—'

'Just a minute,' Luke interrupted. 'The telephone wasn't connected. I told you I tried to dial 999, but it was dead.'

'It was connected,' the tall, more sombre man said, 'but in the struggle for possession of the instrument, the cable was damaged. That was the reason you were unable to make your call to us. Now, Mr Latimer, there is an important question we would be obliged if you would answer. You have told us this already, but we wish to be entirely certain we have understood your statement correctly. At what time and place did you first see Mr Arne this morning?'

'In the bus,' Luke said. They had been over this ground before, but he knew that this was how policemen worked, going over and over the same ground to see if you would contradict yourself. He did his best to be patient.

'In the bus itself?' the short man said.

'Yes, he followed me in and sat down beside me.'

'You did not see him in the station?'

'No.'

'But you told us that he telephoned you when you were in Miss Garvie-Brown's flat, so you knew he was in Edinburgh.'

'Yes.'

'But not how he knew you were there.'

'No, you'd better ask him about that, hadn't you?' Luke said. 'I tried to get it out of him, but he wouldn't tell me. I can only guess he was somehow keeping an eye on me in London.'

'Suppose he was not,' the taller man said. 'Suppose Miss Garvie-Brown's friend who let you into their flat, decided she ought to let Miss Garvie-Brown know what she had done; that she telephoned Miss Garvie-Brown here, but obtained no answer, Miss Garvie-Brown and her mother having gone out for an early round of golf and the doctor, we're told, having been called out to a patient, the house therefore being empty; and suppose the girl had then called the elder Mrs Garvie-Brown with a message for her friend, might not Mr Arne, had he been out here at the time, have learnt at that point where to find you?' The long sentence wound to an end, grammatically faultless.

'You're suggesting he telephoned me from here, from the bungalow, before the murder?' Luke said.

'It would not necessarily have been before the murder,' the tall man said. 'Having learnt where you were, he might have called you afterwards, telling you—as he did, did he not?—that he was in Waverley Station, simply to plant that thought in your mind and build up a picture in it that he had spent the whole morning in Edinburgh. Then, surmising that you would come out to Blackhope when you discovered Mrs Garvie-Brown had moved from Heriot Row, he might have taken the bus back to Edinburgh and waited in the bus station until you appeared.'

'So you've fixed on him already as the murderer?'

Luke discovered an extraordinary mixture of feelings in himself as he realized that the steel jaws of the law were apparently closing on Gilbert Arne. Perhaps it was just that he hated the thought of a steel trap closing on any living creature, even on the Mephistophelian black poodle, who had been such an unwelcome visitor when he first came slinking into Luke's life. A sense of protectiveness, which deeply surprised him, welled up in him. Poor black poodle.

'No, no, Mr Latimer, we have not fixed on anybody,' the tall man said disapprovingly. 'We are exploring the logical possibilities, no more. You cannot yourself see anything impossible in the train of events I have suggested.'

'Impossible, no,' Luke said unwillingly.

'And you find them no more improbable than that Mr Arne should have been keeping you under surveillance in London and followed you here.'

'Oh, I don't know about that.'

'Even slightly more probable, perhaps.'

'Look, the more improbable it is, the more likely it is to have happened in this damned affair,' Luke declared, his voice rising.

'Aye, well, you have something there,' the short man said. 'You do indeed. Now you'll not be leaving Edinburgh for another day or two without letting us know where we can get in touch with you, will you?'

'I don't suppose I'll be leaving at all for the present,' Luke said.

'That's fine then. Thank you for being so co-operative. You'll be staying in a hotel? If you'll just leave the address with us . . .'

Obviously disbelieving at least nine-tenths of what Luke had told them, they waved him politely out.

There was a subtle change in the atmosphere in the house when Lord and Lady Mooney arrived soon afterwards. The Garvie-Browns seemed to regard Lord Mooney as a buffer between them and the police, while the police seemed to tread more softly, to try to change their attitude from one of chill caution to one of wary warmth and sympathy. Not that their attitude before had been threatening, or that the Garvie-Browns had acted as if they felt that they were in need of protection. Yet the change was there, a feeling as if everyone were taking time off to draw a long breath and pause for thought.

Yet Lord Mooney was not in a soothing mood himself. His handsome, florid face was set in hard lines.

'I hope you've none of you been saying too many indiscreet things,' he said acidly when he appeared in the drawing-room after he and his wife had had a brief talk with the detective downstairs, 'but I assume that's too much to hope. Let me tell you, it's a safe rule, when you're being questioned by the police about anything, from a parking offence to murder, to tell them as little as possible.'

'Oh, Charles, this is no time for your flippancy,' Dr Garvie-Brown said. 'We've naturally told them everything we could.'

'It was no flippancy,' Lord Mooney said. And indeed he did not look in the least as he had when Luke had seen him before, a man who drinks heavily in the happy confidence that he will never go that little too far, and who makes jokes for the sake of being able to enjoy his own laughter at them. 'It's common-sense. Remember I've been on both sides of the fence in my time, and I know that if a man I was supposed to be defending poured his heart out to the police before I ever got near him, there wasn't much I could do for him.'

'Who needs defending here?' Frances asked.

'You all do,' the judge answered crisply. But his gaze settled frowningly on Arne. Luke supposed that the police had told him of the uncertainty concerning Arne's movements. 'From the Press, if not the police, since I understand someone here has already spilled some nonsense about old Duncan keeping a diary in which he described a lot of murders he's supposed to have committed. I also understand, and thank God the police do too, that neither this person nor anyone else has a shred of evidence that such a diary ever existed. So from now on keep your mouths shut about it. I think the police will, if you do.'

Lady Mooney had sat down beside Frances Garvie-Brown and taken one of her hands and was limply stroking it, as if she felt that Frances were the person there most in need of comfort.

'Don't take any notice of Charles,' Lady Mooney said in her amiable, empty voice. 'Of course no one believes there was a diary.'

Casper wagged a finger at Luke and Arne. 'They do. And as it happens, so do I. At least, I believe there's something. You've only to look at Latimer to see he's one of us, and Christina hired a detective to dig him up and there he was, he existed. So she had something to make her think of looking for him, hadn't she?'

'That's what I was going to say,' said Giles. 'And as it happens, we know who's got the thing. Latimer or Arne. Or perhaps Latimer *and* Arne. Well, can't we buy it from them?' He turned on Luke. 'What'll you take for it?'

'No!' Vanessa said shrilly. 'Don't, Giles!'

'Giles, don't be a fool,' his father said impatiently. 'Don't you see, whoever has it can't use it now. The possession of it could amount to an admission of murder.'

'I don't understand that,' Arne said. 'Why should anyone want to kill Mrs Garvie-Brown because they'd got this thing away from her? I should have thought she was the goose that was going to lay golden eggs for someone.'

'Except that she would never have laid eggs for anyone,' the judge said. 'If anyone had asked her for money for this diary, or whatever it was, under the threat of publication of it, she'd have grabbed the telephone straight away to call the police. And that's what I believe happened this morning. Her conscience would never have allowed her to pay blackmail. Given time to think things over, it might have allowed her to bury an old scandal, particularly if between us we'd agreed to do something helpful for Latimer, but to yield to intimidation, never!'

'Oh dear, yes, that terrible conscience of hers!' Casper

180

said with a sigh. 'I loved her, you know. I thought she was dear and sweet. But I often found her a very irritating woman. She made me feel so inferior morally.'

'I know,' Lady Mooney said. 'She could look at you as if you had a large smut on your nose which she was too kind to mention.'

'Well, of course, she had that effect on everybody,' Frances said. 'She seemed to be so tolerant, yet she always managed to make me feel a debauched slut. Not that I wasn't fond of her too.'

'That's what I mean. She had a certain aura of moral snobbery,' said Casper.

'She married too late in life,' the doctor said. 'Not a real marriage at all. Got soured and over-compensated by being too good to be true. Poor woman.'

As if flood-gates which had been kept closed in fact with some difficulty had suddenly given way, criticism of the dead woman began to pour out of all her relations by marriage, revealing the mixed feelings that exist between the members of most families. But Luke felt that if he, a stranger, were to agree with anything they said, they would turn and rend him.

The flow was cut short by the judge, who demanded to be told where everyone had been at the probable time of the murder. Abrupt questions soon elicited the information he wanted.

Vanessa and her mother had been out on the golf course together until the fog had driven them indoors. Other golfers had certainly seen them and would be able to corroborate what they said.

Dr Garvie-Brown had hoped for a quiet Sunday morning at home, but had been called out at about ten o'clock to attend to a child who had just come out in a violent rash, which had turned out to be German measles. Then he had no sooner returned home through the fog which had already rolled into the village, than he had been called out again to a bad accident on the main road, in which a car and a van had had a head-on collision. The driver of the car had been killed, while the van driver had been suffering from shock and cuts and bruises. Dr Garvie-Brown had just seen him into an ambulance when the police had come to tell him that he was needed at the bungalow.

Lord Mooney said that he and his wife had not got up until nearly nine-thirty, when, it being Sunday, a day when their daily maid did not come and the au pair girl went out, Lord Mooney had got the breakfast, taken his wife's upstairs to her in bed, then returned downstairs to eat his own in the kitchen, and had still been there, in his dressing-gown, doing the crossword puzzle in his Sunday paper, and Lady Mooney had been having a bath, when the telephone had rung, summoning them to Blackhope.

'Not much corroboration, of course,' he summed up his own story. 'Giles went out about ten o'clock—I heard him leave just as I was going downstairs—so he can't say for sure where I was. It's the truth, though. We had sausages and bacon. I'm good at sausages.'

'And there was that telephone call from your Aunt Hannah in Kirkcudbright,' his wife said. 'That was about eleven o'clock. I listened in on the extension in case it was something interesting.'

'Yes, yes, of course,' he agreed, 'so for once her passion for getting legal advice without paying for it may be of some profit to me.'

Giles said that he had left the house at half past nine. He had driven out to Blackhope for a round of golf with three friends, which had been arranged the day before. He had gone to the club-house, and had met his friends, but almost immediately the fog had come in, they had given up the idea of a game, and he had come to see Vanessa. They had been together until Arne had arrived at the door.

'Where were you during that time, Frances, after you got in?' Lord Mooney asked.

'Doing odd jobs about the house,' she answered. 'Why? I thought it was the earlier time that was important.'

'It's just as well to know as much as possible,' he said. 'What about you, Casper?'

'Much the same as your own story, Charles,' the professor said. 'The long lie-in and a late breakfast. Only no sausages. Porridge and a kipper in my case. And no Aunt Hannah, but a chat with the young couple who live in the flat above as I was fetching in my milk, about ten-thirty, I think.'

Luke and Arne each told his own story.

The Firth was visible by now, though the hills on its far side were still hidden. The sun was low enough in the sky to strike no sparkle from the waves, which looked an oily grey. Golfers had emerged once more on to the golf-course.

There was a pallid redness in the sky by the time that the police allowed the people in the house to disperse. Walking out into the garden with Arne, whom Luke, without being aware of any change in himself, had begun to accept as an ally, he saw a long, wavy ribbon of wild geese go by overhead, making, Lady Mooney remarked, for the bird sanctuary at Aberlady. She then surprised Luke by offering him and Arne a lift into Edinburgh, and so it was in the Mooneys' Rolls, after an almost silent drive, that they were presently delivered at Luke's hotel.

Perhaps it surprised Arne almost as much as Luke had been surprised by Lady Mooney's offer of the lift that Luke then volunteered the suggestion that Arne might stay in the same hotel and have dinner with him.

They had a drink together in the bar before they had dinner. But before they had the drink Arne said that there was a telephone call that he had to make to London.

He made it from the call-box in the lobby and was a long time about it and when he came into the bar his face had the particularly blank look which Luke had come to realize it wore when Arne was worried.

They both drank whisky, sitting at one of the small round tables which were ranged in dead straight rows in the curiously prim-looking room, which somehow conveyed the impression of being dusty and cold, in spite of the fact that it was actually perfectly clean and quite well heated. This effect was something to do with the lighting, which all came from a many-branched copper object which hung from the centre of the high ceiling and cast a pallid gleam, like a wintry, wet dawn, on the almost empty room. It took the malt whisky, spreading its splendid glow through Luke's weary body, to convince him that he was not as chilled as he thought.

Arne, savouring the whisky, said, 'You know, you can't buy stuff like this in England. They keep the best for themselves here.'

'Can you blame them?'

'Not at the moment. Not as long as they've got plenty of it here. I'm going to need several of these.'

'Several will go a long way.'

'After a day like we've had, does it matter? If I'm not fit for questioning next time they start on me, I shan't be the one to complain. You realize they think I did the old woman in, don't you, Luke?'

In the last few minutes they had become Luke and Gilbert to one another. The sheer peace that resulted from having no police or Garvie-Browns in the room had made their intimacy ripen swiftly.

'And did you, Gilbert?' Luke asked.

'I did not, Luke. I may not be all I ought to be. I may have done this and that in my time of which I'm ashamed in my better moments. But I have never committed a murder.'

'Were you out at Blackhope when you phoned me this morning?'

'No.'

'Where were you?'

'In Waverley Station, like I told you.'

'But then how did you know where to find me?' Luke's voice was benign and full of anxious helpfulness as he asked this question. 'As things are, you aren't doing yourself any good by refusing to explain. It makes it look as if you must have been with someone whom that student told about me.'

'Look,' Arne said patiently, 'I was on that train with you. That was just by chance. I was coming here to see Mrs Garvie-Brown again. But then I saw you in the station and I thought we might as well have a talk first, so I followed you out into the street. And I saw you get on to a bus for Morningside. It was easy enough then to guess where you were making for, so I went back into the station, gave you some time to get there, then phoned. If I was wrong and you weren't there, no harm done. But I wasn't wrong. So then, although you wouldn't talk to me, I guessed you'd be making for Blackhope sooner or later, so I went to the bus station and hung around till I saw you.'

'You must have waited around quite a while.'

'Yes, I did.'

'Then there'll be people who noticed you there, and you'll have your alibi.'

'Maybe, maybe not. I'm good at making myself inconspicuous, and I wasn't trying to draw attention to myself, hanging around for so long. I told the police all about it, of course, and they may find someone who saw me. I told them something else too. I told them that golf ball could have been driven deliberately through the window from the garden long after the fog came in. It could have been done just to make things look as if the old woman was killed before the fog.' He emptied his glass, carefully sucking the last golden drops out of it. 'Of course, they didn't need telling.'

'They didn't? They'd thought of that already?'

'Of course. They aren't fools. A very shrewd couple of characters, those two. They're quite as interested in where everyone was after the fog stopped play on the golf course as where they were before.'

'They didn't say anything to me about it.'

'They wouldn't. Nor to me either. But it's the truth. You'll see. But I'm not hoping too much from it. Everything's gone wrong on this case since I started on it. You, to begin with. Most people would have been glad to be discovered by rich relations and find they were in a position to make a good thing out of it. But you—I don't understand you—you just got offended. You know what's wrong with you, Luke? I'll tell you.' Arne stabbed the air in front of him with one of his little white fingers. 'You're either an uncommonly clever crook, which is what I thought till today, or else you're what that professor said the old lady was, you're a moral snob.'

'I'm sorry, Gilbert,' Luke said. 'I'm really sorry. Perhaps the trouble is I've never met a blackmailer like you before. It hadn't dawned on me they were human.'

'A blackmailer isn't human, he's a vampire,' Arne replied austerely. 'I'm not a blackmailer. I just wanted to get that diary back from you and return it to the old lady for a normal fee for a job of work well done. That isn't blackmail.'

'I see. I'm sorry. But you've got that diary yourself, haven't you, Gilbert?'

Luke spoke without any anger. The whisky and the quiet of the sombre room were making him feel relaxed and uncritical, and a strange sense of calm had come to him from having abandoned his enmity to Arne. He was too tired to wonder just then if there could be any danger in this. When he saw anger spark in Arne's cold eyes, he felt surprised.

'You've got to believe me, I haven't got it,' Arne said, dropping his voice to a fierce whisper, though there was no one there to hear them. 'And I'm more or less ready to believe you haven't either, and if that's so we've both been wasting our time, because it's obvious who has got it if neither of us has, isn't it, and he's not going to pay a fee to anybody for anything.'

'Is it?' Luke said in confusion. 'Who?'

'Old Mooney.'

'*Mooney?*'

'One minute, I'll get us some more drinks,' Arne said. He stood up and picked up their empty glasses. 'One thing my father taught me—he didn't teach me much, but that's one thing he did—"Always stand up before you pick up the glasses, Gilbert," he said. And I always do, even when there are only a couple. It's automatic.' He went to the bar.

When he returned, Luke said, 'You don't mean Lord Mooney, Gilbert. You're tired. What you need is a good night's rest.'

'Oh, Luke, boy, think,' Arne said, sitting down again. 'You saw what happened this morning. When I came back to the bungalow with the doctor's wife and the young folks, what did she do? She let herself in with a key old Mrs Garvie-Brown had left with her in case of emergencies. Well, do you think she wouldn't have left a key with someone in Edinburgh too, when she was living all by herself up all those stairs in Heriot Row? Well, who are the people in her family who lived nearest to her in Heriot Row? The Mooneys. They're in India Street, just round the corner from where she lived. That's the part of the town most of the legal profession live in. Of course she'd have left a key with them.'

'And one of them . . .' But it would not have been Lord Mooney, it would have been Giles, Luke thought, and probably without the knowledge of his parents. 'One of them got in that evening when she was out to dinner and searched the place, and she thought it was me, and that's why she turned on me. And if that's what happened, you're quite right, you can say goodbye to any hope of getting your hands on it. It's been destroyed by now.'

'That's right,' Arne agreed unhappily. 'Time and money wasted. As I said before, everything's gone wrong with this case since I started on it. The only thing is, if the diary's been destroyed, why was she murdered? She could talk all she liked, if she hadn't proof to back it up, she couldn't harm anybody.'

'Perhaps she was murdered by someone who didn't know the Mooneys had it.'

Arne looked interested. 'Luke, boy, that's a bright idea. The professor, for instance.'

Luke thought it over, then suddenly leant forward and, thumped the table so that the glasses rattled.

'I don't believe a word of it!'

Arne's pouchy eyelids blinked rapidly. 'You don't believe what?'

'That you haven't got the diary yourself. That you weren't out at Blackhope this morning. That you didn't telephone me from there. That you just happened to come to Edinburgh on the same train as me and catch sight of me in Waverley Station. I simply don't believe it. No, you've got to give me a better explanation than that of how you knew I was in that flat in Morningside.'

Arne gave a heavy sigh. 'And I thought we were just beginning to understand one another. The trouble is, Luke, you won't use your brain. You've a much better brain than me, but you won't use it. You're well educated, you're a professional man, but you just aren't accustomed to thinking for yourself. All right, suppose it wasn't by chance

I came to Edinburgh on the same train as you and saw you in Waverley this morning. Suppose I've been keeping an eye on you in London. Suppose that phone call of mine just now was to someone in London who's told me she's made a thorough search of your flat and there's no sign of anybody's diary in it, only a lot of manuscript that looks as if it might be a novel—'

'She?' Luke interrupted, shouting. All his earlier dislike of Arne came surging back. 'You sent someone to search my flat—to break into it, to read my private papers! Who? That awful woman in your office, the one with the thick thighs?'

'No, no, no,' Arne said gently. 'No one you'd mind at all. Matter of fact, you like her quite a lot. Just my Stephanie.'

'Your—?' Luke felt as if he had been hit hard somewhere near the top of his spine.

'Stephanie. My kid,' said Arne. 'And that's just another case of the way you don't use your brain, Luke, boy. Not to boast, but in your place I'd have got it in one. Didn't she come into your life just after you first met me? Didn't she keep on saying no to all the nice rooms you found for her and keep you hanging around her, telling her everything you were doing? Wasn't it easy for her to tip me off that you were coming to Edinburgh last night, when you cancelled a date with her to do it? And doesn't the way I've kept her at it mean I haven't got the diary, because I was sure you had it? There you are, you see. It's all quite simple really.'

CHAPTER XVII

YES, IT WAS all very simple, and the simplest bit of it all was a certain Luke Latimer. That was something to have learnt. The falling tree, his brush with death, his retreat into himself to try to find out what it was that death had spared, had all led up to this moment and the discovery that he was so simple.

Anyone could deceive him. Anyone could lead him by the nose. Anyone could make him think anything.

Didn't that mean that it was time to stop this playing about with his life and get down to a plain job of work? They had promised that they would take him back at Curt and Broadley if he did not take too long making up his mind about whether or not he meant to return to them. They had really treated him very decently.

'What's amusing you so much?' Arne asked uneasily.

'I'm not amused,' Luke said.

'Well, you're grinning.'

'Am I?'

'The kid's all right, you know. Stephanie. She really likes you.'

'And I like her.'

'There you are, then.'

'Yes, there I am.' Luke was not sure where Arne thought he was, but was beginning to feel that he knew more about this himself than he had for a long time. 'Tell me about Stephanie,' he said. 'Has she got a mother?'

'She had once, naturally,' Arne replied. 'Matter of fact, her name was Rackham. But she didn't stay around long.'

'So you brought Stephanie up all by yourself? That's admirable, that's touching.' Luke almost meant it, although, of course, the whisky was helping him to take a generous view.

'And it hasn't always been easy,' Arne told him earnestly. 'A smashing girl like her. But I've a sister who's helped a lot. You'd like my sister.'

'You never married again.'

'No, thank you—once bitten.'

'Where do you live?'

'Look, what's all this about?' Arne asked. 'Why all this interest in me, all of a sudden?'

'It isn't sudden,' Luke said. 'As a matter of fact, it's one of the first things I wondered about you after we met. What sort of private life has a man like you? I'd never met anyone before I felt I knew so little about.'

'There's nothing much to know about me,' Arne said with an oddly convincing simplicity. 'I haven't much time for a private life. But as it happens, I've a very nice flat in Brighton, which my sister takes care of, and that's where Stephanie grew up and went to a good school, and in my opinion she's a credit to me.'

'And does she really want to go to a university, or was that just part of her cover, like the parents I was told were doctors in Brighton?'

'*I* want her to go,' Arne said. 'I think she owes it to herself, a bright girl like that. But she's got ideas of her own. She likes working with me. Not that it'll make much difference in the end. She'll marry and that'll be that. And some sound training in detective work won't be a dead loss. Lots of married women like getting back to a job once they've got their kids off their hands, and there'll always be plenty of openings for intelligent, middle-aged women in my line of work.'

'Now that's the view of a really prudent father,' Luke said admiringly. 'That's really thinking ahead.'

'Oh, no one can ever say I haven't taken my responsibilities seriously,' Arne declared. 'That's how I am about my work too. There's no lengths I won't go to to protect the interests of a client. That's why I came to Edinburgh today, of course. I was going to warn Mrs Garvie-Brown you'd come here and were going to be starting your little game of blackmail.'

'You don't think that now?'

'Oh no, of course not. I got you all wrong and I'm sorry. But that was just because you got me all wrong. You wouldn't seem to understand I meant you no harm.'

'Well, think of it from my point of view,' Luke said. 'You come walking into my life one day and probably you change the whole course of it, yet I don't know the first thing about you.'

'I wish that was true—about changing the course of things,' said Arne. 'You're just sliding downhill, living as you are, d'you know that? I'd like to help you stop it. Stephanie said the same, "He's just sliding downhill," she said, "and it's a pity, because he's a good sort of boy really, only he seems to think he's got some special sort of privilege to waste his time. Wait a little and he'll start getting grubby, then he'll always be in debt, then it'll be drink or drugs or something—" '

'Just tell me one thing more about yourself,' Luke interrupted, 'then we'll go and eat.' Arne had touched on a very faint secret fear of his that had been troubling him increasingly lately. 'That picture in your office, the one of the birds and the sunset, how did it get there? Did someone give it to you, or did you choose it yourself?'

Arne gave the shake of his head which made it look as if it might be about to roll off his shoulders. 'Now I know you're crazy,' he said. 'That accident really did do something to you. That explains a lot, I suppose. Poor chap.'

'All right, but humour me just this once,' Luke persisted. 'How did you come by that picture?'

'I forget. Took it over with the office furnishings, I

think. Why, have you taken a fancy to it? You can have it, if you want it.'

'No, no,' Luke said quickly. 'I was just interested in what it meant to you.'

'Not a damned thing. I never look at it. What about another drink?'

'In a minute. That picture doesn't mean anything to you, you just let it hang there. Well, what does mean something to you? What do you like? What do you care about?'

'Well, I don't know why you're so interested, but I suppose I do sort of like that picture in a way,' Arne said. 'I don't know why, except that I'm used to it. I was keen about art once. I took up photography. Only as a hobby at first. It wasn't what I wanted to do. I wanted to be a policeman. Everyone said with shoulders like mine I was going to be a big man. But when I was about thirteen, I just stopped growing. I don't know why. Both my parents were big. So I went on with the photography and got pretty good and got in with a detective agency, and that's how I learnt my job and later on I set up on my own, because I like to be independent. Anything else you want to know?'

'But what do you *like*?' Luke asked. 'What matters to you?'

'My job matters to me. And Stephanie, of course.'

'Nothing else?'

'Isn't that enough? Look, I'm not a brilliant sort of man. I'm not even clever, not half as clever as you. So I've got to make do. What's wrong with that?'

There was nothing wrong with it that Luke could see, and perhaps because of this, or perhaps because of the capriciousness induced in the mind by strong drink, Luke's interest in the other man suddenly ran out.

'Let's go and eat,' he said.

They ate almost in silence. Afterwards they muttered good night to one another and went to their rooms.

Luke was very tired. Even when he was not, his mental and physical reactions were often somewhat slow and at any time, on opening his door and finding what he did in his room that night, he might have stood staring for several seconds without saying or doing anything. Now, worn out as he was, he seemed unable to do more than go on and on staring from the doorway in a dazed stupor at the scene before him.

It was a scene of complete disorder. His own few belongings had been so widely scattered over the room that they seemed to have multiplied themselves, as if they could not possibly have come out of the small suitcase that lay open and empty on the floor. The sheets and blankets had been pulled off the bed, the mattress tilted off it. Drawers were open, with their white lining paper ripped out of them. Even a rug had been lifted and left in a rumpled heap. The search had not merely been a hasty one, but gave the impression of having been an angry one. Someone might almost have been taking a fierce satisfaction in letting Luke know what had been done and in leaving as much devastation as possible behind him.

Advancing uncertainly into the room, Luke bent and picked up a single sock that lay by itself near the door, looked at it vaguely, dropped it and sank into the one armchair in the room. He thought of Arne keeping him waiting in the bar to make a telephone call, the call that had been to Stephanie. It had seemed a long call at the time. But in fact it must have been a brief one, if he had come up here to search so frantically immediately on hearing that Stephanie had not found the precious diary in Luke's London flat.

Probably Arne could not have made the search if only Luke had troubled to lock the door of his room. He would hardly have had time to force it. But forgetting to lock the doors of hotel rooms was one of Luke's bad habits. The key of this room was in his pocket now and was only too likely to remain there until after he got home. Luke had as fine a collection of hotel room keys as any man in the country.

But why such savagery in the search? Arne was a trained detective. He could have made the search swiftly, efficiently, and left hardly a trace behind. This mess, instead of being deliberate, might simply have been an amateur's doing. Luke turned this thought over in his mind for a moment, then got up, went downstairs to the receptionist's desk, and asked if she happened to know if anyone had come looking for him during the last hour or so.

She answered, 'Only the young gentleman who brought you here. He said you'd left some papers behind in the car, and when I said he could leave them here and I'd see you got them, he said he thought he ought to hand them over to you personally and would it be all right if he went up to your room. Well, your key was out, so I supposed you were in your room and I was sure it would be all right if he went up. Why, Mr Latimer? Didn't he find you?'

'No,' Luke said.

'Then you didn't get your papers?'

'No. It doesn't matter.'

'I'm sorry. If I shouldn't have——'

'It doesn't matter.' He turned away quickly and went upstairs.

He did not want to tell her of the state that his room was in. He did not want to answer any more questions that day, or give any more explanations to anyone who was not going to believe him. And who was going to believe that Giles Mooney, the son of one of the Lords of Session, had turned Luke's room upside down, hunting for a diary that might not even exist?

But Luke understood now why he had been offered the lift to his hotel in the Mooneys' Rolls. They had wanted to make sure where he was staying so that Giles could return later and make the search. The Mooneys, then, believed in the existence of the diary. That was interesting. But Arne had been wrong when he said that it was in their possession. Obviously it was not. Who had it, then?

In his room Luke re-made the bed, straightened out the rug, shut the open drawers and tidied his own belongings. Afterwards he sat down again in the armchair and stared contemplatively at the lofty ceiling.

Its blankness and remoteness had a hypnotic effect on him. He almost fell asleep. Then all at once he found himself sitting bolt upright on the edge of the chair with a new thought startlingly clear in his mind. He caught his breath. Yes, of course that must be the truth. But could he check it?

Looking at his watch, he saw that it was only a few minutes after nine o'clock. How late, he wondered, did buses run to Blackhope? Perhaps the last had already gone. But he had nothing else to do with the evening, so it might at least be worth while going to the bus station to find out. He had forgotten that he was tired. If fatigue was blurring his judgment, he was not aware of it. Leaving his room, he ran downstairs, having forgotten, as usual, to lock the door behind him. Anyway, it was of no consequence if someone besides Giles Mooney took it into his head to explore the room, for there was nothing to find, nothing worth stealing.

Going out, he took the turning into Minto Street, got on to a bus that would take him to Princes Street, then made for the bus station and went to the platform from which the Blackhope bus had left that morning. He found a small queue of people waiting there, joined it and asked his neighbour in the queue at what time the next bus would leave. In about five minutes, he was told. That meant, he calculated, that he would reach Blackhope between a quarter past and half past ten. It did not occur to him to ask if there would be any buses back into Edinburgh after that hour.

The fog had quite gone. A blustery wind had sprung up, clearing the air, and driving rags of dark cloud across the night sky. When the bus left the built-up area behind and travelled along the shore road a line of faint lights in the distance marked the coast of Fife. The water of the Firth had roughened and the lights of passing cars sparkled on the white froth of breakers along the beach.

Luke got off the bus when it reached the stop where the signpost pointed towards Blackhope. The road was unlit and for a moment, after the lighted bus, he could see barely anything. But then his eyes accustomed themselves to the darkness and he started walking along the grey ribbon of the road that stretched before him. The air was damp and smelled of the sea. Ahead there were the lights of the village. He began to be aware of his tiredness again and to wonder what lunacy had made him set out on this expedition. For what hope was there that the police would have left Mrs Garvie-Brown's car keys in the car, and without them, what could he prove? Besides, he ought to have a witness with him to the experiment that he wanted to make. Why hadn't he thought of asking Arne to come with him?'

Luke also began to think now of that return journey and of the certainty that the last bus back to Edinburgh had already gone. He would have to try to hitch a ride back, or even walk, or find a call-box in the village and telephone to Edinburgh for a taxi to come and fetch him, which would cost the earth. Gloomily he began to consider again the amount of money that he had spent during the last week or two, and how very expensive his involvement with the Garvie-Browns had turned out to be.

Yet all of them thought that he was in it for profit. Even Vanessa had thought so, trying to buy him off with two hundred pounds. Later, when he had time to think about it, that was going to hurt a good deal. It already hurt, in a dead sort of way, though not enough to keep his mind on it. It was again of the car keys that he was thinking as he turned in at the gates of the bungalow. Unconsciously he trod softly, as if he might disturb the spirit of the woman who had so briefly lived there. He went to the car-port.

The keys were not in the car any more and the car was locked.

He stood there feeling futile and ashamed of his own impulsive stupidity. It would have been different if he had been one of those mechanically-minded people who could have started the car simply by lifting the bonnet and doing something clever with fuses and wires, but he was almost as unable to cope constructively with what went on in the inside of a car as he was to perform an operation for appendicitis on a human being.

Because he felt embarrassed at his own ineptitude, he began to hum softly under his breath, standing there with his hands in his pockets.

The sound of his humming was interrupted by the sound of a door opening.

'What is it?' a voice asked. 'Who's there?'

It was Vanessa. She was standing in the doorway of the bungalow, too shadowy a figure for him to have recognized her if he had not known her voice. The open door yawned dark behind her.

'It's only me,' Luke said.

'Whatever are you doing here?'

'What are you?'

'I came over because I couldn't stand the house any more. My mother won't stop talking and my father's taken to snarling at her for it, and what I want is some peace.' She came towards him across the gravel. She was in the slacks, sweater and anorak that she had worn earlier, and looked very slender and insubstantial in the darkness. 'Nobody seems to be thinking about poor Christina, they're

198

only thinking about that damned diary. Why have you come back, Luke?'

'It was just an idea I had,' he said. 'Not a bad idea, actually. Only I didn't think it out properly, so I can't do anything about it. I suppose you haven't got a spare set of Mrs Garvie-Brown's car keys, have you? She'd given you one of her house.'

'I'm not sure. We may have. But I'd think she'd probably have a spare set herself somewhere,' Vanessa said. 'We could look and see. Why?'

'It's rather complicated to explain.'

'Come inside, then. It's cold out here.'

She turned back to the open doorway. Luke followed her. Inside it was all in darkness.

'Why haven't you turned on any lights?' he asked.

'I don't want people to see them and come investigating what's going on. I just want to be by myself.'

'I'm sorry I came, then.'

'Oh, I didn't mean you.'

An ambiguous remark. It meant either that he was welcome, or else of no account at all. He followed her into the sitting-room. Here it was not wholly dark, but filled with the red glow of the electric fire, which, however, gave off a soft enough light, that with the curtains drawn, as they were, no one outside would have guessed that there was anyone in the bungalow.

Vanessa knelt down on the rug in front of the fire. She gave a convulsive shiver and held out her hands close to the shining elements.

'I've felt frozen all day,' she said. 'I can't stop shivering. It's shock, isn't it? Tell me why you want the car keys, Luke.'

CHAPTER XVIII

HE PUSHED a chair towards the fire and sat down near her. The furniture was where it had been in the morning, standing here and there, not yet arranged, with the bookcases empty and heaps of books on the floor and pictures in a stack on the sofa. Only the telephone had vanished. Luke supposed that it had been removed to some forensic laboratory.

'I had an idea about Mrs Garvie-Brown's windscreen wipers, that's all,' he said.

Vanessa gave him a puzzled look. The glow from the fire gave her pale face a rosy tinge.

'Why should they matter?'

'Well . . .' He wove his fingers together, as if he were trying to capture his own idea between his hands and offer it to her. 'You see, we don't know for sure that it was really a golfer who drove that ball through the window this morning. Arne suggested to me it could have been thrown in by someone who wanted to make it look as if she must have been killed before the fog stopped play—in other words, someone who had a perfect alibi for the earlier part of the morning, but none for later. And to know which it was, a real golfer or a fake, and whether she was killed before the fog came or later—wouldn't that be interesting?'

'But how do the windscreen-wipers come in?'

'Don't you see, if she set off for church in the normal way —and she at least meant to, she'd put on her hat, and her bible was in the car, and she'd changed her shoes— and then if she turned back later because she couldn't face driving through the fog, and as she came up the drive, she saw someone, say, letting himself in here, or breaking in, or doing something that made her excited and angry, and she jumped out of the car as soon as it stopped and came running in—which she must have done, because she didn't wait to change her shoes, and she left the keys in the ignition—well, she might easily have forgotten to switch off the windscreen wipers, which she'd certainly have been using in a fog like that. So if we could switch on the engine now and see if the wipers start up, we'd know that's how it happened. We'd know if she had her car out in the fog . . .' He paused. It all seemed unreasonable now, and unconvincing, and ultimately, not his business. 'Don't look so frightened,' he said. 'It's probably all nonsense.'

She dropped her voice as if there were someone there to overhear them. 'But don't you see what you're saying?'

'I know. That if she was killed after the fog started—'

'Then it could only have been my mother, or my father, or Giles. The people I love most. Or me, of course. Because Uncle Charles and Aunt Lucille have alibis for the later part of the morning, and so have Arne and Uncle Casper.'

'I don't think it was you,' Luke said. 'I think Mrs Garvie-Brown was killed by someone who came here to look for the diary when he thought she'd be away at church, and you thought you knew where the diary was. You thought I had it. That's why you sent me the money.'

'Only I didn't,' she said.

'You didn't?'

'Oh, I got hold of it. I'd a hundred in my own account and I borrowed the other hundred from Christina. She lent it to me, she thought, to help me furnish the flat. But it was Giles who sent it to you. He said you'd written him a blackmailing letter and that he couldn't lay his hands on the money straight away, and would I lend it to him.'

'But I didn't write to him at all!' Luke said indignantly.

'I know you didn't. I knew it as soon as I saw you this morning with my cheque-book and the money and in that quiet rage about it all.'

'But why did he do it?'

She made a sound between a sigh and a laugh. 'Oh, Luke, you're rather slow, aren't you? Suppose Giles just wanted to discredit you?'

'To you?'

'Of course to me! He's always thought I belonged to him, and I—I said something to him the other day about wanting to get away from my family and looking for a job in London, and he was scared. Silly of him to be scared, wasn't it? Why should I want a job in London?' She sprang to her feet. 'Now let's look for those keys, because you're wrong, Luke, and I've got to show you you're wrong. I can't have you trying to put the blame on innocent people. Christina never left for church this morning. She didn't drive through the fog. She was dead before it started, and we all know who killed her. It was that man Arne.'

'But if the windscreen wipers—'

'Damn the windscreen wipers! Come on, help me look for those keys.'

She began to pull out the drawers of a bureau and to rummage inside them.

Luke came to look over her shoulder.

'Won't you need lights?' he said.

'I can see quite well,' she answered.

'Vanessa, about Giles wanting to discredit me to you—'

'Oh, forget it, forget it!' she said. 'He was a fool, but it didn't do you any harm, did it?' She was poking about in the corners of the drawers of the bureau, among stamps and packets of rubber bands and pieces of sealing-wax and all the other odds and ends that accumulate in the drawers of a writing-table.

'It might have done you some harm if I'd kept the money,' Luke said, 'and Giles must have thought I would.'

'He'd have paid me back then. He's perfectly honourable.'

'He works in a mysterious way then, some of his honourable actions to perform. Do you know he searched my room in the hotel this evening?'

She slammed a drawer shut violently and straightened up. 'Did he damage anything? If so, I'll pay for it.'

'Oh, stop being such a fool! The point is, he still seems to think I've got that diary.'

'Well, perhaps you have.'

He ignored that. 'If he thinks I've got it, then he hasn't got it himself.'

'Of course he hasn't.'

'Then who has?'

'That man Arne.'

'No, he's another of the people who thinks I've got it, or did until a little while ago. He took quite a lot of trouble to have an eye kept on my movements and to have my flat searched while I was away.'

She moved away from the bureau and stood looking round the room.

'Where would you keep spare car keys, if you had any?' she asked. 'I keep mine in my writing-table—that's why I looked first in Christina's. But it seems she didn't. Perhaps she kept them in a spare handbag. I wonder where her handbags are. Packed in a trunk somewhere. I don't know how on earth we're going to find anything in all this mess.'

'Vanessa, did the Mooneys have a key to the flat in Heriot Row?' Luke asked. 'Could Giles have got in there easily when Mrs Garvie-Brown was out?'

'Isn't it car keys we're looking for?' she said. 'Why have you suddenly switched to the key of her flat?' She put her hands to her forehead. 'I'm trying, I'm really trying, to think where she'd have kept her spare car keys.'

'What about trying your home?' he suggested.

'I suppose it's possible . . .'

'But did the Mooneys have a key to that flat? They live just round the corner from it, don't they?'

'Yes.' She seemed to bring her attention back to him with difficulty. 'Do you think Giles searched there too?'

'I think somebody did,' Luke said. 'Mrs Garvie-Brown jumped to the conclusion I'd done it, and told me she never wanted to see me again, and now I just want to know if it was Giles.'

'Well, the Mooneys did have a key to that flat, so it could have been him . . .'

Vanessa dropped abruptly into a chair and covered her face in her hands. Her reddish hair swung forward, catching the gleam of the fire. 'You know what you're trying to do to me. I told you—You're trying to make me think one of the people closest to me killed Christina. You're wrong, of course, because really we've all got alibis for the later part of the morning too. Giles arrived at our house very soon after the fog, so even if Christina had driven off to church and turned back, she wouldn't have been home before he came. And he and I were together for the rest of the morning. Quarrelling. Quarrelling because I kept on saying I wanted to go away. It's so awful at home!'

'But you don't live at home now,' Luke said.

She sighed. 'No. I thought it would be better when I'd a flat of my own, but it doesn't make much difference. None of them leave me alone. Mother's always coming to see me to complain that they've enough money for my father to retire and they could go and live in Malta, or somewhere like that, and have sunshine and servants and enjoy life. And she thinks it's because my father's mean that he won't do it. And he keeps badgering me to come out here to keep my mother company, and doesn't like me living alone in case of my getting into loose ways, or something. And Giles keeps on wanting me to say when we can get married . . . So we were quarrelling. But I don't suppose you believe me.'

'Why shouldn't I?' Luke said.

'Because you'd like to think it was Giles who killed Christina. But he was with me all the time. He didn't do it. And my mother was doing odd jobs about the house. I heard her moving round. And my father was called out to that accident very soon after the fog started, and he wouldn't have wasted time getting to a serious accident just to do a little murder on the way. He may be a bit mean, and a bit of a bore, and too crazy about golf, but he's an awfully good doctor. But what's the use? Your mind's made up it's one of us. You're a terribly cruel person, do you know that? Why can't you leave this to the police? They're trying to find the golfer who hooked the ball through the window. They're going about it in the normal way, questioning everyone who was out on the golf course this morning. That's the right way to do it. Why can't you leave it to them?'

'Yes.' Luke paused for a long time. 'Why not?'

He did not like being called a cruel person. He did not think that he was cruel. He knew that he was actually a little freakishly repelled by the occasional discovery of cruelty or violence in his nature. But perhaps that in itself was a bad sign and Vanessa had just intuitively probed the truth about him. He was his grandfather's grandson, and perhaps his fear of violence in himself arose only from the fact that he had inherited an abnormal amount of it from Duncan Garvie-Brown.

He thought once more of the odd fear that Stephanie Arne had aroused in him by her soft, inviting passivity. Of course, he knew now that it had not been passivity at all, and on the whole he liked her the better for knowing it. She had merely been waiting and watching and listening for anything that he might reveal. But at the time he had not known that. Her quiescence had seemed a danger to him. What he needed in life was someone who would fight him back and help to cure him of his fears of the inner darkness in himself that he had never dared to explore until the tree had crashed upon him in the gale.

If it had really been the tree. Hadn't it in fact been that journalist, Smithson, coming to see him in hospital with his grisly theory of a multiple murderer in Luke's family, that had unsettled his mind and upset his acceptance of life as he had lived it till then?

Smithson had been the tree.

That was the truth.

He had made Luke believe that he was the grandson of a man who had murdered four women, not merely one, and that had made him seem unbearable to himself. Merely four. Good God, and now he was getting used to the idea of seven! And beginning to find that he could stand it. You could get used to anything. And he was not alone in having to get used to it. The Garvie-Browns, the Mooneys, were in it with him. No doubt the whole human race was in it with him, if you counted their wishes and not only their deeds, and ought to be paying their threepences for all the destruction they desired.

'All right, I'll go,' he said.

Vanessa came up out of her chair as suddenly as if she were angry with him for giving in to her.

'Yes, go,' she said, 'go! But we've got to settle this thing about the windscreen wipers first, or you'll never trust me or any of us. I'll go home and see if they've got them there. Perhaps they have. It's just worth looking, anyway. Will you wait here?'

'Yes, I'll wait.'

She shot out of the room and he heard the front door slam behind her.

He waited in the sitting-room for some minutes after she had gone. Then he prowled round the rest of the bungalow, turning lights on without worrying about whether or not they were seen. There was no doubt about it, a search would be hopeless. Though one of the bedrooms had been made just habitable, he found, when he opened one or two drawers, that they were all packed to bursting, not merely with clothes, but with sheets and blankets and old curtains. The kitchen had crockery and cooking-pots stacked on every shelf and all over the floor, amongst a litter of the straw and newspapers that had been used for packing. It would take long enough to find a kettle to make a cup of tea, let alone something as small as a spare pair of car keys, if they even existed.

Why had he come, he wondered. Why hadn't he simply rung up the police with his idea? That was what any practical person would have done. Anyhow, they had probably thought of it for themselves already. If they had not, they were hardly likely to welcome a suggestion from a person who told them crazy stories about missing diaries and ancient murders. It would be idiocy, besides, to tamper with the car without a witness. There would be Vanessa, of course, if she found the keys in her home and returned with them. But would she do either? And was she to be relied upon as a witness? She wanted the murder to have happened before the coming of the fog, when her parents and Giles were all safely equipped with alibis. So even if the windscreen wipers started to move when the engine was switched on, would she ever admit that they had?

But she was an honest person, wasn't she? She wouldn't perjure herself. Or would she?

A few days ago Luke would have been ready to swear that she was as honest a person as he had ever met, but at the moment he was completely without any trust in his own judgment. Look at his absurd mistake about Stephanie. Look at how impossible he found it to make up his mind even now just how much of a crook Gilbert Arne was. That man had got him all mixed up. Ever since he had slipped into Luke's life, Arne seemed to have been manipulating his mind. Even the idea that the golf ball might have been thrown through the window when the fog was already thick had been dropped into Luke's mind by Arne. Even the fact that there had been those seven murders in the past, that documentary evidence of them existed, hadn't that all come from Arne too?

And wasn't Vanessa being a remarkably long time about looking for those keys?

A wild anxiety for her safety suddenly drove all other thoughts out of Luke's mind. Suppose that in the darkness she had walked straight into the person who had already killed one woman that day, and who perhaps had been eavesdropping outside that broken window while Vanessa and he had been talking about the windscreen wipers.

Luke went running to the front door and plunged out into the garden.

His real reason for coming out here this evening, he knew, had been simply to be near Vanessa. He had not expected to find her in the bungalow, but had thought that she would be in the house next door and at the back of his mind he must have vaguely hoped that just possibly he might find some reason for going there. Yet on meeting her, he had let her go off alone to face God knew what dangers. He felt sick with anger at himself and called out her name.

As he did so, he saw something move in the dark shadows of the car-port. A squat, bulky shape. It was surmounted by an oddly shaped little triangle, which in a better light he could have identified as a small tweed hat. The figure was crouched over the bonnet of the car, which was open. The car-port was filled with the sound of the engine ticking over. Even in the darkness Luke could see that the windscreen wipers were swinging from left to right, from right to left.

He rushed towards the car.

He did not see the other figure that moved up behind him, a slim figure in dark slacks, a sweater and an anorak, a woman with red-gold hair that looked almost black in the pale starlight and a pale, wild face, and it was only out of the corner of his eye, and too late, that he saw her lift arms made muscular by playing golf and swing the golf club that came crashing down on his skull.

CHAPTER XIX

IT IS POSSIBLE that Luke's life would have ended there and then if it had not been for Gilbert Arne, who, whatever else he might be, was a hard-working and intelligent detective. If he had not been on the spot, if an hour or two earlier he had not half-expected Luke to leave the hotel, watched for him and followed his bus to Blackhope in a taxi, the golf-club might have descended again and again.

Later it was claimed that of course this would not have happened, that there had been nothing murderous in the attack on Luke. He had been an intruder, after all, unrecognizable in the dark, understandably an object of fear.

Whatever the truth of that, Arne did not wait to find out if the assault was meant to be deadly or merely temporarily disabling. Coming charging unexpectedly out of the car-port, the short, stocky man disarmed the tall, slender woman without any difficulty. When he grabbed her she began to scream. The noise was heard by some neighbour who happened to be passing in the road and who came running into the garden to find out what was going on. Frances did not wait to confront them, but writhing out of Arne's grasp, fled into the night. Arne and the neighbours turned their attention to Luke.

He recovered consciousness in a hospital ward. The hospital was a small and pleasant one in East Lothian and during the two days that a young West Indian doctor insisted he remain there, he was treated with all kindness. It was because of his previous accident, of which the doctor had heard from Arne, that Luke was kept there so long, not because he appeared to have received any serious injury from the blow with the golf club. But he had no objection to spending the two days in hospital. It was restful and quiet and they fed him quite well, except for a superfluity of boiled carrots. His only criticism, and in its way a serious one, was that they kept allowing policemen in to talk to him.

There was one sitting by his bedside when he first came to himself. It was the tall, cadaverous detective from the Edinburgh CID, who spoke in long, complex, grammatical sentences, and one of these had started winding its slow length along, competing with the fret-saw that seemed to be doing some complicated carpentry inside Luke's head, when Luke, feeling that it suited his condition far better to be unconscious than to make the effort to take in what was being said to him, lapsed back into blackness.

When he surfaced again a different policeman was sitting there and Luke found, as he looked at him, that his face did not waver strangely about, as if he were looking at it through rippling water, but remained sanely still. Also the fret-saw had stopped.

Luke answered the questions that he was asked quite lucidly, then fell into a deep, normal sleep which lasted until he was roused irritably out of it by the clanging and banging of early dawn, which so merrily starts the day off in any hospital. He drank the cup of tea that was brought to him and did his best to go to sleep again, only to be roused again almost at once, so it seemed, to talk to yet another policeman.

The first visitor other than a policeman who came to see him was Gilbert Arne. He came treading softly along the ward with his little steps, looking, as usual, both furtive and formidable. On seeing Luke, he rubbed his little hands together in a gesture full of self-congratulation, as if he would be the last person to deny that it was solely due to himself that Luke was evidently so well. Sitting down on the chair by the bed, Arne leant forward and spoke in a whisper, aware that anyone who had frequent visits from the police must be an object of intense curiosity to the other patients.

'You're looking fine,' he said. 'Just fine. You know, you must be a lot tougher than you look. The way you went down when she took that swing at you, I thought you'd had it. Also, d'you know, when she suddenly showed up like that, I thought for a moment it was the girl? I'd seen her go out and I was expecting her back. Didn't you think yourself it was her, or didn't you get a chance to see her?'

Luke gave a slight shiver as a peculiarly vivid memory came back to him.

'Yes, I thought it was Vanessa,' he said. 'It didn't make sense, because I was sure it was Giles who'd killed Christina. He'd no alibi for the time after he'd left his friends in the golf club and before he arrived at the Garvie-Browns'.' Luke might have added, 'And I wanted it to be Giles.' He went on, 'But I did see her for an instant out there in the darkness, and, yes, I thought it was Vanessa. But the first thing that CID chap told me when I recovered consciousness was that it was Frances. I just about took it in, then blacked out again. They're very alike, of course.'

'Yes, in build and general colouring,' Arne agreed, 'and they were dressed alike in their golf things. She's confessed, did you know that? Gone to pieces completely and confessed everything. But she'll get off with manslaughter—what they call culpable homicide up here. Did you know there's no such thing as a charge of manslaughter in Scotland?'

'No, really?' Luke said. 'I didn't know that.'

'Culpable homicide, that's what they call it,' said Arne. 'That's what she's pleading guilty to and I should think it's the truth. I don't believe she meant to kill the old woman.'

'Why did she, then?'

'Because the old woman was trying to get in touch with you to apologize for what she'd said to you when she spoke to you last.'

'That seems a queer reason for getting killed.'

'I don't think Frances was in a state to do much reasoning. Myself, I don't think she has been for a long time. From what they're all saying, she's been getting more and more unbalanced recently. And when she heard old Christina start to telephone, she thought it was to the police, and she rushed at her and grabbed the phone away and they had a struggle for it, and Frances got hold of it and hit out. With a head like yours it wouldn't even have made a dent, but the old woman's heart packed up.'

'Then Frances went outside and hurled a golf ball through the window, to give herself an alibi.'

'Yes, just as I said.'

'What made Frances think Christina wanted the police?' Luke asked. 'And how do the police know she didn't want them but me?'

'Because she'd just asked the operator for your number. That's on record. Then the line went dead, the operator said. That's when the wires were broken. The way it happened was this. When the fog stopped Frances and the girl playing golf, they went back to the house and Frances started those odd jobs about the house she talked about. But presently she had the idea of popping over to the bungalow to see if she could find the diary. She'd got that spare key to the bungalow, so she could get in, and she knew the old lady would probably have started off for church. If she hadn't, if she was at home, no harm done—Frances would just be dropping in to see how she was getting along. Nobody noticed her slip out of the house, because the doctor had been called out to the car-smash in the village and Giles Mooney had shown up and he and the girl had settled down to a nice long quarrel and weren't paying attention to anyone else. You're wrong, by the way, that Mooney didn't have an alibi. By the time Christina had tried to get to church and come back, and then tried to make that telephone call, he and Vanessa were already having their quarrel. And both of them were much too angry with each other to notice when the noise of Frances's little jobs stopped.'

'So if Christina was killed in the later part of the morning, it had to be Frances who did it,' Luke said. 'Yes, I see.'

'But if it was in the first part of the morning, it was me, wasn't it?' Arne said with a grim little grin. 'And even now, you half wish it was. You'll never quite make up your mind about me, will you, Luke boy? D'you know, you haven't even said thank you to me yet for being on the spot when I was needed?'

'I haven't?' Luke said, shocked. 'No, I haven't. That's terrible. Thank you, Gilbert. Thank you from the bottom of my heart.'

Arne twisted his little hands together, looking embarrassed. 'The fact is, I wasn't worrying about you,' he said. 'I was just doing my job.'

'Were you really?' Luke asked. 'Were you still actually employed by Christina, as you told the police?'

'Well, not exactly.' Arne's air of embarrassment continued. 'But I did think till yesterday you had the diary and were coming here to try to sell it back to Mrs Garvie-Brown at a stiff price—if not to do something in the way of blackmailing the whole family. So I thought if I could get it back from you and return it to her without putting a price on it at all, I'd get a fee. Just a normal fee. I thought I could count on her for that. It was taking a bit of a risk, perhaps, but there've been some lean times lately.'

Luke nodded. It would be as well, he thought, to accept that version of Arne's recent activities. It might even be perfectly true. That was something that Luke was unlikely ever to know for certain.

'Let's go back to Frances,' he said. 'How was it she didn't realize Christina was calling me and not the police, if she'd actually given a London number?'

'It was like this. Frances went over to the bungalow, found the car was gone and nobody at home, and unlocked the door and went in. But that was just when Christina came back and she actually saw Frances letting herself in and she was furious at such an abuse of her trust. The people next door weren't meant to use her key like that, it was just for emergencies. She went rushing in, leaving the car key in the ignition, not changing her shoes, and found Frances actually going through the drawers of her writing-table. So they had a row, a real screaming row, so it seems, Frances saying she wanted the diary and would go to any lengths to get it, and Christina saying she was going to call the police and have Frances arrested for trespass. Not meaning it, of course. Probably neither of them really meaning it, except that Frances did want that diary very badly. Not to prevent scandal. She didn't love her husband's family so much that she'd have cared about that. But she did want power over her husband to make him retire, or else give her the money, so that she could go to live in Malta or the Caribbean or somewhere where she thought life would be very gay and very smart and altogether different from Blackhope—though it's probably exactly the same, golf, coffee, bridge and whatnot. But the grass is always greener somewhere else for the Frances Garvie-Browns.'

Luke gave a gentle touch to the area on his head where Frances's golf-club had landed. It was swollen and extremely sore.

'Go on about what happened during the quarrel,' he said.

'Oh, they both calmed down and Christina asked how Frances knew about there being a diary, and Frances told her that they all knew. Giles and Vanessa had worked it out between them after you turned up here, she said, and Giles had already searched for it once in the Heriot Row flat, because none of them trusted Christina not to ruin all their lives with it when the whim took her. So Christina realized it wasn't you who'd done that. And Christina told Frances they had nothing whatever to worry about, they would never hear any more of the diary. She promised it solemnly. And she agreed not to call the police and they more or less made friends again and Frances left. But just as she was letting herself out of the house, she heard Christina pick up the telephone and ask for a number and she thought Christina was calling the police after all and she rushed back and snatched the phone away from her and the disaster happened.'

'And killing someone, even if you don't mean to, is an upsetting business, I suppose,' Luke said. 'She was probably going quietly farther and farther round the bend all day, so that attacking me in the evening seemed a quite ordinary thing to do.'

'The girl told her you were there, of course,' said Arne, 'and your theory about the windscreen wipers. So Frances slammed the door on her and the doctor in that upstairs lounge and locked them in and went rushing over to the bungalow to make sure the windscreen wipers were switched off. She wasn't expecting you to be in the garden, of course, but she took the golf-club in case.'

'Which reminds me of something else I've been wanting to ask you,' Luke said. 'You'd got the windscreen wipers working when I came out of the bungalow. What made you tamper with them? It made them useless as evidence.'

'They were useless all along,' Arne said. 'A car that had been standing like that in an open car-port with anyone able to come and go and tamper with it—how could that be evidence? So I just tried it for my own satisfaction. I'd been eavesdropping on you and the girl through that broken window, you see, and I thought, now that's a really nice ingenious theory, the sort of thing an educated bloke like Luke would think of. I'd just like to go and see if there's anything in it.'

'And there was. I was right.'

'Well . . .' The look of embarrassment returned. 'No.'

'*No?*' Luke exclaimed. 'But you said—'

'No, I didn't. I'm very careful what I say, always,' Arne said. 'You have to be in my job. And I'm talking to you like this now because we haven't a witness, and it was because of your ingenious idea that they caught the murderer. You see, it was her fear that the windscreen wipers had been left turned on that made her rush out and attack you and give herself away and go right round the bend and confess everything. But the old lady had turned them off all right. It was me who turned them on, just to be on the safe side. Not, as I said, that they could be taken as evidence. But there are times when you're worried about yourself when you feel every little helps.'

Luke gave a laugh. 'Oh, you were right when you said I was simple, weren't you, Gilbert?'

'I'm usually right about people,' said Arne.

'Yet you thought I'd got the diary.'

'That's true. Well, nobody's omniscient.'

'Who *has* got it?'

'If you want a guess—but what's the good of guessing? —I'd say the professor. He's probably the brightest of the bunch, and also he's the one who's made the least fuss about it. He hasn't tried searching for it. He's kept very quiet. Yes, I'd say it's him. But that's just a guess. And if he's got it, he can keep it. I want nothing more to do with the business. There's been something about this case I've never really liked. It's gone wrong from the start, with you being so suspicious of me and all. Now you just take it easy and get well, and maybe we'll meet in London one day and have a drink. You've got my telephone number.' He stood up. 'You just give me a ring when you

216

feel like it and you and me and Stephanie could all have a drink together.'

A telephone call, they both knew, that would never be made. A drink that would never be drunk.

'Yes, I'll do that,' Luke said. 'And again, thanks for last night.'

'My pleasure.'

Arne walked softly away down the ward. A black poodle, going as he had come. Only not a poodle. A terrier, perhaps, alert, cocky, a good ratter . . .

Luke lay back and had a pleasant daydream that his next visitor would be Vanessa. He imagined her arriving with a big bunch of grapes and a good book for him to read. But she did not come. He did not expect her to. She would marry Giles and not too long from now, it was to be hoped, Luke would be successful in forgetting that she had ever existed. His next visitor, very much to his surprise, was Casper Garvie-Brown.

He came in looking inquisitively at each patient he passed, rather as if he were not sure that he would recognize Luke when he saw him, and when he did, looked hesitant and vague, as if all of a sudden it had struck him that his visit would take some explaining.

Sitting down on the chair that Arne had left, Casper said that he hoped that Luke was feeling better, that no doubt he had heard about poor Frances and that it was extraordinary how many of the events that went to make up the world's history were totally unnecessary from all points of view. After that he sat silent for a time. Luke waited.

'Well,' Casper said after a little, 'I've really come to say another of those things you may find unforgivable. It's about the diary. If you've got it—'

'I haven't,' Luke said. 'Haven't you?'

'Certainly not. If I had, none of these tragic things would have happened.'

'You mean you'd have destroyed it?'

'No, no, no, certainly not. And what I was going to ask you is, *if* you've got it—and if you have, I respect your motives in keeping silent about it. I suspect nothing sinister, do understand that—well, if you have, *please* don't destroy it. To me it's a terrible thing when documents of historical interest are destroyed simply because a few selfish people, without foresight, without imagination, are afraid of what they may bring to light. And that diary, if it's preserved, will become of immense historical interest. Think what it must reveal of a mind, a period, a place. Oh God, if only I'd known of it sooner . . .'

'As a matter of curiosity,' Luke said, 'what would you have done with it?'

'Oh, concealed it, of course. I shouldn't have subjected my family to the embarrassment of having it published. But I should have concealed it where it would eventually have been found.'

'For instance?'

'The best place I can think of would be the University Library. I'd slip it into one of the less interesting stacks and trust to luck that it would be safe there for a generation or two, but that sooner or later some student, desperately hunting for a subject for his Ph.D. thesis, would chance on it and have the most startling and exciting experience of his life. I like to think of that student . . . Pain and horror all get forgotten in the end, you see, and it takes a far deeper capacity for feeling than most of us possess to resurrect them, but historical interest goes on for ever.'

'I wish I had the diary then,' Luke said. 'I'd give it to you. But I'm afraid I haven't.'

The professor sighed. 'It was just a thought . . . And may I say that if you feel insulted by anything I've ever said or done, I hope you'll forgive me. I have the highest regard for you and I hope we'll make that trip to the Highlands together some day. After all, we're kin.'

His green eyes, so like what Luke's would be when he was twenty years older, smiled through his spectacles as he got up and said goodbye.

That was the last that Luke saw of any of the Garvie-Browns before he left for London. That was two days later. He did not have to give evidence at any inquest, since public inquests are not held in Scotland. Instead he had a private session in the office of the Procurator Fiscal in Edinburgh, then he was free to go. Free to forget the Garvie-Browns and the seven dead women who had been briefly brought to life after their long sleep in obscurity and now could go back to it.

For somehow the newspapers had not got hold of the story. Frances Garvie-Brown had accidentally killed her husband's stepmother during a quarrel over a young man whom the older woman had befriended, that was the version of the story that was solidifying in the minds of journalists, and the friends and acquaintances of the Garvie-Browns. It caused a mild sensation locally, but did not even achieve a small paragraph in any national newspaper.

'And I'll soon be believing it myself,' Luke said to Mrs Doubtfire when he saw her next in her bright little office, with glasses of gin on the desk between them, as well as fresh flowers and the domesticated-looking heap of knitting, which had changed its colour since Luke had last been there. Mrs Doubtfire had finished whatever the last garment had been and had begun on another. Luke had never noticed before that this sometimes happened. It gave him a sense that far more time had passed since his first meeting with Gilbert Arne than he had realized.

'After all,' he went on, 'it's a much easier story to believe than the one about the diary.'

'But it's the diary you still believe in.' Mrs Doubtfire's tone was worried and mournful. Luke had just told her that he was leaving Good Neighbours, Ltd, as soon as she could conveniently let him go, and returning to Curt and Broadley, who had appeared flatteringly pleased to have him back. It had turned out that they had a high opinion of his abilities and had been hoping that he would return once he had fully recovered from his accident.

Mrs Doubtfire had said that she had expected it from the first and that she was sure he was doing the only sensible thing, and that of course there were no hard feelings, and that perhaps he would still fill in for her occasionally when he had nothing else to do with an evening, and Luke's heart had sunk a little, even as he was saying that of course he would help most gladly, for he knew what she could make of an obligation. But he had a deep obligation to her and had no desire at all not to recognize it.

'Yes, I do believe in it,' he replied, 'because Arne found some fragments of it. Want to see them? They came to me by post this morning.'

'*Arne* found it . . .?'

'Yes. It seems that after he'd been to see me in the hospital he got to thinking again, and had the idea of going back to the flat in Heriot Row. There were decorators in the place and they let him drift around, thinking he was something to do with the gas or the electricity or something. And in one of the fireplaces he found a few ashes. The top of the grate looked swept and garnished, but these ashes had slipped through the bars and been overlooked. They were the ashes of burnt paper. And the writing on two scraps of paper was still readable.'

Luke took his wallet from his pocket and extracted two small plastic envelopes and slid them across the desk to Mrs Doubtfire. In each was a piece of yellowed paper, charred around the edges.

She handled them cautiously, reading the very small, crabbed writing through the plastic.

On one were the words, '. . . vie-Brown, being of what I

am accustomed to consider as sound mind, although at times I feel that some of my colleagues on the Court of the University most unreasonably appear to entertain doubts . . .'

On the second scrap, which was smaller, were only the words, '. . . this splendour of experience . . .'

'So he enjoyed it all,' Mrs Doubtfire said as she gave the envelopes back to Luke. 'Wouldn't it be satisfactory to believe in a hell for him to burn in?—though the desire for revenge is really a dreadfully enervating emotion. Few things wear you out so quickly.' She picked up her glass of gin and looked deeply into it, like a clairvoyante into her crystal. 'I was so sure Christina wouldn't destroy the diary. I suppose she did it after she found someone had got into her flat and searched for it. I suppose she got scared then and burnt it in case the searcher found it next time. But where did she keep it till then?'

'I've got a feeling it was in a big crocodile handbag she used to carry around,' Luke said. 'I think she'd only have felt it was in a safe place if she had her hand on it all the time. It wouldn't have occurred to her that she wasn't safe herself. Anyway, I'm glad now we can be sure it went up in flames.'

Mrs Doubtfire gave one of her sardonic grins. 'There'll be times ahead when you won't feel so glad. There'll be times when you wish you'd got your hands on it. You'll think of what you might have got for serial rights from some Sunday paper, and film rights, and a paper-back with a nice lurid cover on all the bookstalls. Yes, even you. We all get more money-conscious as we get older. Though there would have been complications about whom the copyright belonged to. I can see that. So everything is probably for the best. I'm a great believer in the idea that everything, in the long run, is generally for the best. I don't see the point in believing anything else, anyway. Which reminds me . . .'

Luke had just extricated himself from the loving grasp of the Finnish armchair and was standing before her.

She went on, 'I almost forgot. I had a letter this morning, from someone applying for a job here. The girl gave your name as a reference.'

Bewildered, Luke said, '*Mine?*'

'Yes. Her name's Vanessa Garvie-Brown. She says she has commitments which will keep her in Edinburgh for some weeks. I suppose she's referring to the trial of her mother for manslaughter—'

'Culpable homicide.'

'Sorry, culpable homicide, and perhaps to the fact that she has to finish the term at the school where she's teaching. A nice, conscientious girl. But then it seems she'll be free to come here. Well, is she honest, reliable, hard-working . . .?' Mrs Doubtfire's grin broadened. 'Of course, all these girls get married and want to leave. I'll end up in an old people's home yet, and I wonder which of you all will bother to come to see me.'

ELIZABETH FERRARS

ALIVE AND DEAD

Martha Crayle worked for an agency that helped unmarried mothers. She thought she knew all the problems until the blonde girl strayed into her office.

Amanda was pregnant. That at least was clear. She had been married. That was agreed. The baby was not her husband's. Agreed. But here the problems started.

He had died in an air crash three years before. The records bore this out and her parents confirmed it. But Amanda insisted that he was still alive and that she had recently, unexpectedly met him. Her parents claimed that she was emotionally upset by her pregnancy. They further stated that he had been a kind, supportive young man. Amanda described him as a plausible, ruthless crook.

The next day a man was found murdered nearby and the police arrested Amanda. But how can someone be killed who's been dead for three years? Martha Crayle's problems were about to get even more complicated.

HODDER AND STOUGHTON PAPERBACKS

ELIZABETH FERRARS

MURDER AMONG FRIENDS

War-time London. In the evening streets the air raid wardens check for black-out infringements. Behind the heavy curtains of Cecily Lightwood's flat, the guests are gathering for a small party. Many are old friends, most inhabit the artistic and literary worlds, all are awaiting the arrival of the famous playwright Aubrey Ritter.

But his entrance is delayed; irritatingly, distressingly, fatally delayed. Off stage, on the stairway, a sudden wild cry is heard. Ritter is dead. Savagely beaten, his body has been found upstairs.

Almost before it began, the party is over. But the search for a person most probably known to those present is just about to begin . . .

'A rich entanglement of emotional involvements . . . Keep your wits about you for this one'
Bloodhound

'A name I read for pleasure, not just business'
Anthony Price in The Scotsman

'Fascinating . . . Elizabeth Ferrars, together with other writers such as Dorothy L. Sayers have given us a whole new sort of crime fiction'
H. R. F. Keating

HODDER AND STOUGHTON PAPERBACKS